A Distant Music

Book 1 in BJ Hoff's *The Mountain Song Legacy.*

"For this Ken   through
the eastern h   of wood
smoke in the   se brings
to life this ge   nts, who
learn far mor   er points
in the story a   Yet even
in the darkes   el by one
of historical f

—Li   rt

"In the lyrica   t God is
present even   verflows.
A warm and satisfying tale of characters who will live in your memory for
years to come."

—Angela Hunt, author of *The Novelist*

"As always when I open BJ's books I am drawn into a place that is both distant
and at home. The metaphor of music, of lost music especially, so resonates
with those of us who at times feel our voices are lost and long to know that
we will be found. I know I'll love this series as I love her others and secretly,
as I tell my husband, I wish I could create the kinds of characters BJ does
because I fall in love with them and want them always as my friends."

—Jane Kirkpatrick, author of *Look for a Clearing in the Wild*

"I read *The Penny Whistle* years ago and never forgot it. I was delighted to
see that it had become a full-length novel. *A Distant M*   ntains all the
elements—compelling characters, fascinati   r writing—
that I've come to expect from a b   cover."

—Deborah Raney, auth   erish

"BJ Hoff is a master storyteller. With impeccable research, vibrant characters, and historical accuracy, Ms. Hoff weaves a story that's impossible to put down."

—*Lori Copeland,* author of *The Plainsman*

"How do I begin to describe a book that touched me in the deepest parts of my heart? I laughed. I cried. I despaired. I regained hope. *A Distant Music* inspires me to live life well no matter what my circumstances....In *A Distant Music,* miracles do happen but in unexpected ways."

—*Armchair Interviews*

"*A Distant Music* is another captivating book by author BJ Hoff. Ms. Hoff has the ability to create such believable characters that you feel like you know them as friends when you close the book's final page....*A Distant Music* holds such wonderful prose and such realistic descriptions that I felt I was there."

—*Jill Eileen Smith,* reader

"Picking up a BJ Hoff novel guarantees that you will be transported into another time filled with captivating characters. Book #1 of the new Mountain Song Legacy series, *A Distant Music,* is no exception. BJ Hoff's gift of bringing characters to life shines in *A Distant Music.* I found myself drawn into Maggie MacAuley's troubles and shed more than a tear or two with her. *A Distant Music* is an enchanting read that touches the heart. Once more BJ proves that when it comes to the historical voice, she is the master."

—*Vennessa Ng,* book reviewer

"BJ Hoff's latest novel, *A Distant Music,* plays on for me like a haunting melody, even a week after I've finished it. The characters are still very much alive in my mind. This is the first book I read of hers, but I definitely plan to read her others, especially the ones in the Mountain Song Legacy series. Her ability to weave spiritual truths into a great story will keep me coming back for more."

—*Lynetta Smith,* reader

B.J. HOFF

The Wind Harp

HARVEST HOUSE PUBLISHERS

EUGENE, OREGON

Cover by Koechel Peterson & Associates, Inc., Minneapolis, Minnesota

BJ Hoff: Published in association with the Books & Such Literary Agency, 52 Mission Circle, Suite 122, PMB 170, Santa Rosa, CA 95409-5370, www.booksandsuch.biz.

This is a work of fiction. Names, characters, places, and incidents are products of the author's imagination or are used fictitiously. Any resemblance to actual persons, living or dead, or to events or locales, is entirely coincidental.

THE WIND HARP
Copyright © 2006 by BJ Hoff
Published by Harvest House Publishers
Eugene, Oregon 97402
www.harvesthousepublishers.com

Library of Congress Cataloging-in-Publication Data
Hoff, B. J.
   The wind harp / B.J. Hoff.
     p. cm. — (The mountain song legacy ; bk. 2)
   ISBN: 978-0-7369-1458-1 (pbk.)
     1. Family—Fiction. 2. Coal mines and mining—Fiction. 3. Kentucky—Fiction. 4. Domestic—Fiction.
I. Title II. Series: Hoff, B. J., Mountain song legacy; bk.2.
   PS3558.O34395W55 2006
   813'.54—dc22   2006009752

Printed in the United States of America

09 10 11 12 13 14 / RDM-SK / 10 9 8 7 6 5

For "the men in my life—"

Jim...

A husband who sets the standard for all others...

Dennis and Eric...

More sons than sons-in-law...

Noah, Gunnar, and Caleb...

Who give me the right to brag.
You're growing up so quickly!
May you also grow in God's grace.

Acknowledgments

Special thanks to special folks...

Nick Harrison, whose many gifts go far beyond the editorial, and whose steady faith is an inspiration for all those who are fortunate enough to work with him.

The Harvest House "family"—So fully committed to their authors, their readers, and especially to their God. What a blessing it is to work with you.

Janet Kobobel Grant, my agent, my friend...and the one who knows just when and how to apply that extra little push to keep me going.

My readers—You and Christ in you...the reason why I do it.

My family—May God bless you all for putting up with me...especially during the "deadline days."

Prologue

A Decision Made

Home is where there's one to love,
Home is where there's one to love us!

Charles Swain

∼

**Skingle Creek, Northeastern Kentucky
August 1904**

The time had come for Maggie MacAuley to make a decision. She had used up most of the extended leave that Miss Addams had reluctantly granted her. There was no more time for delaying the inevitable. She had to decide, and she had to decide now.

For most of her childhood friends—the ones who had remained in Skingle Creek—there would have been no decision to make. After all, she was a woman grown: twenty-four years old with a hard-earned college degree, a teacher's certificate, and a respectable position at Hull House. To others, a choice between returning to the bustling city of Chicago and the opportunity to work with Miss Jane Addams, or staying here, in the tiny coal town of her birth, would be no choice at all.

And yet lying here in the bed that had been hers when she was growing up, in the same bedroom she had once shared with her two sisters, Maggie felt an unexpected tug at her heart at the very thought of leaving again.

She sat up and began to loosen with both hands her heavy braid of hair, pausing at the sound of raised voices coming from the kitchen. Da and Ray were at it again.

With a sigh, she went on undoing her braid. By now she had become used to these almost-daily arguments between her father and her brother, but her stomach still tightened when she was forced to listen.

Today was Sunday, so the two had time to square off in the kitchen before church. During the week, what with Da leaving for the mine before daybreak, they didn't see each other until evening, so they usually waited until after supper to pitch their battles.

No matter what time of day they went at it, they were loud, increasingly hostile, and a constant distress to Maggie's mother.

As for Maggie, she hated arguments of any kind, but especially between members of her own family. One thing was certain: Her brother, Ray, was cut from a different bolt than she and her two sisters. Not one of them would have dared to argue with their father when they were Ray's age.

The truth was that not one of them, women grown though they were, would dare to argue with Da *today*. Matthew MacAuley was simply not a man to suffer backtalk from his children, no matter if they were now adults.

Maggie slipped out of bed and padded in her bare feet to the window. It was open, but not the slightest breeze stirred the curtains. The air was already muggy and thick, heavy with the acrid smell of coal dust. Trying to ignore the quarrel in the kitchen, she drew the curtain enough to look out on the narrow side yard, faded to a dull brown from lack of rain and the heat wave that had held steady for nearly three weeks.

A clothesline sagged from the side of the house to a limb on the gnarled old maple tree across the lot. A shovel leaned against the wall of the cellar near two overturned coal buckets, both empty. From here she couldn't see Dredd's Mountain, where the mine dug into the hillside, but she was aware of its hovering presence all the same.

The coal company still owned the town, and the mine still spilled its ash and dust over the entirety of Skingle Creek, painting it a relentless gray. The house next door, which Tom Quigley religiously painted white every five years, wore the same smoky coat as her parents' home and every other house in town.

Her sisters, especially Eva Grace, the older, hated Skingle Creek. Even as children, she and Nell Frances had spent many a night whispering from one bed to the other about the day when they'd be old enough to escape. And they had both followed their dreams. Eva Grace now lived in Lexington with her husband, while Nell Frances, also married and with two little girls, had moved even farther away, to a farm in Indiana. Only Ray, the youngest of the four, remained at home, and no doubt he was already planning his own flight.

Maggie's feelings about Skingle Creek had never been as bitter or as sharply defined as those of her siblings or many of her now-relocated schoolmates. She too disliked the drabness, the oppressive veil of dust and grime that colored the town, where boredom bred mischief or worse trouble among the young people, and where heavy spirits were all too prevalent among the parents.

But Skingle Creek was home, and in a way she couldn't begin to understand, she had never lost her sense of belonging to this place. Her roots seemed to have grown deeper and stronger than those of her sisters, and although she'd eventually gone away, she had never quite shaken free of the town's hold on her. Skingle Creek was a part of her, and no matter how long she stayed away, she never felt a total separation from her hometown.

Where her sisters saw hopelessness and an intolerable monotony of days, Maggie had always sensed the heart of the town and believed in the goodness of its people and in a way of life that, hard as it was, was meant to be valued and preserved.

She jumped as a sudden shout bounced off the walls of the kitchen. Then the door slammed and silence fell.

With a sigh, she turned away from the window and went to make her bed. She found these continuing disputes between her father and brother exhausting. The irony in the situation was that the dissension between them had been generated almost entirely by Ray's resolve to help ease the family's financial burdens—and Da's equally fierce determination to prevent him from doing so.

Though Maggie loved them both and hated this rancor between them, she could see both sides and thought she understood each. She, like her da, did not want to see Ray working in the mines. But at fourteen, her brother was already close to their father in height and on his way to being just as thick-muscled and sturdy. Most likely Ray felt it only right that he take his place in the mine to supplement Da's wages. To their father, however, Ray was still a boy who needed all the education he could get so he wouldn't be dependent on the mine for a living.

According to her mother, ever since the cave-in last year when Da suffered a broken back and a shattered knee, he'd been living with constant pain, which had slowed him down considerably. While Ray admitted that he didn't want to give up his education, it seemed to trouble him even more to see their father, given his condition, carrying the full weight of supporting the family.

From all appearances, the conflict was a draw. An encounter between two equally stubborn males whose intentions were the best—but whose emotions were highly inflammatory.

Maggie had tried talking privately with each of them with no visible results. And when she discussed the situation with her mother, she knew for a certainty that it was wearing her down, too. Last night, after one of the hottest bouts of quarreling so far, she had heard her mother quietly weeping in the bedroom.

Long after silence settled over the house, Maggie searched her thoughts for something—anything—she might do to help ease the problem. Although an idea had been lurking at the edge of her mind for several days now, last night it appeared in full force, giving her quite a jolt.

She had wrestled with her emotions and prayed for guidance most of the night. Small wonder she felt so dull and weary this morning. But she finally knew what she had to do, as unsettling as it might be. There was no way of knowing what it would accomplish, if anything, but in the bright light of morning she realized her decision had been made.

She plopped down on the side of the bed, sitting very still, the knot in her throat tightening even more. She would write to Miss Addams this morning and tender her resignation.

Maggie was aware that she might give up her position at Hull House only to eventually find that it had been in vain, that she had made no difference after all in what admittedly seemed to be an unresolvable conflict between her father and brother. Any sign of change would almost certainly be slow in coming. But she simply could not leave her family. Not now. If for no other reason than to be here for her mother, she had to stay.

Besides, if she were to be brutally honest with herself, the hostility between her father and brother wasn't the only reason she was staying in Skingle Creek.

But that was another concern, one she wasn't ready just yet... perhaps would *never* be ready...to confront.

Chapter One

A Sunday Surprise

Write his merits on your mind;
Morals pure and manners kind;
In his head, as on a hill,
Virtue placed her citadel.

William Drennan

September

Maggie had almost forgotten how a big family dinner could wreck a kitchen. Even though they were a *small* family these days—only four of them—it seemed as though every pot and pan and most of the tableware had been used. She glanced around from the sink, relieved to see they finally had things under control. The table was cleared, the linens shaken, the dishes dried and put away. All that remained was to scour the stove and clean the sink.

She tugged the sleeves of her shirtwaist up a bit higher, though they were already soaked, and swiped a hand over her forehead to blot the perspiration. The day was hot for September; the kitchen so steamy it was nearly intolerable. Most of yesterday had been spent in the same sweltering heat, helping her mother can tomatoes and corn. At the moment all she could think of was a cool bath, the quiet of her bedroom, and the book about Miss Helen Keller that she'd brought with her from Chicago. She was definitely ready for a rest—and some peace and quiet.

"I'll finish up, Mum. You go on out in the front room with Da and Ray. It'll be cooler in there."

Her mother shook her head. Kate MacAuley wasn't one to leave her kitchen until the last spot had been wiped clean. "Ray was going over to Tim's, and your da will be napping by now."

But obviously her father wasn't napping at all, for just then he appeared in the doorway. "Maggie? Jonathan Stuart is here wanting to see you."

Maggie stared at him. "Mr. Stuart? To see me?"

"Aye. Says he has something to discuss with you."

Maggie frowned. What in the world would Mr. Stuart want to talk with her about? She glanced down over herself and groaned. Her apron was stained with gravy. She felt damp to the bone from dish-water and perspiration. And she knew without looking that her hair was a disaster. "I can't let Mr. Stuart see me like this! I'm a fright."

Her mother was already tugging at the strings of Maggie's apron. "Oh, you're fine now! You mustn't make Mr. Stuart wait while you take time to primp. Go on and see what he wants."

"Mum! Look at me!" Maggie threw her apron off, scarcely missing the dirty dishwater.

"If the schoolteacher has come to the door on a Sunday afternoon," her da broke in, "then he has something important on his mind. Come along now."

For no explicable reason, Maggie suddenly felt like a child again. A child whose teacher had come to call and found her playing in the mud.

"You and Da come too."

"I'll be finishing this kitchen first," said her mother. "Then I'll come and say hello. Go *on*, Maggie."

"I've already said my hellos," Da told her. "I'll be helping your mother."

Still Maggie hesitated. She fumbled with her hair, tugged her sleeves down past her elbows, and ran a hand over her skirt, which, of course, was badly wrinkled.

Shooting her parents one more uncertain look, she sighed and left the kitchen.

She stopped short just inside the living room—the "front room" as her parents still called it—trying not to stare at Jonathan Stuart, who was sitting on the edge of her father's overstuffed chair. In the few weeks since she had last seen him, he had grown a mustache. It was a neat and closely trimmed mustache, but a surprise all the same.

He smiled and stood as soon as he saw her. "Maggie. I'm sorry if I've come at a bad time. Your father said it was all right—"

"Oh no. I mean, it's not a bad time at all, Mr. Stuart. Please, sit down."

He hesitated, clearly waiting for her to take a chair. Maggie plopped down on her mother's rocking chair, still feeling absurdly childlike and at a loss. She wouldn't have been surprised to find that her feet weren't touching the floor but swinging above it, as they had when she was six years old.

She couldn't have looked worse, she was sure of it. Damp and disheveled, she probably smelled like fried chicken and gravy. A touch of her hand to her temple confirmed that the steamy heat of the kitchen had caused her hair to frizz about her face.

Mr. Stuart was, of course, his usual natty self. Trust the man to look unwrinkled and totally unfazed by the sultry day. Not a fair hair out of place, as always, with his snowy white shirt starched and crisp, his pale blue tie perfectly knotted.

The man had no wife, so how did he manage to always appear so impeccably groomed and spiffy?

It occurred to Maggie that while her former teacher had always been a well-favored man—half the girls in school had had a terrible crush on him, herself included—he had grown even more handsome with age. What was he now? Thirty-five? No, he'd have to be older than that. She had been out of school for eight years. He must be nearing forty if not more. Not for the first time, she was struck by the reality of how young he'd actually been all those years ago. Because his illness at that time had taken such a dreadful toll on him, she hadn't realized just *how* young.

It occurred to her that she was being rude. He was just sitting there, watching her with an uncertain smile while she indulged in her bad habit of woolgathering.

"If you're busy, Maggie—"

"No, not a bit. I mean, I was. But I'm not now." She was actually *stammering*. "Isn't it—hot?" she managed to say. Well, that would certainly convince him that she was the same clever girl she'd been under his tutelage.

He nodded. "I'm quite ready for fall."

Come to think of it, Mr. Stuart didn't seem to be all that comfortable himself. Perhaps he was embarrassed for her, given her appearance?

"Maggie, let me get right to it. Ray told me you're staying in Skingle Creek, that you're not going back to Chicago."

Maggie nodded. What Ray couldn't have told him, of course, was that she was already regretting the decision she'd made, already missing her friends and the children at Hull House in the worst way.

"I was surprised, to say the least. I thought you were happy working for Miss Addams."

"Oh, I was. I loved it there. But it—well, it just seems that this isn't a good time for me to leave again."

"You're worried about your father."

Maggie glanced around to make sure her father was out of earshot. "I am, yes. But that's not the only reason I decided to stay."

Although he had touched on an awkward subject, Maggie finally relaxed a little. This was Mr. Stuart, after all. The one adult she had trusted as much as her own parents when she was a child. She sensed he hadn't changed. There was the same steady kindness in his dark eyes, the same concern he had always held for his students, the same low gentleness in his tone of voice.

Clearly he was waiting for her to say more.

"It seems to me that my mother needs me here." Again Maggie glanced around before going on. "She didn't ask me to stay. In fact, I'm afraid she felt bad that I insisted. But Da can't do as much as he used to, and that puts more on Mum. She's...in truth, Mr. Stuart, I don't believe she's all that strong anymore. All these years of working so hard every day—perhaps it's catching up with her. She doesn't keep up as well as she used to."

He gave a slow nod. "No doubt you're right, although it's difficult for me to think of your parents as being any different than they've always been. I can't see that your mother has aged a bit over the years. And Matthew—" he smiled. "Well, he's still a fortress of a man."

"I'm afraid the fortress has crumbled a bit," Maggie said. "Da has a lot of pain, Mr. Stuart. Mum says it never quite goes away. And then there's this...terrible tension between him and Ray."

She stopped, unwilling to breach the privacy her family held so sacred, even with Jonathan Stuart, although she knew nothing she said would ever be repeated outside of this room.

But again he nodded, as if he already knew at least a little about the situation. "Ray thinks he needs to quit school and go to work in the mines."

"He told you?"

"No—your father did."

Maggie shouldn't have been surprised. She knew her da and Mr. Stuart had become good friends over the years. Still, it wasn't like Matthew MacAuley to confide in anyone except Maggie's mother... and sometimes not even her.

"Then you probably know that Da hates the very thought of Ray going into the mines. And so do I. Ray's bright—*very* bright—and he should get as much education as possible. Poor Mum! She's caught in the middle. She wants the best for Ray, but she worries herself sick over Da having to work so hard, given the way his back and leg plague him."

Maggie felt a drop of perspiration trickle down the side of her face, and she reached to dab it. "I can't leave. I'd not draw an easy breath if I did. So I'll be staying. At least for now."

He studied her for a moment. "So—it wouldn't do for me to try to convince you that you deserve to live your own life? You're what now, Maggie? Twenty-two, twenty-three?"

"Twenty-four. And no, I don't suppose even you could change my mind, Mr. Stuart, although I value your opinion as I always have. I've already written to Miss Addams to tell her I'm not coming back."

He searched her face for another moment, and then got to his feet and went to stand with his back to the window, still watching her. "Well then, that's that. I wanted to make sure your decision was final before I offered you a job."

Maggie stared at him. "A job?"

"A teaching position."

"You mean…at the school?"

The corner of his mouth twitched. "I should think so."

"But I thought you already had a second teacher."

His expression sobered somewhat. "Carolyn Ross, you mean. Here's the situation. Mrs. Ross originally hired on as school secretary, expecting to work only half-days. When she saw that I was getting farther and farther behind, what with trying to maintain the position as principal and being the only teacher, she agreed to work full-time, taking the youngest students in the morning and tending to her secretarial duties in the afternoon. We've reached the point, however, where we actually need another teacher so Carolyn—Mrs. Ross—can function as a full-time secretary."

Maggie hoped her excitement wasn't too obvious, but this was more than she had hoped for. A teaching position—and one with Jonathan Stuart at that! "The town has grown that much?" she asked, forcing a note of calm into her voice.

He nodded. "It may not look like it, but it has. I imagine the student enrollment is half again what it was when you were in elementary. There are a number of things I'd like to implement both as principal and teacher, but I can't find time enough for everything. I can't tell you how pleased I was when the board recently authorized the hiring of another teacher."

He stopped, lifted his head a little, and looked directly at her. "I'm hoping you might consider the position, Maggie. No doubt the money wouldn't be what you're used to, but I expect it would pay better than most anything else you'll find in Skingle Creek—if you're planning to work, that is."

"Of course I need to work," Maggie said. "In fact, I've already been going about from place to place, looking for something. But so far the only offer I've had was from Mr. Ferguson at the company store. And that would be only a few hours a week."

"Well, naturally, I don't need your answer today," Mr. Stuart said, "but I hope you'll give it serious consideration."

Maggie knew she probably should at least *appear* to be more professional, more mature. But then, this was Mr. Stuart, and if he remembered much about her at all, he already knew that a cool head had never been one of her strengths.

"Oh, I don't have to consider it, Mr. Stuart. I'll take the job."

It gratified her no end to see his expression brighten. "Well, that's wonderful! But are you quite sure you don't want to think about it...perhaps talk with your parents?"

Maggie shook her head. "No. In truth, I've been praying for days for a job—anything at all that would allow me to earn my keep and help my parents so Ray can stay out of the mines. This is far better than anything I hoped for. I can't tell you how much I appreciate your thinking of me."

"You're the *first* person I thought of, Maggie. How often does a town the size of Skingle Creek manage to come across a teacher with your qualifications?" He paused. "When do you think you might start?"

"As soon as you want me. Tomorrow's Monday. What about tomorrow?"

He laughed. "You always were decisive. I'd love for you to start tomorrow. But are you sure you don't need more time?"

"Wouldn't it be good to start as soon as possible, before things get too far along?" Maggie asked. "School's been in session, what—only a week?"

"Exactly a week. And if you're serious about starting tomorrow, I couldn't be happier. It might be good if you could come early, perhaps an hour or so before class takes up, so I can help you get settled. Would that be possible?"

By this point, Maggie could scarcely control her excitement. "Mr. Stuart, I'm so eager to get back to teaching again I'll be there before the sun comes up if you want! I've been missing my children at Hull House terribly. I can't wait to have a class again."

His gaze went over her face, and Maggie fervently wished she could have been freshly groomed—and more composed. And she probably should have at least *pretended* to be less eager.

But when his smile came, she didn't regret that she'd allowed her feelings to show. It was the same slow, fond smile that had always made her feel special.

Not that his smile had ever been for her alone. In truth, Jonathan Stuart had a way about him that could make even the most timid and retiring child feel favored and important. *All* his students believed they were special to him. No doubt they still did. As his student, Maggie had thought Jonathan Stuart a great man, a man with whom she would have trusted her life. And now, more than a decade later, the depth of kindness reflected in his eyes, the strength engraved upon his good, lean face, told her the years hadn't changed him.

The thought of working each day under the supervision of this man, a man who had had such an incredible impact on her life, who had played such a significant part in her becoming a teacher to begin with, made her catch her breath.

If her sisters had been here, no doubt they would have teased her about being "sweet" on the teacher. Well, perhaps she did still have a bit of a crush on Jonathan Stuart. He had once been her hero, after all, when she'd been an impressionable—and wounded—child. And he'd just made himself a hero in her eyes again by offering her a job that would certainly appear to be an answer to her prayers.

Jonathan Stuart was entirely deserving of her admiration. Even so, she would make quite sure he never caught her acting like a smitten schoolgirl. She would be professionalism itself. She would be such a good teacher—an *outstanding* teacher—that he would soon realize his faith in her had in no way been misplaced. Indeed, she intended to waste no time in proving herself worthy of *his* admiration.

Chapter Two

Autumn Afternoon

Dream not of noble service elsewhere wrought;
The simple duty that awaits thy hand
Is God's voice uttering a divine command,
Life's common deeds build all that saints have thought.

Minot F. Savage

Jonathan Stuart knew this scene by heart. Every day for two weeks now he had stood at the schoolhouse window watching Maggie and the younger students at their afternoon recess. He never tired of the picture they made. Maggie, tall, slender, and as graceful as a young willow, could move as quickly as any one of her young charges. At the moment they had her surrounded under the old hickory tree, no doubt pestering her for yet another race across the school yard.

She shook her head, laughing as she gathered little Iris Gundy into her arms and swung her around. Jonathan smiled with her as he watched. Maggie's hair had escaped the clasp that usually secured it at her neck, and the late September sun glanced upon it, setting it ablaze in a flash of copper fire.

Jonathan lost his smile, quickly turning his attention across the road where the early autumn sun had glazed the hills a brilliant crimson and gold. Despite the season's beauty, something about this time of year, when the shadows grew longer and the days began to grow shorter, never failed to evoke an aching sense of melancholy in him. Old, all-but-forgotten dreams and nameless longings that lay buried throughout the other seasons parted the veils of memory and nagged at him again.

The sound of the children's laughter—and Maggie's—drifted through the partly open window, and he made an effort to shake off the encroaching gloom to his spirit. The older students had congregated together near the pump, claiming their last drinks of cold water while they could. He should ring the bell soon to call them back inside, but he was reluctant to let go of the scene before him.

"Jonathan? Do you have a moment for a question?"

Jonathan wheeled around to find Carolyn Ross standing just inside the room, watching him. He felt an unreasonable flush of embarrassment, as if he'd been caught eavesdropping.

"A question? Of course." He motioned that she should come in, then went to his desk. Her eyes never left his face as she walked the rest of the way into the room. He liked Carolyn, he really did, but at times she made him inexplicably uncomfortable.

She had a way of scrutinizing him as if she were trying to see inside him, past a shuttered window. She was an attractive woman. Well, more than attractive if he were to be altogether honest. In her mid-thirties, she had the kind of creamy smooth skin that would age slowly if at all, and eyes so dark they seldom betrayed any hint of expression. Graced with a face and figure that a man couldn't help but notice, she also possessed keen intelligence and a generous sense of humor. Moreover, she was efficient to a fault, a stickler for detail, and somehow made even the largest tasks seem ridiculously easy to tame. Jonathan sometimes wondered if she shouldn't be principal instead of him.

Carolyn Ross and her husband had moved to Skingle Creek about five years ago, when they bought the Dunbar family's mill and surrounding property. Unfortunately David Ross died the same year. After selling the mill back to Milton Dunbar, Carolyn moved into town.

At the time, Jonathan wondered why she'd stayed on. She had no family in the immediate vicinity, no children in school, no other ties to the community. He couldn't help but admire the woman. Certainly he enjoyed working with her, even though at times he felt a prickle of annoyance at the way she seemed inclined to...*hover* over him. As if perhaps he couldn't quite manage things on his own. She noticed the slightest lapse on his part: such as not wearing a muffler on a cold day or not always using his eyeglasses for close work. Sometimes she would chide him for the careless quality of his lunches, and for the next two or three days she might bring in an extra apple or a pastry and put it on his desk.

In truth, her attentions confused him. On occasion she made him feel as young and awkward as one of his adolescent students; other times he felt so old and absentminded he needed monitoring. His friend and pastor, Ben Wallace, had unknowingly added to Jonathan's confusion by observing that "Mrs. Ross seems to have taken quite a shine to you."

Jonathan had been too taken aback to manage more than a startled stare.

"Oh for goodness sake, Jonathan! You've been a bachelor so long you don't even notice when a beautiful woman is warming up to you? You need to take off the blinders, my friend," Ben had commented.

"Maggie's very good with the children, isn't she?"

Carolyn's voice jarred him back to his surroundings. Given the direction of his thoughts, he couldn't quite bring himself to look her in the eye. "Maggie...oh yes, she's doing a fine job."

"I confess I wondered at first if she'd be suitable," Carolyn went on, "young as she is. But she's working out well."

Jonathan nodded. "I couldn't be more pleased."

"Didn't you tell me she was your student years ago?"

"She was, yes. In fact, all of the MacAuley children have been my students. Maggie's two older sisters and her brother, Ray, of course."

The tiniest frown crossed her features. "Can we hope that his older sister's influence might have a positive influence on Ray? Perhaps along the lines of self-discipline and tidiness?"

Now Jonathan frowned. "Ray's not a discipline problem."

Carolyn lifted her eyebrows.

"Oh, he's been in a few scrapes, I know. That business with the pig on the first day—but he wasn't alone in that, you know. Besides, the boy is fourteen, after all. He's really not as much of a troublemaker as some of the others his age. As for his appearance—" Here Jonathan sighed. "He's simply at that clumsy age, I expect. Ray's a big boy. I've watched him over the years, and I suspect he's not quite comfortable in his own body yet. He's grown quickly, and he's…ungainly because of his size. At heart, he's a good boy. And he comes from good people."

Carolyn smiled. "Jonathan, I do hope these children realize how fortunate they are to have a teacher like you. Although I wonder if your kind heart isn't somewhat *too* soft toward them at times."

Jonathan shrugged off her compliment. Or *was* it a compliment?

Just then the sound of stamping and giggling erupted in the hallway. Maggie bringing in her charges, although he hadn't rung the bell yet. An early return from recess usually meant she had one or more who had become too rowdy to contain outside.

She stopped just long enough to look in. Her face was flushed, her hair windblown. "Sorry for the ruckus, Mr. Stuart," she said with a sheepish smile. "They're wild today for some reason—"

She stopped at the sight of Carolyn Ross. "Oh I'm sorry. I didn't mean to interrupt."

"It's all right, Maggie," Jonathan assured her. "In fact, we were just talking about what a good job you're doing."

Maggie's eyes lighted on Carolyn, and then went back to Jonathan. "Not so good today, I'm afraid. I don't know if it's the nice weather or just mischief working on them, but they've been a handful, let me tell you." She paused. "Well, I'd better stay close on their tails."

And off she went. Jonathan couldn't stop a smile as she went flying out the door and down the hall.

"Was she a good student?"

Jonathan removed his eyeglasses. "Maggie? Probably the brightest I've ever had."

"Then why in the world didn't she stay in Chicago and make something of herself?"

Why did he find Carolyn's remark so annoying? It was probably a reasonable enough question.

Before he could answer, she gave a quick, dismissing motion of her hand. "I didn't mean that the way it sounded. Her job here is just as important as whatever she was doing in Chicago. I'm simply surprised that such an obviously intelligent young woman would be content to settle in a small town like ours."

"I'm sure she has her reasons," Jonathan said, having no intention of divulging anything to do with Maggie's family problems. It occurred to him that Carolyn's question about Maggie could just as well be asked of her.

Carolyn looked at him. "Well, in any event, it's our good fortune that she *did* decide to stay. I'm especially thankful she's here. It's allowed me to get back to my own job—for which, if I do say so myself, I'm far more suited than that of being a teacher."

"You do anything you attempt very well, Carolyn," Jonathan replied almost automatically. "You did a good job with the younger students, and your willingness to work with them until we hired Maggie certainly made my life a great deal easier." He paused. "You said you had a question?"

She studied him for a moment and then glanced at the book she'd been holding in her hand. "I noticed the little Lazlo boy has been absent for four straight days this week. Maggie said the older sister told her that Huey has a cold. Four days is somewhat excessive for a cold, isn't it?"

Unease stirred in Jonathan. He lifted a hand and kneaded his temple. "I'd best stop by and check on him."

"Shouldn't Maggie do that? Huey is her student."

Jonathan continued to rub his temple. "No. She wouldn't know the Lazlos. They moved here only last year. I'll go myself."

Carolyn closed the ledger, watching him. "Is there a problem there?"

"I hope not."

In spite of his reply, Jonathan had begun to wonder about the Lazlo family. By the end of the last school term, both Huey and his sister, Selma, had missed too many days of school. He'd called at the house twice, but both times the mother—a gaunt woman with flat, impassive features—had informed him that the children were ill, practically closing the door in his face.

The school term was nearly over by then, so he let the matter go for the time being. But he'd promised himself that if the problem started up again this year, he would make it his business to find out what was going on.

It seemed he would be required to do just that.

Mrs. Ross didn't like her very much. Maggie had reached that conclusion not long after she hired on at the school, and nothing had changed her mind in the interim.

While her small charges rested their heads on their desks for ten minutes of quiet time, Maggie went about her afternoon routine of watering the sweet potato plant in the window, arranging homework papers to pass out, and straightening the students' supply shelves. As she worked, her mind played over the way the school secretary invariably made her feel awkward and out of place.

Carolyn Ross had made enough remarks about Maggie's youth to convince her that the woman found her wanting in both experience and ability. It would be tempting to write off Mrs. Ross's remarks as the sarcastic barbs of an older woman who perhaps resented a younger, seemingly less-qualified coworker for gaining an undeserved advantage. But Carolyn wasn't all that old, and Maggie was *not* unqualified for her job.

Mr. Stuart wouldn't have offered her the position in the first place if he hadn't believed her capable. He simply wasn't the kind of man to hire someone, former student or not, unless he genuinely thought she was adequate. And she *was*. She was a good teacher, and she knew it.

So then, just what was Mrs. Ross's problem? Oh, the woman was civil to her, at least most of the time. *Always* when Mr. Stuart was around. She was never actually rude. To the contrary, if Maggie were to single out any specific example of the school secretary's dislike, she would find it difficult to do so. It wasn't so much what the woman said as the *way* she said it and the way she sometimes looked at Maggie—as if she were a troublesome child who didn't quite measure up, an annoyance imposed upon her good nature to be tolerated in spite of her better judgment.

Maggie plunked a book down on her desk with a little too much force, and a couple of small heads came up. She put her finger to her lips to caution silence, but the rest period was almost over so she sat down and began to mark the remaining few papers that were going home with the children today.

The absence of work from Huey Lazlo turned her thoughts away from Carolyn to the solemn-faced little boy with the evasive eyes. She'd neglected to mention Huey's extended absence to Mr. Stuart, and she needed to remedy that. He tended to be quite strict about the school's attendance policy. If a child were out more than three days with no explanation, either from the family or another student, it was considered excessive and called for a home visit.

Huey had been absent all week. Uncertain as to whether she should call on the family or if Mr. Stuart would prefer to make the contact himself, she decided to talk with him yet today after dismissal. Hopefully without Mrs. Ross in attendance.

Chapter Three

A Buggy Ride with Mr. Stuart

Is your place a small place?
Tend it with care—
He set you there.
Whate'er your place, it is
Not yours alone, but His
Who set you there.

John Oxenham

∼

Much to Maggie's surprise, Jonathan Stuart asked her to go along on his visit to the Lazlo family the following Sunday.

The only chance of catching a miner at home was either late in the evening or on Sunday, so that afternoon the two of them set off in Mr. Stuart's buggy to "the Hill," as most of the townspeople referred to Dredd's Mountain.

The day was chilly but bright and crisp, with the feeling of an early fall in the air. The maple leaves were turning yellow, and goldenrod hugged the fence posts. At this time of year, the autumn foliage glazed the encompassing mountains with some of the most breathtaking colors one could ever hope to see. Although the air was always overlaid with the smell of coal dust, the more pleasing aroma of wood smoke also filtered through the light wind that had blown up.

This part of the state, which some called the *Cumberland,* was coal-mining country. Rugged and wild, it ran along a plateau made up of ridges and valleys and rivers, all of which were a part of the Appalachians. Skingle Creek was lazily quiet, Sunday afternoon being the only day of the week when no whistles blew or train cars rattled from the mine, the one day when the miners managed a few hours of extra rest and free time to spend with their families. Maggie and Jonathan passed one or two young couples out walking along the way, and every now and then a pack of children would chase each other into the road and run alongside the buggy. But for the most part, the town was hushed.

Maggie's family had gone to visit Da's niece, Martha Taggart, and her family at their farm south of town. Unless things had changed, Da would be in one of his dark moods when they returned. A visit to the Taggarts usually left him uncommonly somber and quiet. It wasn't that he begrudged his niece and her family what they had. Maggie's mother said it was just that the time they spent at the Taggarts always reminded Da of his dream that he would one day have a farm of his own—a dream that seemed more unlikely with each passing year.

Her father had longed for his own land for as long as Maggie could remember. It was a part of being Irish, he said, the desire for one's own place. To be a landowner meant never having to face eviction from someone else's property, never having to fear the specter of homelessness. It represented freedom to an Irishman in a way that nothing else possibly could.

Maggie hadn't heard him mention his old dream since...well, she couldn't remember when. Had he finally given up hope then? It seemed her folks had never managed to get ahead. For as long as she could remember, they had lived mostly from hand to mouth, never managing to save much. The company paid the miners what they pleased, and any man foolish enough to speak up against the paltry wages was likely to find himself with *no* wages soon after. Even when a miner managed to eke out a small amount and put it by, something always seemed to happen to make it disappear.

She sneaked a glance at Mr. Stuart. Rumor had always had it that the schoolteacher came from a wealthy family. Indeed, it didn't seem likely that a small-town teacher's salary would stretch far enough to pay for the nice house he owned or the extras he sometimes bestowed upon the school and his students.

On the other hand, the stories about his family's wealth might be just that: rumor. He wasn't a man to talk about himself, so his life before Skingle Creek remained pretty much a mystery. Probably the only person in town who might know something of Mr. Stuart's background was Pastor Wallace, for the two men had been the closest of friends for years.

Mr. Stuart and Maggie were nearing the edge of town now, and the horse readied itself for the climb up the Hill. A rough road had finally been cut through to make the houses perched on the side of the hillside more accessible. Years before, when Maggie had made her frequent visits to her best friend, Summer Rankin, she'd had to climb a rocky footpath strewn with brambles and weeds.

Summer. To this day Maggie couldn't think of her childhood friend without her heart turning. Summer had been only nine years old when she died, and Maggie twelve. But the age difference had never interfered with their friendship. In many ways, they had been as close as sisters—so close that for a long time after Summer's death, Maggie had felt as if a part of her had died too.

Again she looked over at Mr. Stuart, remembering how he'd tried to help her during that awful time, how kind he had been to her, how patient and understanding. And now here she was, grown-up and a teacher herself, riding along with the man who had been *her* teacher, on their way to the home of a student. *Her* student.

A buggy ride like today's was an event for Maggie. Her family had never owned such a convenience. They either walked or made use of the battered old farm wagon Da had bought years ago from Jeff Taggart. No doubt Maggie would have enjoyed it more if she wasn't finding it so difficult to make conversation. Of course, Mr. Stuart being the quiet-natured man that he was, probably didn't mind the silence. Still, Maggie felt compelled to at least be sociable.

"Fall has always been my favorite season," she offered, pulling at a strand of hair beside her ear. "It's like the town gets all dressed up this one time of year. Usually it's so dreary, what with the coal dust and all."

Mr. Stuart glanced over at her and smiled. "This is my favorite season too. But do you really find the town all that drab the rest of the year?"

"Don't you? It's always so gray. Even the snow looks dirty in the winter."

He was silent for a moment. "Has it been difficult for you staying here instead of going back to Chicago? I remember how eager you used to be to get away from Skingle Creek."

Maggie mulled his question over in her mind. "It hasn't been as hard as I thought it would be. Being able to teach is what's most important to me. I'd miss teaching something fierce. I suppose I *was* anxious to leave for a time, but once I left, I never stopped missing my folks."

She stopped and then admitted, "I missed Skingle Creek too. Living in the city wasn't quite everything I'd thought it would be."

Mr. Stuart nodded. "I expect one reason I've been so content here is that even though I grew up in the city, I never really liked living there. It didn't take me long to realize I was better suited for small-town life."

Still fiddling with her hair, Maggie turned to him. "May I ask you something?"

"You never used to need permission to ask me a question," he commented with a wry smile.

Maggie rolled her eyes at that. "I didn't, did I? Was I a terrible nuisance to you?"

"You were never a nuisance, Maggie. You were quick-witted and curious. What's more, you were the best student I ever had."

"Mr. Stuart! I never was!"

"Indeed you were," he said, keeping his eyes on the road. "I had all I could do to keep you interested much of the time. You were a challenge to teach—but a delightful one."

He seemed to be completely serious. How much it meant to hear praise from this man who had been a hero to her for most of her growing-up years! For the life of her, Maggie could think of no reply.

"You were going to ask me something?"

"Oh…yes. I just…I've always wondered what brought you here to Skingle Creek."

He said nothing. Had she offended him? Perhaps his reasons were private, too personal to air.

"I'm sorry," she said quickly. "It's none of my business—"

He shook his head. "No. No, it's not that. But it's somewhat difficult to explain."

"Oh, that's all right, Mr. Stuart. I always did ask too many questions, I know. It's just that with your education—and you being such an exceptional teacher, truly you are—you must have had all kinds of opportunities in better locations than this."

"Hardly," he said, his tone dry, although he was smiling. "There were…circumstances. Poor health—but you already know about that. A broken engagement. And I suppose I was getting restless, feeling the need for a change. But it was more than that. The truth is that I've always believed God called me here."

He looked over at her, as if wondering whether he should say more. He hesitated another moment, then went on. "When I was still teaching at the university, a missionary came to speak to the students and faculty. Not a foreign missionary—his field was the mountains of Appalachia. He spoke about the enormous need in most of the rural regions for doctors and teachers. He had a list with him, and Skingle Creek was one of the districts in need."

The buggy swayed a little on the rough road, but the horse maintained its footing. "Something…took hold of me in the auditorium that day and wouldn't let go," he continued. "I fought my feelings for two months before I finally gave in. But I think I already knew the matter was settled. Over the years, I've come to realize that God doesn't always speak in specifics, but He has a way of impressing His will upon us until we respond.

"Even after I came here and talked with the school board, however, I was reluctant to take the position. I wasn't exactly…captivated by the appearance of the town."

"I can certainly understand that," Maggie said.

"Nevertheless, I accepted the job. Almost in spite of myself. The truth is that I simply couldn't refuse it." He expelled a long breath, adding, "I knew it was where I was meant to be."

Although Maggie had heard every word he said, her mind locked on the fact that there had been a broken engagement. *Did that mean he'd been jilted? Surely he had been the one to break it off?* She couldn't imagine any woman being so foolish as to reject a man like Jonathan Stuart. Whatever had happened, it might answer another part of the mystery as to what had brought Mr. Stuart to Skingle Creek. There had always been much speculation about why he'd remained single all these years. Now she could only wonder if it was because he had never recovered from the pain of a lost love.

Maggie flinched as her old flair for melodrama reared its head. Still, it seemed such a terrible waste, that a man who loved children as much as Mr. Stuart so obviously did would spend his life caring for everyone else's children but his own.

"I'm so sorry, Mr. Stuart," she said quietly.

"Sorry?"

"About…what happened. Your engagement—"

He smiled and shook his head. "That was a long time ago, Maggie. I was just a boy. It was all for the best. And what about you?" he asked, still smiling. "I find it difficult to imagine that you didn't leave behind at least a few broken hearts in Chicago."

Maggie quickly glanced away. There were no broken hearts in her wake. In fact, she hadn't even been kissed since she'd said goodbye to Kenny Tallman just before they went their separate ways to different colleges. But she wasn't about to tell Mr. Stuart that.

"No broken hearts for me," she said, her tone light. "Unless you want to count a pair of ornery, freckle-faced twins who imagined they had a terrible crush on me. Bernie and Brian Callaghan. Seven years old, and holy terrors they were. They used to brawl in front of the entire class over which one would pound the erasers for me."

"Ah. I always knew you'd grow up to be a heartbreaker one day."

She glanced over to find him watching her with a teasing glint in his eye.

She grinned back. "Miss Addams gave us little time for lollygagging with the fellas. Bernie and Brian were all I could handle."

They rode along in silence until he brought the buggy to a halt in front of an unpainted shack. Grayed from the elements, its front steps sagging, and a part of its tin roof pulled away from the sheathing boards, it had the grim look of abandonment.

There were no curtains at the windows, only brown paper replacing a missing pane in front. Tall weeds and grass had grown wild, but there were no flowers to provide even a touch of color. On a clothesline at the side of the house hung a pair of men's overalls and a few pieces of girls' clothing. Nothing pointed to even the slightest effort to make the place a home.

Maggie's breath caught in her throat at the sight of the place.

"Yes, it's bad, isn't it?" said Jonathan Stuart.

It was worse than bad. It was appalling. The thought of wee Huey and his sister living in such a forlorn-looking hovel wrenched Maggie's heart. Most of the houses in Skingle Creek, her own home included, were company houses. Erected quickly and as cheaply as possible, they were entirely without adornment. But many of the families who lived in those houses did what they could to make them more attractive inside and out. They painted the exteriors every few years, planted flower and vegetable gardens, tended their yards, and kept things neat and presentable. A few, like Maggie's father, obtained permission to add improvements: a porch, a storage shed for tools, shrubbery, stone pathways, and other niceties.

The Lazlo place looked as if it had not been inhabited for years. And yet a family lived here. A family with two young children. Huey Lazlo, Maggie's student, was a thin little boy with enormous, sorrowful eyes partly concealed by a shock of dark, untidy hair. The boy's clothing, and that of his older sister, always appeared heavily patched and none too clean. Huey's uncertain smile and timid manner had endeared him to Maggie. It was an unpleasant shock, seeing the crude conditions in which he lived. And yet, to be objective, she had to remember that most of her students lived with little more than the basics required to sustain life. There were no wealthy mining families in Skingle Creek. For the most part, life was hard for every child in town.

She could only hope the inside of the Lazlo home would be a marked improvement over its exterior.

Chapter Four

Prayer Is No Small Thing

But the child's sob in the silence curses deeper
Than the strong man in his wrath.

Elizabeth Barrett Browning

⌒

At first Jonathan thought it was going to be the same scenario as before, that the Lazlo woman would block him from entering. She stood staring, her flat, broad features impassive, her small eyes devoid of any expression except perhaps a glint of confusion.

Uneasiness crept over him. Perhaps the woman simply didn't know what to make of two teachers showing up on her doorstep on a Sunday afternoon, but there was something more than a little troubling about that empty stare, the opaque eyes.

Jonathan was puzzling over what tack to take when a man came up behind her, edging her out of the way.

The children's father, Jonathan assumed. "Mr. Lazlo?"

He was a big, dark-haired, black-bearded hulk of a man with thick shoulders, a paunch, and a wide, angry scar that lined his forehead and wrapped around his right eye. The look he settled on Maggie and Jonathan was less than friendly, but at least he seemed to be more alert than the woman.

"You're the teacher?"

"Jonathan Stuart. I'm Selma's teacher and the school principal." He extended his hand, but the man ignored it. Jonathan hesitated, then nodded in Maggie's direction. "And this is Miss MacAuley, Huey's teacher. Would it be all right if we came in and talked with you for a few minutes?"

The man took his time replying. Without looking directly at Jonathan, he stepped back and finally, with a short nod indicated they could enter. The woman's expression never changed.

Inside, Jonathan looked around for the children but saw no sign of them. What he *did* see was a sight he had encountered before on the Hill. This was worse than some, but not quite so bad as others. Standing there, breathing in the close, fetid air of rooms shut up too long with no ventilation—and heavy with the odor of cheap cigar smoke—he made an effort to squelch a threat of dizziness.

There were almost no furnishings in the room—only a stained, overstuffed chair with the batting spilling out from a torn seat; two beds with iron bedsteads and thin, sagging mattresses, carelessly covered over by quilts that appeared none too clean; and a faded picture of a field with a hunter and a dog on the wall next to the door. The bare, plank floor had gaps as wide as a man's foot in some places, and its corners were cluttered with items of clothing, papers, and other odds and ends.

Out of the corner of his eye he caught a glimpse of the woman watching Maggie, her eyes no longer quite so dull, though still showing only a minimum of interest in the younger woman. He saw that the man's gaze had also turned to Maggie, but his was an entirely different expression, one that made Jonathan decidedly uncomfortable.

Instinctively he moved closer to Maggie. She surprised him by taking his arm, and he realized then that she also was aware of the man's dark, clinging stare. Lazlo's gaze followed Maggie's movement before darting back to Jonathan.

"If you want to sit, th' only place is th' bed," said Lazlo. His voice was low and rough, as hard as a blow, with a hint of an accent Jonathan didn't recognize.

"We'll stand, thank you," Jonathan replied quickly. The idea of sitting on one of those two dingy looking beds, much less allowing one to touch Maggie, made him cringe.

The man shrugged and rested his hands on his paunch, both thumbs braced behind his suspenders.

He was a disreputable-looking sort. That thicket of a beard and untamed hair gave him a wild look. But the ashen skin tone that made him look unwell and the air of defeat and failure that hovered round him negated any real sense of threat. In that instant he saw that Lazlo's hands were scarred far worse than the slash on his face. Jonathan couldn't be certain, but he thought they might be burn scars.

The man's clothes were clean, which was more than could be said about his wife. Her long, black skirt was torn and soiled with what might have been grease, her bodice stained in several places. A few tangled strands of hair had escaped the knot at the back of her neck and hung limply around her face.

"Are the children at home?" Jonathan asked abruptly, remembering why he had come.

The man's eyes met the woman's for a fraction of a second before he shook his head. "Out somewhere," he said shortly.

Jonathan looked around. The house was eerily silent, the only sound that of a dog barking somewhere outside. Something made him wonder if Lazlo was telling the truth about the children being gone.

Maggie had dropped her hand away from his arm, but stayed close as she spoke. "I've been concerned about Huey. He was absent four days last week. Has he been ill?"

She directed her question to the mother, but it was Lazlo who replied, his gaze again roving over her in a way that made Jonathan want to get her out of the house as quickly as possible. "Th' boy was sick."

Maggie hesitated and then said, "But...he's well enough to be outside?"

"He's better now. Be back to school next week."

Jonathan attempted to engage the woman in their conversation. "Mrs. Lazlo, you'll recall that last term both children missed a great deal of school. I hope that's not going to be the case this year."

The woman's eyes were like dark caves, her expression unreadable as she looked at her husband, who again answered in her stead.

"If they sick, they stay at home. When they well, they go to school."

Jonathan studied the big man standing across from him. Lazlo's expression wasn't exactly belligerent, but close to it. "May I ask where you're from, Mr. Lazlo?"

Lazlo's eyes narrowed slightly. "Ashland first. Then here."

"You're from Europe originally?" Jonathan prompted.

"We come from Ukraine. Two years ago, maybe more."

That might account for the man's defensiveness. It wasn't unusual for some of the immigrants who worked in the mines to be guarded, even suspicious. A new country could be daunting, and they weren't always treated the best, after all.

Jonathan sensed it was time to go. It was clear they would learn nothing more about the children today and for Huey and Selma's sake he didn't want to alienate their parents by seeming to pry.

"Well, we'll leave you to the rest of your afternoon," he said. "We'll look forward to seeing Huey back in school tomorrow." He paused, then added, "You have fine children. We're glad to have them with us."

Lazlo was paying no attention to him whatsoever, but instead was watching Maggie with that same dark, furtive expression that Jonathan found unnerving if not downright offensive. He clasped Maggie's elbow and moved her toward the door.

Outside he looked around but saw no sign of Huey or Selma.

Neither he nor Maggie spoke until they pulled away and started down the Hill.

"Do you think the children were really outside?" Maggie said.

Jonathan looked over at her. "I don't quite know what to think. The place is small enough that it would be difficult to keep them hidden for any length of time. There looked to be only two rooms. On the other hand, there seemed to be no sign of them outside either."

"We weren't there all that long. Only a few minutes."

"You think they were in the house?"

She frowned. "I don't know." She pulled in a long breath as if to steady herself. "What a terrible place. The whole time we were there I felt something wasn't...right. I *did* think the man might be lying. And that woman—"

She shuddered visibly.

"I know. I wonder—" Jonathan stopped, uncertain as to whether he should voice what he was thinking.

"What?"

"It sounds unkind—and I could be wrong—but I wouldn't be at all surprised if the mother isn't...slow."

Maggie began to rub her arms, as if a chill had seized her. "This Mrs. Lazlo—she reminds me of another woman," she said. "There was a family who used to live on the outskirts of town. I remember going with Mum once to take a basket of food to them. The man had been injured in the mine, and they had all these children—"

"The Teagues."

"Yes! You remember them, too."

"I called on them a few times, trying to convince them to send the children to school. But they never did."

As soon as Jonathan thought of Elsie Teague he understood why Maggie had mentioned her.

"You might be right about Mrs. Lazlo," he said. "There's a similarity there to Elsie Teague."

"Mum said Mrs. Teague was feeble-minded," Maggie said, watching him.

A sour taste rose to Jonathan's mouth. The thought of just how dismal Selma and Huey Lazlo's living conditions might actually be made his stomach knot. "I don't know if that's what it is or not, but there's something wrong there, no doubt about it."

"Oh." Her soft word sounded more like a sob. "Those poor children. If their mother really isn't right and their father—"

She broke off.

"Maggie?"

She turned toward him.

"I don't know why you would have reason, but please don't ever go up there alone. In fact, you needn't go at all. If the need arises again for a call, I'll take care of it."

She frowned. "But that's my responsibility. I'm Huey's teacher."

"And I'm *Selma's* teacher and the school principal, so both children are my responsibility. I mean it, Maggie. I don't want you going up there alone." A heavy knot of dread settled in his chest at the very thought.

He felt her studying him, but finally she agreed. "All right," she said, her tone reluctant but resigned.

They rode the rest of the way in silence. As they finally pulled up in front of the MacAuley's house, Jonathan wondered what Maggie was thinking. She had to have seen the way Lazlo had looked at her. She was young, yes, but surely she wasn't so naive that she hadn't noticed the man's insolence.

She avoided his eyes as he helped her out of the buggy.

Jonathan stood watching her for a moment. "Maggie?"

Finally she looked at him.

"Huey and Selma will be all right."

He regretted the words the instant they left his tongue. Maggie MacAuley had never been one to be soothed by empty words, even as a child. Why would he make the mistake of being glib with her now?

She searched his gaze, and Jonathan found himself unnerved by the depth of her intensity.

"No, Mr. Stuart," she finally said, her tone hard, even bitter. "Most likely they *won't* be all right. We both know that. It's doubtful that Huey and Selma will ever have a chance to be all right."

When she would have moved past him, Jonathan stopped her with a hand on her arm. "Perhaps *we're* their chance."

She frowned.

"Maggie, do you pray for your students?"

"Of course I do. But there have always been some—not just here in Skingle Creek, but in Chicago as well—that I don't know *how* to pray for. For some children life seems so hopeless that you begin to believe nothing you can do will ever make a difference."

Jonathan knew all too well what she meant. He had faced that seemingly impenetrable wall of hopelessness too many times himself to be anything less than completely honest with her.

"Maggie, I've been a teacher now for a very long time, and I've come up against some altogether desperate situations. Situations that tested my faith more times than I can count. It's not likely to be any different for you. But I know you well enough to know that you became a teacher because you love children and you want to make a difference in their lives. Am I right?"

She nodded, her expression puzzled.

"Then believe me when I tell you that the longer you work with children, the more faith will be required of you. You're going to encounter situations that will force you to realize that sometimes praying for your children is the only thing you *can* do."

Again he paused, struggling to find the right words. "You'll find that most times praying for them will be the *most important* thing you can do. There's nothing small about prayer. The more you cover your students with it every day, the more you'll eventually help to deliver them—and yourself—from the heartbreak of hopelessness."

Her gaze, troubled and uncertain, again searched his, and Jonathan wished he could somehow imbue her with the kind of strength he knew she was going to need to carry her through the years ahead.

She had always been so quick to hurt for others, so determined to staunch their wounds and right the wrongs all around her. Even when she was a child herself, she had mothered the younger children, defended those weaker or less fortunate, often growing frustrated and even angry when her fierce attempts were somehow thwarted. And today he had seen that this part of her hadn't changed. This fire in her soul to rescue, to heal, to bring things right for those who couldn't do it for themselves—it was still the very essence of Maggie and all that made her so special.

His own spirit groaned for the pain she would face. And yet he knew without a doubt that it was that very passion in her, that zeal to change and redeem and restore, that would bring to Skingle Creek's children a hope they might otherwise have never known.

He hadn't realized that he had taken hold of her until he saw her glance travel down to his hand on hers. He released her at once, saying, "You're a good teacher, Maggie. A fine teacher. And your students will be blessed for having you in their lives." *You are going to be one of the best things that ever happened to this town and its children, Maggie MacAuley. I know that, even if you don't....*

She gave him one of her quick, slightly tilted smiles. "Thank you, Mr. Stuart. And thank you for taking me along. I enjoyed the buggy ride!"

He held the gate open for her, and with a small wave, she hurried up the stone pathway to the house.

Jonathan stood watching her, waiting until she'd gone inside and closed the door before getting back into the buggy. Before driving off, he tugged the collar of his jacket more snugly about his throat. For the first time since they'd left earlier that afternoon, he felt the chill of the day.

Chapter Five

When the Night Is Long and the Questions Are Many

Night grows uneasy near the dawn....

W.B. Yeats

⟋∼⟍

Maggie opened the back door that led directly into the kitchen. She took only one step inside before stopping. The entire family was sitting around the table: her mother and father, her brother, Ray—and her older sister, Eva Grace.

"Evie!"

Her sister smiled at her surprise, stood, and moved to hug her.

"What in the world? When did you get here? Why didn't you tell us you were coming?"

Eva Grace laughed and held her at arm's length for a closer look. "Whoa. Slow down. I got here about an hour ago, but Mum and Da just came in not long before you did. And I *did* write that I was coming, but apparently I beat the letter here. How are you, little sis?"

They hugged again before Maggie shed her coat and took the chair her brother gave up to her. Then everyone started talking at once.

The first thing that struck Maggie as she studied her sister was that, for the first time she could remember, Eva Grace wasn't reed slim and picture perfect. In fact, she looked as though she'd put on a surprising amount of weight, and her always impeccably styled blonde hair appeared carelessly wrapped into a topknot.

As she studied her more closely, she realized that Evie didn't look well at all. Her eyes were shadowed, and that and the extra fullness of her face gave her a somewhat puffy appearance. She was still extraordinarily pretty, of course; Eva Grace had always been the beauty of the family. The beauty of the *town*.

Maggie glanced around. "Where's Richard?"

Her sister waved a hand. "Oh, he couldn't come this time. He's too busy. Board meetings and the like."

Eva Grace had "married up"—their mother's way of putting it. Evie had met Richard Barlow at an extension meeting for young people. Not long after they married, he'd taken a job with a large firm in Lexington, where they had lived ever since.

Although Maggie had spent some family time with Richard, she learned more about him from her mother's letters. Richard came from a well-to-do family, was ambitious, and, more recently, had started his own company. She would have been surprised if Eva Grace *hadn't* married well. Just about every eligible boy in town had either courted her or tried to, but her sister had never been interested in the local fellows. She'd made up her mind early on that she was going to marry a man who would take her out of Skingle Creek.

And so she had. But now she was back, and in spite of the way they'd fussed at each other when they were younger, Maggie couldn't have been happier to see her. Even the thought that she would have to give up her privacy and share a bedroom again didn't mar her pleasure for more than a second or two.

That night, Kate MacAuley lay in bed, watching her husband take the pain medicine for his injured back and knee.

As always, he frowned as he drank the last of it. He hated the taste of the stuff. He said it was vile, but Kate knew that what he hated even more was his need for its relief, his dependence on it. Every few weeks, he would try to go a night without it, but after an hour or two of tossing and turning, he'd throw off the covers and fix himself a dose. He refused to take it in the morning. He went to work in pain and returned home in even greater pain, giving in at night only because he knew he could not go without sleep and continue to work.

Kate hated seeing him this way as much as she knew Matthew hated *being* this way. Ever since the cave-in last year, she had watched him change from his former brawny, good-natured if somewhat stubborn self to a man who was often impatient and sharp, even with those he loved, and who refused to admit the severity of his pain, even to his own wife.

Only a year ago her husband had been one of the strongest men working the mines, as well as a man to whom others looked for level judgment and advice. Nowadays, however, it seemed that even the minor tasks drained him of his strength, and she feared his impatience and short temper were beginning to keep former friends—and his own son—at arm's length.

Lately Kate was finding it more and more difficult to force an optimism she didn't feel. If she countered one of his dour remarks with an attempt at cheerfulness, he would turn a withering look on her that made her feel a fool. Yet if she gave in to his glum mood, thinking perhaps he wanted her to sympathize with him, he would draw in on himself and grow more morose than ever. She had reached a place where she truly didn't know what to do for her husband.

If only he didn't have to work so hard…perhaps that would help. But what choice had they? If Matthew didn't work, they would lose everything they had. Certainly, the portion of her wages that Maggie faithfully handed over every payday helped, but it wouldn't keep them, nor did they have any right to expect more of her than she was already giving. And even if Matthew were to relent and allow Ray to go into the mines, they would still need Maggie's share. The young boys were paid as little as management could get away with when they first started out.

Besides, Matthew would kill himself digging coal before he agreed to let his son go below ground.

"It's nice having both Maggie and Eva Grace home at the same time, isn't it?" she said as Matthew slipped into bed beside her.

"Nice, if they don't take up spatting the way they used to."

"Oh, they won't, I'm sure. They're all grown-up now. Our girls are women now, Matthew. And wives themselves, except for Maggie. No doubt it won't be long before she's married too."

He gave a short sound of derision. "And where do you think a husband for Maggie is going to come from? I can't see that one settling for anyone around here."

"Matthew! Sure, and there are still some good men in Skingle Creek."

"The good ones are already taken. If it's marriage the girl's wanting, she'd have been better off staying in Chicago."

Kate pushed herself up on one arm to look at him. "You know why Maggie didn't go back. She stayed to help us. And I can't pretend I don't like having her here. And Eva Grace, too, for that matter, though I know she'll not stay long. Not without Richard."

He curled his lip. "Mr. Hoity-Toity."

Kate studied him. "You've never liked Richard."

"Have I ever said I don't like him? I don't recall saying an unkind word to him or about him."

"Even so, you don't like him."

He shrugged, then blinked hard, as if the movement had pained him. "It's neither here nor there whether I like the man. He was Eva Grace's choice."

In truth, Kate had also had a bit of a problem warming to her son-in-law. Richard had a way of making her feel like shanty Irish. Anytime they visited, which was seldom, he acted as if he couldn't wait to get away. Not once before or after he and Eva Grace were married had he made the slightest effort to build any sort of a relationship with her or Matthew.

Still, there was no denying that Richard had done well by the girl. According to Eva Grace, they had a fine home in Lexington with all the refinements they could want. It seemed that Richard was a hard worker and was also a deacon in the church, a man held in the highest regard by their acquaintances.

The girl could have done worse. A lot worse.

Matthew reached to snuff the oil lamp beside the bed. After giving Kate a quick kiss on the cheek, he turned away from her. Kate knew he would talk no more. He was becoming more and more withdrawn these days, a clear indication that the pain was growing worse. When nighttime came, he was exhausted and seemed to crave sleep, no doubt as a means of escaping the assault against his body.

She lay staring at his broad back, listening to his deep, even breathing. Another moment and she moved closer, close enough to touch her face to his shoulder without waking him, drawing comfort from his warmth, from the strength that, even in sleep, gave her shelter and eased her own pain.

Maggie would have thought that the familiarity of having her sister back in the bed next to hers, sharing the same room that had been theirs throughout their childhood, would have encouraged sleep to come easily. Instead, she was beginning to wonder how she was going to get through what promised to be an exceedingly long night.

Of the three girls, Eva Grace had always slept more deeply than Maggie or Nell Frances. At times their mother would become so exasperated with Evie that she threatened to pour water straight from the well on her if she didn't get up when she was called.

Apparently marriage had changed all that. At least, *something* had

changed it. It seemed as if her sister had been in motion ever since
they'd gone to bed, well over an hour ago.

Having been apart for so long, they'd talked the first few minutes,
catching up on each other and their parents. Although now that she
thought about it, Maggie realized that *she* had done most of the talking. For once, Eva Grace had had little to say—a few remarks about
her house and the city of Lexington, but nothing more. Even when
Maggie asked questions, her sister seemed disinclined to answer. At
one point, Maggie was tempted to ask if something was wrong, but
Eva Grace had chosen that moment to say goodnight and turn her
back.

She'd been quiet for a while, leading Maggie to think she was
asleep. But then she turned restless, changing positions, tossing the
bedclothes, occasionally making the little clicking sound in her throat
she'd made as a child when she'd had too much johnny-cake and
couldn't sleep.

By now Maggie was restless too. She could feel herself growing
frustrated, reaching that pivotal point where she'd be too irritable to
sleep the rest of the night. That was no way to face Monday morning. With a deliberate effort, she turned onto her other side, her back
toward Eva Grace, and willed herself to lie motionless and breathe
deeply until sleep came.

She finally did doze off, but in what seemed only a short time, she
stirred, listening. At first she thought the sound was outside, perhaps
from a night creature that had come near the house. She waited,
listening closely. She realized then that the sound was coming from
Evie's side of the room.

Maggie struggled to focus her eyes in the darkness. Finally, framed
by the dim glow of moonlight filtering through the window, she made
out her sister's form. Huddled under the blankets, her shoulders rising
and falling, Eva Grace was sobbing.

Alarmed, Maggie slipped out of bed and went to her sister. Even
with the hooked rug, the floor was cold on her bare feet and she
shivered.

"Evie?" She put a hand lightly to Eva Grace's shoulder, and her sister turned to look at her. "Evie? What's wrong?"

Her sister stared up at her. "What?"

"You were crying. What's the matter?"

Eva Grace lifted a hand and wiped it across her eyes, then shook her head. "I'm not crying."

"I heard you, Evie."

Again her sister shook her head, glancing away from Maggie. "No, I wasn't…I must have had a bad dream."

There was just enough light seeping in beneath the window shade for Maggie to see her sister's evasive expression. She was deliberately refusing to look at her.

Uncertain, she dropped her hand away from Eva Grace's shoulder.

"Go back to bed, Maggie." Evie's voice sounded ragged and phlegmy.

Torn, Maggie hesitated. "You're sure?"

Eva Grace nodded, turning onto her side.

Stung by this gesture of dismissal, Maggie again touched her sister gently on her shoulder before going back to her own bed. By the time she finally heard the sound of Eva Grace's even, shallow breathing, she was wide awake. Had Evie lied to her? She had been so sure she'd heard her weeping. That was what had awakened her in the first place. But why would she lie?

Of the three of them, Eva Grace had been the only one who cried easily as a child. Easily and often. In fact, Maggie and Nell Frances had more than once grumbled about the way their older sister seemed to be capable of turning on the tears at will, either to get her way with one of her beaus or else to coax a bit of sympathy from a family member—usually their mother. And it almost always worked.

As accustomed as she'd once been to using tears to her advantage, why would she try to conceal a bout of weeping?

Maggie curled up on her side, just barely able to make out the outline of her sister in the other bed. Maybe Eva Grace and Richard had had a fight. For the life of her, she couldn't imagine Richard

Barlow raising his voice, but then she hardly knew her brother-in-law. She didn't think she'd ever been around the man more than an hour or so, and then never alone.

Richard had always struck Maggie as a bit of a stuffed shirt. Whenever Mum would bluntly ask Eva Grace whether there was a grandchild on the horizon yet, Maggie would almost strangle at the thought of the tediously proper Richard summoning enough emotion to sire a child.

Her face burned in the darkness, not only at her totally inappropriate thought about her sister's husband, but also because she knew she was being unfair. She had never heard Eva Grace utter a disparaging word about Richard. To the contrary, her sister had never seemed anything but ideally happy with him. Of course, that was in the early years, when she rarely spoke of him in anything but glowing terms and an almost annoying spiel of lovestruck adulation. She had seldom been with Evie over the past few years. Their contact had been almost entirely through letters.

Well, it wasn't her place to approve or disapprove of her sister's husband. She didn't have to live with him.

There's a mercy...

She bit her lip, impatient with her own pettiness. Deliberately she turned her thoughts back to the afternoon, but the memory of the meeting with Huey Lazlo's parents unsettled her so much she grew more tense and wakeful. Even though Mr. Stuart's caution not to go back to the Lazlo's alone had at first made her feel childish, in truth she was grateful for his concern. She didn't *want* to go back to that house ever again—certainly not by herself. Should the occasion arise that she had to, she definitely would want Mr. Stuart at her side.

What was there about Jonathan Stuart that had always made her feel so safe—and *still* made her feel safe? When she was a child, he had been dreadfully ill for a long time: thin, even gaunt, lacking any real physical strength or stamina. Yet despite his failing health, his students had looked to him as a protector, as a rock. And she had been no exception.

Indeed, for Maggie, he had been her safe place to go when everything else seemed to be falling away. She had trusted him as she had never trusted another soul, other than her own parents. And he had never failed her.

As was the case with many of the older girls at school, Maggie's admiration for Jonathan Stuart had eventually bloomed into a full-blown crush. In spite of the fact that she and Kenny Tallman had been considered a "couple" until they graduated, Maggie had spent most of her adolescence and teen years half in love with her teacher, as only an ingenuous schoolgirl can be. The hopelessness of her infatuation served only to make him loom larger in her estimation.

Increasingly restless now, she pitched onto her other side. She knew her thoughts had taken a treacherous turn, but she allowed herself to indulge them anyway. She almost wished Jonathan Stuart didn't seem so much *younger* than she'd remembered him. Probably because he had been her teacher for years—she had practically grown up under his watchful eye—she always thought of him as being much older than he actually was. But it took only a moment of figuring to realize that when he had first come to Skingle Creek, he couldn't have been much older than she was now!

One facet of her memory hadn't failed her: He was still as handsome as ever.

Enough. She wasn't a schoolgirl any longer, and she needed to stop thinking like one. Hadn't she promised herself when she accepted the teaching position that she'd behave like a woman grown instead of the child she used to be?

Besides, Jonathan Stuart was as far removed from her today as he had been all those years ago. There was a considerable age difference between them, after all. Not that that would make a tad of difference to her, but it probably would to him, his being ever the gentleman.

Then, too, she wondered if there might not be something more than a professional relationship between him and Mrs. Ross. She'd speculated more than once as to whether they might not be romantically interested in each other. Well, she didn't know about Mr. Stuart—he was almost impossible to read. But Mrs. Ross was more transparent, and unless Maggie was badly mistaken, the woman would like to be more to Mr. Stuart than just the school secretary.

And given the fact that Mrs. Ross was not only closer to Mr. Stuart in years but was also enviably attractive, Maggie figured the likelihood of his ever seeing her as anything other than the skinny little red-haired schoolgirl she'd once been could hardly be more remote.

Disgusted with herself, she flipped onto her back, gave the bedclothes a couple of thumps, and expelled a sharp breath. Wasn't she going to be in fine fettle tomorrow, though? Not only would she start off the work week with no sleep, but she hadn't bothered to braid her hair, so it would be as wild as a grass fire. An hour later she was still staring at the darkened ceiling, wide awake and wondering if it had been folly entirely that had convinced her to stay in Skingle Creek instead of going back to Chicago.

Chapter Six

From Girl to Woman

When youth, the dream, departs,
It takes something from our hearts,
and it never comes again.

Richard Henry Stoddard

~∽~

Monday went just about the way Maggie had feared it might.

Tired and touchy because of her lack of sleep and troubled thoughts about Eva Grace, it was all she could do to keep her mind on the children and their lessons. As if they sensed her struggle to stay focused, they behaved like little savages most of the day. Maggie actually had to break up a free-for-all in the school yard during recess between two little seven-year-old girls—Dottie Russell and Sissie Miller—who went after each other over a squirrel tail one of them had grabbed from the other. They were going at it like two mean little pigs in a barnyard brawl when one of the boys came running for Maggie. She was on her knees at the time, trying to clean some horse dung off the bottom of little Timmy Neal's shoes. Apparently the child had been carrying it around all morning. A souvenir from home.

It was just her luck that Mr. Stuart had spotted the ruckus from the window of his room. He had the two girls separated and on their way to stand at the front of the building before Maggie could concoct a reasonable-sounding explanation as to why she hadn't managed to settle the problem herself.

In retrospect, she supposed she must have appeared somewhat wild-eyed, because when Jonathan Stuart returned to her, his quizzical look made her feel like a troublesome child herself.

"I'm sorry Mr. Stuart. I was helping Timmy Neal clean the horse droppings of his shoes. I didn't realize—"

"Why didn't you simply have him wipe it off on the wet grass?" he interupted.

She looked at him.

Indeed. Why hadn't she? Where *was* her mind today?

"I...suppose I didn't think."

Something flickered in his eyes. "I see. And our two little scrappers? What was that all about?"

"As I understand it," Maggie said with a sigh, "both of them wanted the same squirrel's tail."

He tilted his head slightly, his gaze intensifying. "Yes. Well, that would be worth fighting over, I suppose."

"If you're seven years old."

"Indeed."

"Mr. Stuart?"

"Yes, Maggie?"

"I'm sorry. I should have kept better control."

He raised his eyebrows as if surprised. "There's nothing to be sorry about. You can hardly manage to be in two places at once." After a pause, he added, "The children seem unusually...boisterous today, don't you think?"

Maggie nodded. "They are. But it's probably my fault. I'm...I've been somewhat rattle-brained myself. They probably picked up on that."

"Is something wrong?"

"No. Well—" Maggie hesitated. "No. It's just that Eva Grace came home yesterday, and we had a late night. Talking and catching up, you know. And I'm feeling the effects of too little sleep."

He smiled. "That must have been a nice surprise for your family. Or were you expecting her?"

Maggie shook her head. "She arrived before her letter."

"Well, I'm hoping to see her. She's well, I hope?"

Maggie hesitated, but only a second or two. "She seems fine. She's by herself though. Richard couldn't come this time."

Something in her tone or her expression must have caught his attention because he stood as if waiting for her to say more. But Maggie could hardly tell him she'd heard her sister crying her first night home. Instead she forced a cheerful note into her voice, saying, "I'd best get my wee rascals back inside. It's blowing up quite a chill."

Still smarting from the feeling that she had disappointed him, Maggie hurried to herd the children into the building

Jonathan watched her gathering her little ones like a young mother hen collecting her chicks. She moved much as she always had, quickly and efficiently, her expression set in a look of firm purpose.

Maggie in charge. That was how he had often thought of her when she was wearing that look. The problem these days was that he *too* often thought of her. Sometimes she would do something, say something, that would remind him of the child she had been. Other times he would find himself surprised and dazzled by the woman she had become.

Until her recent return to Skingle Creek, Maggie had stayed a schoolgirl in his mind. Not a little girl, of course; she had graduated at sixteen, no longer a child, but not yet a woman. Certainly not the woman she was now. When he thought of her during that time between her graduation and her return—and he *had* thought of her—he never pictured her as she was now, but only as she had been then.

In many ways, she was still the same. The intensity and resolve of the young Maggie MacAuley still hovered about her, and she had the same mercurial mind and relentless curiosity she'd always had. Her natural leadership ability and the sense of fairness that had been hallmarks of her girlhood were very much in evidence, and she could grasp a situation and a practical solution almost instantaneously.

But in other ways she was noticeably and disturbingly different. Never flighty or careless, she seemed more optimistic and happier than she had been as a child. She'd lost some of the solemnity that had once characterized her personality.

Her earlier awkwardness had completely disappeared. Jonathan couldn't quite stop a smile. Maggie as a youngster had been tall for her age and often reminded him of a young colt, one that hinted of a future grace and panache, but for the time being was all long legs and ungainly movements. She still had a spattering of light freckles bridging her nose and high cheekbones, and the red hair she had always detested still blazed and worked its way out of control most of the time. But what had appeared wild and incorrigible on the young girl seemed a fiery glory on the young woman.

She has become quite lovely. Quite lovely indeed...

Jonathan balled his hands into fists so tightly his knuckles hurt. A painful tightness gripped his throat. It took an effort to get his breath. He had allowed his thoughts to roam into forbidden territory. His mood suddenly went dark and angry—angry at his carelessness. He dared not let himself go down that road.

Years ago—her last year in Skingle Creek—that same constriction in his chest had seized him when he least expected it. It was the week of her graduation, and it had suddenly dawned on him that she would soon be leaving Skingle Creek. Maggie was one of six students he had managed to keep in school past the time their classmates had left. Somehow he had compressed two final years of education into one so that those who desired to go on to college were prepared to do so.

Maggie had been his star student for years. Because of her hard work and high grades—and with the help of a friend on faculty—Jonathan had been able to arrange nearly a full scholarship for her at the University of Cincinnati.

On the day he still remembered with some chagrin, he'd been going over some of the course offerings with her, trying to answer her questions. He was seated at his desk with her standing beside him, bending over slightly to follow the list he'd made for her. It was a warm springtime day, and she'd been outside with the younger children earlier. He turned to look up at her, and at the same time her hair accidentally brushed his temple. Suddenly the warm scent of sunshine from her hair fell over him like a veil. He couldn't breathe, nor could he tear his gaze away from hers.

Something sparked in her eyes—surprise, but something else too…something that at the time, at least, he interpreted as fear. To this day humiliation still washed over him at the thought that something in his expression might have frightened her.

For his own part, what had gripped him that day had been the dizzying realization that he was attracted to her. Strongly attracted. To a student. And to a student who was very special to him, at that.

Until that moment, he hadn't named the attraction for what it was. He had believed himself incapable of anything of the sort. The years between them, his situation as her teacher and a person in authority over her had enabled him to pretend that he could keep any improper feelings well in check.

Obviously, he'd misjudged himself. What seemed to make matters worse, he had always been genuinely *fond* of Maggie MacAuley. As a child, she'd been a bright and challenging student who grew into an even more challenging adolescent, one who knew her own mind and was determined to make something good of her life, something more than Skingle Creek could offer her. Jonathan's regard for her had always been complicated. He liked and respected her for her strong individuality, but also for the exceptional person he sensed she would one day become.

To this day, he honestly believed that mere physical attraction to a pretty teenager wouldn't have shaken him to the depth of his being had it not been for that special fondness he held for the girl, the affection and respect he'd always felt toward her in spite of her youth. Even so, there was no denying that those last few weeks—perhaps even *months*—before she'd gone off to college had been a time of confusion and distress because of the impossible appeal she held for him.

A sudden cold blast of wind from the darkening sky roused him from his unsettling train of thought, reminding him that he was standing outside alone in the school yard, foolishly leaving his entire class to enjoy an extended period of unaccustomed freedom. If he dawdled any longer, Carolyn Ross would soon come marching out the door to make sure he hadn't fallen in the creek or hit his head on a rock.

He sighed and started toward the building.

Chapter Seven

Uneasy Thoughts

Silence has its victories,
But peace is seldom one of them.

Anonymous

Every day for a week Jonathan watched Selma Lazlo for a sign of what he had begun to suspect after his visit to her home. He asked Maggie to do the same with little Huey. By Friday, however, he was beginning to doubt his suspicions. While Corey Duggan rang the afternoon dismissal bell, Jonathan stood, reminded the class of their book reports due Monday, then went to the door to send them on their way for the weekend.

He watched the Lazlo girl, as usual the last to leave, trudge partway down the school yard and then turn to wait for her younger brother. Until Huey met up with her and took her hand, she stood alone. Quiet and slow in her movements and responses, the ten-year-old Selma typically kept to herself. In fact, she seemed to have no friends.

It was almost as if she faded in the presence of others, absorbed by the group.

Jonathan had often noticed her standing off by herself in the school yard while the other girls played tag or jumped rope. More than once he encouraged some of the other children to include Selma, and at first they tried. But Selma refused them too many times, and eventually they stopped asking.

Her lack of participation in any activity both puzzled and troubled Jonathan. Selma was a plain child, somewhat larger than the other girls her age, with light-brown hair cut short and straight. Her clothing was drab, worn, and usually patched. She was typically solemn. Although Jonathan frequently tried to coax a smile from the girl, he rarely succeeded. She seldom met his eyes and, instead, kept her gaze fixed on her desk except to concentrate on the chalkboard during a lesson.

He had seen no indication of severe punishment or beatings, nor had Maggie in young Huey. But experience had taught him that the signs of mistreatment were easily concealed by a child's clothing; he had learned to look for more than visible evidence. Selma's withdrawn, evasive manner had put him on the alert, and his meeting with the children's parents had set off all manner of alarms.

When a situation like this arose, he had to steel himself to not overreact, to not rush to judgment. He couldn't go accusing parents of something so heinous simply because they were "different" or because a child seemed particularly shy or solitary. And yet in all the years he had been teaching, only on one occasion had he come close to judging a man guilty when he'd been innocent—at least of any *physical* maltreatment.

There had been widespread rumors about Judson Tallman, the mine superintendent, in part because of the suspicious disappearance of his wife—a disappearance that even today remained a mystery. Tallman's son, Kenny, had raised Jonathan's suspicions by certain aspects of his behavior, but as it turned out, the only physical violence Kenny had suffered had been at the hands of two of his classmates, which the boy had endured in an attempt to protect his best friend, Maggie MacAuley.

Jonathan shook off the memory. His concern was with the present. So strong were his instincts that he had to struggle not to act on them. But he had nothing to go on except his own suspicions, so for the time being he could only keep a watchful eye on the children.

Maggie looked up to see Jonathan Stuart standing in the doorway of her room, watching her with a smile. Instinctively she put a hand to her braid to see if it was still secure. For once it was.

"Mr. Stuart?"

"May I have a moment, Maggie?"

"Of course. In fact I was about to come looking for you," she said.

He walked the rest of the way into the room. "Something wrong?"

"No. Not at all. Mum wanted me to invite you for Sunday dinner this weekend. She thought you might want to visit with Eva Grace a bit, and Da was saying it's been too long since you've come for a meal."

His face creased into an even wider smile. "I can't think of anything I'd rather do than enjoy one of your mother's Sunday dinners."

Pleased, Maggie tucked away the last of the children's homework papers in her satchel. When she looked up, his expression had changed.

"Oh, Maggie, I'm so sorry—I'm afraid I've forgotten something. Another engagement. It completely slipped my mind."

He seemed to be genuinely disappointed, as was Maggie. But he also seemed embarrassed, so Maggie hurried to reassure him. "Why, that's all right, Mr. Stuart. Maybe next week. You can let me know later."

He nodded, his face still flushed. "Yes. Yes, definitely next week. If it's all right with your mother, that is. I do apologize…"

"Don't give it another thought, Mr. Stuart. I expect you get a lot of invitations out, what with you being…"

It was Maggie's turn to be embarrassed. Perhaps he would just as soon not be reminded of his bachelor status.

But he merely smiled and shrugged. "As a matter of fact, I *do* get my share of invitations. I suppose being one of the few bachelors in town has certain advantages. I eat rather well. But to tell you the truth, your mother's cooking can't be matched…nor the company around her table. You thank her for me, Maggie. And if next Sunday is convenient for her, it's good for me. Will Eva Grace still be here?"

"Oh, I think so," said Maggie. "She hasn't said anything about leaving yet."

"Well, then—" He hesitated, looking around the room. "Is there anything you need before I leave?"

"No. Thank you, Mr. Stuart. But was there something you came to see me about?"

"Oh, yes! I almost forgot. I wanted to ask you about Huey Lazlo. I noticed he's been here every day this week. How has he seemed to you?"

Maggie thought for a moment. "He's been quiet, but he always is. I suppose he's well enough."

"All right then. Just keep a close watch, would you? And you have a good weekend, Maggie."

He seemed in a hurry to leave. As she watched him go, Maggie couldn't help but wonder what his other Sunday engagement was. Not that it was any of her business.

Still, she couldn't altogether dismiss the disappointment she felt at the thought of not seeing him for two days.

Jonathan was still berating himself when he got home. Maggie's invitation had appealed to him far more than the one he'd already accepted. He looked around the dim entryway before shrugging out of his coat and loosening his tie. After a moment he headed for the kitchen to get a glass of milk. He felt strangely at odds, even a little irritable as he stood looking out the kitchen window onto his back-yard.

He didn't like Fridays. There was something about coming home to an empty house at the end of the week that was different from other days. More and more lately he felt restless and even somewhat out of sorts Friday evenings. He stayed fairly busy on weekends, work-ing around the house or helping out with something or other at the church. Sometimes he had dinner plans or took in a social at the town center. But there was a loneliness that settled over him on Fridays before he even left the school building. He had an idea what was responsible for his mood, though he didn't like admitting it…even to himself.

Most everyone looked forward to the weekend. The children, especially, couldn't wait to get out of school on Friday afternoons. They usually raced down the school yard to the road after dismissal as if they were trying to outrun a barrage of fireballs at their backs. The weekend was a time for doing things with others. Families met for meals. Young couples went walking out. Often there was a square dance or a church dinner going on. It was a time when people came *together.*

Unless, that is, you were a bachelor approaching middle-age with no family nearby and whose friends were all married.

He walked into the living room and lighted the oil lamp by the sofa. It was cold enough for a fire, but instead of starting one he sat down and put his feet up and his head back. Most of the afternoon light was already fading, making way for dusk. He thought he might take a nap, but instead he sat staring into the cold fireplace.

He'd been thinking about getting a dog for companionship, but every time the thought occurred to him he would reach the same conclusion: it was unfair to leave an animal alone all day while he was at school.

Of course, he could always get *two* dogs. They could keep each other company when he was gone and liven the place up a little when he was home. Make some noise. Stir up a little dust. It would give him an excuse to clean on the weekends. The way it was, he could go for days if he wanted, scarcely lifting a hand around the house other than to pick up the papers and wash his few dishes.

It seemed only right to clean one's house, but it also seemed a foolish waste of time when there was no need.

He would ask around next week. One of the local farmers ought to be able to help him find a dog...or two.

The thought cheered him a little. He wasn't really hungry, but he supposed he ought to eat before too much longer. Food might get rid of the headache that had been nagging at him since noonday.

Perhaps he'd walk down to Blanche Hubbard's place for a light supper. "Hubbard's Cupboard," she called the diner.

One side of the building was a restaurant, the other side a dry goods store, where Blanche sold mostly material, buttons, and other accoutrements. The coal company had fought against the dry goods establishment, claiming everything the townspeople needed could be purchased at the company store. But Blanche had stood her ground and, to most everyone's surprise, her determination had won out. Both the store and the diner had been in business for nearly four years now, and from all appearances did a healthy trade.

Jonathan was always glad to see a private enterprise survive in Skingle Creek. The coal company owned and controlled almost everything, including the bank, the one general store, even the health care services provided by Lebreen Woodbridge. The Company could be a formidable adversary to anyone who dared to attempt the establishment of a privately owned business. Blanche Hubbard was one of the few who'd met their bluff—and won.

His thoughts turned from Blanche to Sunday and the reason he'd declined Kate MacAuley's dinner invitation. He had almost forgotten that he'd promised to attend Carolyn Ross's recital for her music students early Sunday afternoon.

He'd just as soon spend the day digging rocks, but Carolyn had caught him off guard, pointing out that her music students were also *his* classroom students, and that the event would be brief, given the scarcity of children in Skingle Creek with the means to study anything outside the schoolroom. Jonathan had fumbled for an excuse, but he hadn't been able to come up with a legitimate one. It wasn't that he had no interest in the children or in music. To the contrary, he was exceedingly fond of both. He simply had an inexplicable lack of interest in Carolyn Ross, a situation he found regrettable. There was no denying the woman's appeal: She was attractive, talented, intelligent—and if his friend Ben Wallace was right, she might even be interested in more than a professional relationship.

What was wrong with him anyway? There weren't many unmarried women in town to begin with, certainly none as attractive or as interesting as Carolyn. Ben was probably right when he told Jonathan that he ought to get his head out of the sand and court the woman. Instead, he found himself avoiding her except at school, where it was impossible to keep his distance for any length of time.

Obviously, it was this lack of interest that had allowed him to forget his commitment to attend Carolyn's recital. He would much rather be spending the afternoon with the MacAuleys.

With Maggie...

He tried to force his thoughts in a different direction. He was thinking entirely too much about Maggie lately. But no matter how he tried, he couldn't seem to keep his mind off her. Sometimes when he least expected it, she would invade his thoughts with the sound of her laughter, nearly as mischievous now as when she was still a schoolgirl...or her smile, the way one corner of her mouth turned up a little more than the other...or the way the morning sun would set her hair on fire when she took the children out for their recess.

She was still awkward around him, as if she was never quite certain of his approval. Sometimes she actually jumped when he came into her classroom.

Jonathan wished he knew a way to put her more at ease with him, so they could at least be friends rather than continuing with this awkward teacher–former student relationship. But in truth he wasn't all that comfortable with her either. He was still trying to come to grips with the young woman she had become rather than the girl he remembered. He was finding it difficult to move past his role as her former teacher into this new capacity as her colleague, and, eventually he hoped, her friend. He didn't dare allow himself to think about becoming more, although sometimes...

He squeezed his eyes shut, firmly willing himself to turn his mind onto any subject but Maggie. Finally, little by little, his thoughts grew vague and drifted off into the mist of an uneasy sleep.

Chapter Eight

Friday Night in Shingle Creek

There is no pleasure to me without communication:
There is not so much as a sprightly thought comes to my mind
That it does not grieve me
to have produced alone,
And that I have no one to tell it to.

De Montaigne

∽

Kate, I declare if you had nothing at all to worry about, you'd invent something."

At any other time, her da's words would have been meant as a good-natured teasing. But sharp-tempered and impatient as he was of late, they cut through Maggie like a jagged blade, and she knew they must be wounding to her mother as well.

Maggie wasn't deliberately eavesdropping. Indeed, she'd been on her way to fetch a coat so she could leave the house and the tension inside it for a time. But she stopped short outside the kitchen when she heard the tone of her father's voice and the strain in her mother's.

"I'm telling you, Matthew, the girl isn't well. She moped about the house all day, scarcely talking at all. And didn't you see how she could hardly wait to leave the table and get to her room tonight?"

"Eva Grace is no girl, Kate. She's a woman grown…and a married one at that. Don't be fussing at her now. She's perfectly fine, you'll see."

Silence. Then her mother spoke again. "She doesn't look a bit well, either."

Her father groaned. "Let it *be,* woman! I'll have another slice of that cake, if there's enough."

"There's plenty."

Her mother's tone was tight, but Maggie sensed the two had backed off from an argument. Thanks be.

She hurried into the kitchen while things were calm and took her coat from the hook by the door.

"Where are you going?" her father snapped.

"Just for a walk, Da. I thought there might be music at the square since it's Friday night."

"Did you ask your sister to go with you?" her mother said.

Maggie nodded. "She said she'd rather not, that she just wanted to stay here where it's warm."

"I don't like you being out alone at night, girl," Da said with the same sharp edge in his voice.

Maggie gritted her teeth but kept her tone even. "Everyone's out and about on Friday evening, Da. I'll be fine. And I won't be late. I just need to unwind a bit after being in the classroom all day."

He said nothing else, so Maggie darted a quick smile at her mother and made a hasty exit. She was still chafing when she reached the gate and started toward the square. Would Da never stop treating her as though she were still in leggings? At least tonight he didn't tell her to be home by eight! No doubt she *would* be, but it would be her own doing, not in response to her father's command.

Every day it seemed something happened to remind her how

difficult it was to be an adult living under her parents' roof. Da, especially, treated her much as he always had: as a little girl to be told what to do and when to do it. He had always been severely protective of his daughters, and in truth Maggie wouldn't have wanted him to be any other way. But he couldn't grasp that she no longer needed to be ordered about in almost every situation.

It wasn't quite the same with Eva Grace, of course. She was the married daughter, there only for a visit. With Maggie, however, Da had reverted to treating her as if she were a schoolgirl under his protection…and his authority. Even her mother seemed predisposed to treat her as if she had never left home.

To be fair, the present circumstances had to be as difficult for her parents as they were for her. Although both of them had seemed relieved when she'd told them she wasn't going back to Chicago, Maggie knew they were uncomfortable with the *reason* she wasn't going back. In their minds, perhaps her desire to help out actually fostered a feeling of dependency that was foreign to both their natures. And to feel dependent on one's own child, even when that "child" was living under the same roof, no doubt could be a bitter pill to swallow.

On weekends and in the evenings, Maggie sensed that they all invaded each other's privacy, except perhaps in the case of her mother. Mum had always thrived on having the entire family around her. If truth were told, she was probably overjoyed to have both Maggie and Eva Grace home again by the fire. But Ray was at an age where he surely disliked being under the scrutiny of three women, not to mention the way Da quizzed him about every part of his life, from his schoolwork to his friends. She had seen the cornered look in her brother's eyes more than once, a look that plainly said he wanted to cut and run.

Maggie was already beginning to wish she could afford her own place and at the same time continue to help her parents financially. Even a single room of her own in a boardinghouse sounded good to her. In fact, the idea was rapidly progressing past wishful thinking and taking on the shape of necessity.

She shuffled along, her hands tucked in her pockets as she neared the square. It was an unusually cold night for early October. There was a sharp breeze, for which Maggie was grateful. The wind lifted the acrid coal dust away from the town and carried it up the mountain, leaving the more pleasant odor of wood smoke and the faint scent of evergreen in its wake.

She made a deliberate effort to turn her mind away from her family, uncomfortably aware that lately she'd caught herself too often dwelling on her own problems. And they weren't even real problems. Problems were what her da had, with his need to go on working in the mine even though he lived in constant pain. Problems were what some of her students had, particularly those from large families where it was difficult to keep food on the table and decent clothing on their backs. And then there were the Lazlo children. Who knew what those two had to put up with?

She was fairly certain that Eva Grace had real problems too. Problems that made her cry in the night long after she believed Maggie to be asleep.

No matter how many times Maggie asked what was wrong, the reply was always the same evasive "nothing." But in Maggie's experience a body didn't cry for no reason. Something was weighing on her sister, something so troubling it was breaking her heart. And whatever it was, she was adamant in her refusal to talk about it.

Maggie sighed so deeply it came out more like a sob. It would be such a help to have a close friend nearby, a friend like she'd found in Sally Ogleby in Chicago. The two of them had quickly become close, working together, rooming in the same boardinghouse, and spending what little free time they could manage in each other's company. It had been such a comfort to have someone with whom to share the fears of living in a strange city, the problems and discouragement that came with working among the poor, many of whom were illiterate, often ill, and lacking even the most basic of necessities.

The truth was that sometimes even in the midst of her family, Maggie felt lonely. There was Mr. Stuart, of course. He had been a friend to her most of her life, until she went away to college. But he had been a part of her childhood. Things were different now that she was grown up. And he was her *principal*. She couldn't very well confide personal matters to him. She was no longer a little girl in need of a strong shoulder and wise advice.

Although sometimes that's exactly how she felt.

She heard the sound of music now, and her spirits lifted a little. Normally she didn't much like crowds, but tonight the thought of being among people seemed more desirable than usual. She picked up her pace as she headed toward the square.

The Company had cleared a small piece of ground—the "square"— for the town's few activities: fairs, bake sales, the occasional tent meeting. On most Friday nights until the weather turned bitter, a few of the local men would come together with their musical instruments and play for two hours or more. They almost always drew a crowd. There wasn't that much going on in the way of weekly entertainment in Skingle Creek, so folks tended to congregate for almost any event.

Maggie recognized the musicians right away. The lanky Dewey Easter was fiddling up a storm, with Chester Rydell and his oldest son backing him up on banjo and guitar. These three were favorites around town and always drew the largest Friday night audiences.

Maggie made a place for herself in the midst of the crowd, smiling at those who greeted her. In no time at all her foot was tapping along with the beat. She loved music and had often thought she might like to play an instrument herself, but there had been neither the time nor the money for such things when she was growing up. Even so, her lack of musicianship in no way diminished her enjoyment of the talents of others.

She tucked her coat collar more snugly around her throat and tugged her cap down as far as it would go. Soon she was smiling, her troublesome thoughts caught up and blown free by the driving, irresistible mountain music.

Jonathan made no attempt to make her aware of his presence, not just yet. He was enjoying watching her from where he stood, well behind her and off to the right. He couldn't stop a smile at the sight of her. Her cheeks were flushed from the brisk night air, her hair peeking around her cap and falling over the collar of her deep-blue coat as she hugged her arms to herself and swayed to the rhythm of the music.

His gaze went to the musicians, who at the moment were deep into the Celtic type of music commonly expected from them. He glanced back at Maggie and saw that she was now tapping her foot to the energetic beat. In that instant, he was struck by the awareness that, like the majority of the town's populace, Maggie was thoroughly Irish. Yet not since she was a little girl had he given any real thought to the fact. But as he studied her, it came to him that everything she was, everything that made her so undeniably special could never be separated from the part of her that was linked to her family, to the heritage of a distant island about which he knew too little.

Unexpectedly the need to know more, to know everything about Maggie, pressed in on him and set off a kind of yearning. He wished he could walk up to her and take her arm, even hold her hand, and ask her all the things he wanted to know about her.

He swallowed hard and clenched his hands. But after another moment he could stand it no more and began to move, threading his way through the crowd until he came up next to her.

He touched her lightly on the arm to get her attention, but quickly dropped his hand away. "Maggie." His voice sounded strained to him, unfamiliar.

She turned, and he was pleased to see her face light up, as if she was glad to see him. "Mr. Stuart! I didn't know you were here."

"I was over there." He motioned to where he'd been standing. "They're very good, aren't they?" he said, gesturing toward the trio in the middle of the square.

"They are! I can't stand still at all when they're playing."

They stood without speaking for a time, taking in the music, occasionally looking around at their neighbors.

"You're here alone?" Jonathan finally asked.

She nodded. "I tried to get Eva Grace to come with me, but she wouldn't budge."

"Still doesn't like the cold?"

She studied him. "How do you remember things like that? And you're right. Eva Grace always hated cold weather."

Jonathan shrugged and smiled a little. "Her dislike for winter was never exactly a secret. The classroom was never warm enough for her. In truth, it was never warm enough for *anyone*, myself included."

"It's better now though."

"It's the new furnace," Jonathan said. "A long time coming."

For some reason he was finding it difficult to manage an intelligent thought and wondered if she sensed his awkwardness.

He glanced down at her to find her staring directly into his eyes. Disconcerted, Jonathan glanced back toward the musicians, who had stopped playing and were rubbing their hands together as they conferred.

"I think they're about to stop for a bit," said Maggie. "It's probably difficult to play very long at one time, what with the cold."

Jonathan turned to look at her. Did he dare ask? Well, why shouldn't he? They worked together, after all. They were friends, weren't they?

"Maggie, I…I was on my way to Hubbard's to have some dinner. Have you eaten?"

The instant the words left his mouth Jonathan wondered what had possessed him. Had he actually just invited her to have dinner with him?

She stared at him, her surprise obvious. Or was she embarrassed?

"Have I—oh yes. Yes, Da likes to eat early, soon after he gets home."

"Of course. I should have realized. Well, I thought if you hadn't—" He was stammering! How foolish he must seem to her.

"But I could keep you company, if you like," she offered.

Jonathan found his breath. "I'd *love* the company." He felt himself grinning like a smitten schoolboy, but he couldn't stop. "You'll at least have a piece of pie, won't you? Blanche Hubbard makes a really *fine* pumpkin pie, you know."

Without thinking, he tucked her arm inside of his and began to steer her through the crowd, his mood suddenly lifting away from the usual Friday night discontent to an uncommon exhilaration.

Chapter Nine

The Beginning of Something New

Nature's law is that all things change and
turn, and pass away.

Marcus Aurelius

~

How very odd this was!

Maggie sat across from Jonathan Stuart, trying, with little success, not to stare at him. Had she ever imagined that she would one day sit across the dining table from her former teacher—the hero of her childhood—not as a student but as a woman grown?

Hardly. She forced down another taste of pumpkin pie, which under any other circumstances would have been delicious, but under present conditions nearly choked her with every bite.

If she could have imagined this night, she would have thought she'd enjoy it. Here she was, being treated like an adult by someone she admired beyond all telling. She was finally the recipient of his undivided attention, free to listen to and savor the low, mellow voice she had always, even as a child, found so soothing. Yet so anxious was she to be thought of as a woman rather than his former student that she couldn't relax and simply be herself.

At least she'd learned some things about him, things she might never have known had it not been for this night. Before now she had known him only in the way a child, or, later, a teen, can ever know an adult, given the years between them and the different places they occupied in the world. Always he had compelled her respect, her gratitude, and a kind of schoolgirl adulation. But she had never really known him as a person, as a man. As a most *attractive* man.

She had noticed in the classroom that he often used his hands to elaborate or emphasize. During his illness, she'd been aware that his hands sometimes trembled. But not until tonight, when he rested his hands on her shoulders as he helped her out of her coat had she realized the strength those hands could convey.

She vaguely remembered that he had an older sister named Patricia, but only tonight did she learn that his sister was married with grown children, that she was several years older than he and consequently had been influential in his upbringing, and that he admired her tremendously.

She knew that her former teacher greatly respected his parents, but not until tonight had she known that they had been middle-aged when he was born. She discovered they had done their best to take an active role in his life, and that he still found it difficult to talk about his mother, who had died while Maggie was at the university.

She knew his father was an attorney, that he now shared his home with his daughter in Lexington, and that in spite of needing to use a wheelchair much of the time because of near-crippling arthritis, he maintained his independence as much as possible.

She had always thought of Jonathan Stuart as an extraordinary teacher, but not until tonight had she known that he very nearly had gone into the ministry instead of education. She also learned that he had a peculiar interest in the weather. Even as a student she had seen him often go to the classroom window and look out, but not until tonight did she discover that thunder and lightning—and snowstorms—held a great fascination for him.

As a child, she'd been aware that his dark, deep-set eyes—such a surprising contrast to the fairness of his hair—conveyed an incredible depth of kindness. But only now did she experience the way those eyes could make her heart swell or warm her skin like a physical touch.

And not until tonight did she realize that the smile that could bathe even the most woebegone child in approval and encouragement could also find its way to the loneliest, emptiest part of her, stealing her breath as something new and wonderful gradually opened and bloomed in celebration of her senses.

Nothing had ever made her feel this way before.

Whatever he'd been saying, he suddenly stopped. "You're not making much progress with that pie," he said, a touch of humor pulling at the corners of his mouth.

"Oh! It's very good. I was just…listening."

"And I've given you far too much to listen to," he said dryly.

"I'm sorry?"

"You've managed to get me to talk about myself a disgustingly long time. It's your turn now."

Maggie shook her head. "There's nothing to tell. You probably know everything about me there is to know, and none of it is very interesting."

"I rather doubt that either is the case." His tone was mild, even casual, but his gaze was almost unsettling in its intensity.

For a time he asked her the kind of questions any acquaintance might ask after an extended absence: about her work in Chicago, her family, her plans for the future. Then he caught her off guard. "What do you hear from Kenny these days? Or *do* you hear from him?"

"Kenny Tallman? Goodness, I haven't heard from him in years."

"Not at all?" He looked up from his plate, his expression questioning. "That surprises me. There was a time when everyone thought the two of you would probably…marry."

Maggie felt heat rise to her face. "It wasn't like that with Kenny and me. We were too young to know what we wanted. We were mostly just good friends."

The truth was that although she and Kenny had been "boyfriend and girlfriend" all through school, once he decided to go to seminary and the mission field, he'd made it clear he had no intention of cleaving to anyone or anything in Skingle Creek. He wanted to be "free to follow God's plan" for his life.

And God's plan didn't include Maggie.

"Any regrets?" Jonathan Stuart asked, his voice soft. "Or should I not ask?"

Maggie fumbled for a truthful reply, yet one that wouldn't reveal more than she wanted him to know.

"No, I don't mind," she said, managing a smile. "I'm just not sure how to answer. I did miss Kenny at first. He was such a special part of my life for so many years. He was a *good* friend to me. But eventually we stopped writing, and finally we just drifted apart. I'm sure it was best that way. Kenny had a strong sense of God's call on his life, and by then I knew I had to go in a different direction."

What she didn't say was that by then she had also known it wasn't Kenny she wanted to spend her life with. It had never been Kenny. She simply hadn't wanted to face the truth that she wanted something...*someone*...she couldn't have.

When had she realized that Jonathan Stuart meant too much to her, that he had become more than a revered teacher, a mentor, or the object of a schoolgirl crush? It might have been during the week just before she graduated from high school. She'd had questions about some of the university courses and had stayed after class one day so he could help her with the syllabus.

The room had been quiet, the breeze sifting through the open window warm and fragrant from all the springtime blooms and buds outside. He was seated at his desk; she was standing beside him.

Maggie leaned over his shoulder for a moment to point something out, when he suddenly turned and looked at her. Their eyes locked and held, and in that instant something turned in Maggie, something new and unfamiliar and so unexpected it was as if he'd touched her. With a fleeting but piercing clarity, she realized she *wanted* him to touch her.

Shaken, she took a step backward, and just as quickly he turned back to his desk.

Later she told herself that she'd only imagined the feeling that had seized her. And of course she'd imagined what she thought she'd seen in his eyes. Even so, she knew she must never again risk being alone with him in such close circumstances.

At that time in their lives, as her teacher with several years standing between them, he was as forbidden to her as if he'd been married.

And now?

Now...she wasn't so sure she was willing to relegate him to that same safe place. True, the years still stood between them. And even though he was no longer her teacher, he was still her supervisor. But she was no longer a child.

And she was no longer convinced that he was forbidden.

Suddenly the question that gnawed at her was how *he* saw *her* after all these years. Would it be possible for Jonathan Stuart to change his conception of her? To look past what she had been all those years ago to what she was today? Or would she forever be the child-Maggie instead of the woman she knew herself to be?

"I'd hoped Eva Grace would stop by the school. It seems I may have to come to *her* if I'm to see her before she leaves."

So deeply had Maggie been immersed in her thoughts that it took her a moment to take in what he was saying.

"Maggie?"

"I'm sorry," she said. "In truth, I'm a little worried about Eva Grace.

He frowned. "Is she ill?"

"No. At least I don't think so. But—" She stopped, but her need to confide in someone she could trust was too strong. "There's something wrong with Eva Grace, Mr. Stuart. I *know* there is. But she won't talk about it—not to me, and not to Mum either."

She told him about the late-night weeping, and how Eva Grace neither looked nor acted like herself. "She's made no effort to see any of her old friends. She won't even leave the house. Mum says she mostly just sits around during the day. That's not a bit like Evie. She's always wanted to be on the go, to be doing things and to be with people."

He nodded slowly. "You're right, it doesn't sound like the Eva Grace I remember. But people do change. Your sister has been married and living away from home for several years now. Couldn't that be all it is?"

"I suppose," Maggie said reluctantly.

"But you don't think so."

"Just being married and living away from home wouldn't make her cry herself to sleep every night, would it?"

His frown returned. "No. No, it wouldn't." He paused. "Is there anything I can do?"

Maggie shook her head. "I don't know what it would be. But you've already helped by just letting me talk about it. I'm trying not to worry Mum any more than necessary. And Da—well, I don't think he feels up to talking much at all anymore."

"Matthew is no better?"

Again Maggie shook her head. "No. But with Da, at least I know what's wrong. Mum says the pain has worn him down something fierce."

He nodded. "Matthew needs the kind of medical help he's not going to find in Skingle Creek, I'm afraid."

The drift of the conversation toward her father prompted Maggie to glance at the large clock on the far wall. "I should be going, I expect," she said reluctantly. "Da still fusses if I'm not home when he thinks I should be."

He smiled a little as he got to his feet. "Once a father always a father?"

"Oh, Mr. Stuart, you've no idea!"

Maggie stood and reached for her coat, but before she could slip into it, Jonathan Stuart came round the table and held it for her.

Oh, my. I could get used to this!

"I'll see you home," he said.

Maggie turned around. "You needn't do that, Mr. Stuart. I'll be just fine."

But he had already taken her by the arm, stopping only long enough to pay Mrs. Hubbard.

Outside, the musicians and crowd had dispersed, though several people were strolling along ahead of them as they started up the road.

"Really, Mr. Stuart, you don't have to do this."

Maggie knew her protest to be a feeble one, and the fact that he was still clasping her arm pleased her no end. Even so, she wasn't mindless of the curious looks they encountered as they went on.

There might be much to be said for a small town, but there was also the fact that when one had grown up in the same place a move couldn't be made without someone noticing. She had the annoying feeling that everyone they met still thought of her as "little Maggie MacAuley" and wondered what in the world she was doing walking along with her teacher after the sun went down.

Mr. Stuart, however, seemed oblivious to the inquisitive glances. He spoke easily to all they passed and even stopped to exchange a few words with Mr. and Mrs. Riley from the church, and then again with Mr. Gibbon, the bank president, who seemed friendly enough in spite of the questioning looks he kept shooting at Maggie.

She was almost relieved to get past the main part of town and start down the more isolated road toward home. Mr. Stuart made a few comments about the poor condition of the road and the need for more gas lamps along the way, which, of course, would never happen because of lack of funds. Maggie mostly listened and nodded her agreement.

When they finally reached her house, he opened the gate and walked up the yard with her. At the porch Maggie stopped. "This was

awfully nice of you, Mr. Stuart. The pie, and then seeing me home
and all...."

He was studying her with a faint smile. "Maggie—do you know
my given name?"

"Your name? Why, yes—yes, of course I do."

"Then do you think perhaps you might use it from now on?"

Is he serious? Can I ever think of him as anything but "Mr. Stuart"?

The look in his eyes told her that he *was* serious. And after another
moment, she realized how pleased she was by his suggestion. So
yes...yes, she *could* use his given name. In fact, she *wanted* to.

"I expect so, if that's what you'd like," she said, clearing her
throat.

His smile warmed even more. "I would, Maggie. I would like that
very much. And thank you for tonight, for keeping me company. I
enjoyed it."

"So did I, Mr.—" Maggie stopped and swallowed hard again.
"Jonathan."

He took her hand, and then released it. "Goodnight, Maggie."

At that moment the door flew open.

Chapter Ten

Night of Secrets

A man's most open actions have a secret side to them.

Joseph Conrad

⌁

Ah, there you are! I was getting—"

Matthew MacAuley stood in the doorway, his hair ruffled as though he'd been raking his hands through it. He looked from Maggie to Jonathan.

"Why, hello, Jonathan. I wouldn't have been worried if I'd known Maggie was with you."

Jonathan sensed Maggie's tension and was aware of her watching him. He felt more than a little awkward himself but tried not to let on. Instead he moved to ease the situation for Maggie.

"Matthew," he said with a nod. "Yes, I ran into Maggie at the square and talked her into keeping me company at supper. I hope that's all right."

"Oh, aye. Of course it is. Good of you to see her home. I don't like the girl out alone after dark."

"Da—"

Jonathan heard the level of Maggie's discomfort in that one word and knew that the kindest thing he could do for her was to make as quick an exit as possible.

"Entirely understandable. You can't be too careful. I hope I didn't inconvenience you. I was enjoying the chance to catch up with Maggie and lost track of the time."

Matthew nodded and glanced at Maggie, who stood looking as though she'd like nothing better than to drop through the porch.

"Won't you come in for a spell, Jonathan?" Matthew asked.

"No, but thanks. I'm sure you need to get to bed early. I'll just say goodnight to both of you and be on my way."

He turned to leave and was halfway down the yard when Maggie said, behind him, her voice thin and obviously strained, "Goodnight... *Jonathan*. And thank you."

He hesitated, turned back, and gave a quick wave before going on, the sound of his name on her lips echoing all the way.

In spite of the brief moment of awkwardness back at Maggie's house, his spirits remained high as he walked home. There was something about being with Maggie that could always cheer his heart.

Even as a child, she'd been good for him. During his illness, when he'd had to struggle to make it through each day, something about her no-nonsense, take-charge nature had never failed to give him a lift. And she seemed to sense his "bad days"—when his heart faltered nearly as much from discouragement as the illness itself. He could count on her to look for ways to help, either by working with the younger children or doing small tasks about the schoolroom.

After what he still thought of as his "miracle," when his health—and his hope—had been restored, he could always depend on her to lend a hand in the classroom. During her teen years she became almost as much his assistant as a student. She'd been such a help to him that after she graduated and went away to college, he'd been disorganized for weeks, badly missing the order she'd brought to the school.

The truth was that he hadn't realized how much she'd done until she was no longer there to do it.

Tonight had been a pleasant reminder of the little things he'd missed. Her unexpectedly husky voice that sometimes caught in her throat when she was under stress or taken off guard. The smile, tilted at one corner, that could be impish and warm at the same time. The uncommon green eyes that marked most of the MacAuley children, passed down from their father—eyes that could dance with amusement or flame with indignation. Her way of looking at him as if he were a mythical hero...and making him wish he were. That riot of fiery hair that always had a will of its own, yet never failed to intrigue him.

He suddenly realized his thoughts were leading down a treacherous path—and not for the first time. He slowed his pace, wishing he had the right to think about her as much as he did think about her. He caught himself wondering how she would feel if she knew the way she occupied his thoughts, if she realized that she held an appeal for him that had nothing to do with her once being his student.

Was that altogether true, though? Perhaps what he felt for Maggie had more to do with their past than he realized. How did he separate the child he'd been so fond of from the fascinating young woman she had become? Would she be repelled by his present interest in her, by his affection for her? Was he wrong in hoping that the reason she was so exasperated by her father's treating her like a child was because she wanted to be seen as older and more mature—in the hope that her former teacher would no longer think of her as a child?

Was he being altogether foolish to assume that she cared one way or the other how he thought of her? Perhaps it had never occurred to Maggie that he thought of her at all. There was always the possibility that she wouldn't relish the idea if she *did* know. A man—how many years...fifteen or nearly that at least—older than she, unable to get his mind off her.

He groaned to himself, slowing his pace even more. *Fifteen years...*

But was that really so much? He wasn't quite forty yet, after all. Not exactly in his dotage.

He fumbled for some reassurance. Yes, what about Herb Danson and his wife? Herb was a good twenty years older than Maryanne, and from all appearances they were an ideal couple. For that matter, look at Ben and Regina Wallace. At least a dozen years or more accounted for the difference in their ages. And to anyone who knew them, they set an example for the perfect marriage.

Marriage?

Jonathan shook his head as if to lose a bothersome insect. He had to stop this. He might not be exactly doddering, but he was no schoolboy either. A little common sense was called for, and the sooner the better. And he hadn't missed the glint of fire in Matthew MacAuley's eyes when he'd first seen his daughter standing on the porch with a man. Until he realized who she was with, he'd looked as if he might have been about to fetch a shotgun. He and Matthew might be friends, but if Maggie's father sensed anything amiss in a man's behavior with his daughter—especially an *older* man—Jonathan suspected friendship wouldn't count for much.

Disgusted with himself and frustrated with the entire situation, he expelled an impatient breath and turned his thoughts toward home.

Matthew faced his daughter. "Since when do you call Mr. Stuart 'Jonathan'?"

Maggie headed toward the kitchen, answering as she went. "He asked me to call him that, Da."

He was on her heels like a bloodhound on the scent. "That doesn't seem right to me, Maggie. He may not be your teacher anymore, but he's still your employer."

Maggie stopped just inside the kitchen. Unfortunately there was no sign of her mother or Eva Grace to deflect his attention. "He's really *not* my employer, Da. I'm employed by the school board, just as Mr.—just as Jonathan is. He's my superior, of course, being the principal. All the same, it was his idea that I call him by his given name. Not mine."

Her father's lips thinned, and he clearly had a mind to say more when Maggie's mother walked into the kitchen. "Oh, you're home, Maggie! Good. We were getting worried."

Thoroughly exasperated by now, Maggie looked from one to the other. "You can't be worrying about me anymore, Mum. Nor you, Da. I'm not a little girl any longer. I'm perfectly capable of looking out for myself, whether it's daylight or dark."

Both stood staring at her, Da's face rapidly darkening to a thunderhead.

Her mother merely looked confused. "We know that, dear. But still—"

"Jonathan Stuart saw her home," Da said, his tone grudging. "So she was in good hands." He turned back to Maggie. "But we had no way of knowing who you were with until you showed up at the door, girl! No matter how old you might be, we still worry."

"That was good of Mr. Stuart," said her mother. "But I hope it wasn't a bother."

By now Maggie had all she could do not to grind her teeth. "He *insisted* on seeing me home, Mum. He didn't seem to consider it a bother. Not at all. We met up with each other at the square, and he invited me to supper—"

"But you'd already had your supper—"

"Yes, I know," said Maggie, pulling in a deep breath. "But he wanted some company while he had his, so I had a piece of pie with him."

"Oh, well, that was nice then," her mother said vaguely.

Hoping to change the subject, Maggie asked about Eva Grace.

Her mother made a palms-up gesture. "She stayed in the bedroom by herself all evening again. Maggie, have you tried to talk to her?"

"I told you I have, Mum. I get nowhere."

So far she had kept her silence about her sister's nightly weeping. Her mother had enough to worry about these days without fretting over Eva Grace. The searching look her mum now fixed on her made

Maggie wonder if she wasn't suspicious that her daughter was keeping something from her.

Maggie was relieved when Da cleared his throat and announced he had to get to bed. Which meant that *everyone* had to get to bed. His assumption that the entire household would keep to his schedule, including bedtime, didn't bother Maggie as much tonight as it did most other times. At least he wouldn't be nagging her about coming home late, and her mother wouldn't be able to question her further about Eva Grace.

Truth to tell, the thought of the dark, quiet bedroom was inviting. Finally she'd be able to think about the strange…but not unpleasant…evening she had spent with Jonathan Stuart.

On her way to the bedroom, she silently tested his name on her lips again, wishing she could say it aloud.

Jonathan…

She half hoped Eva Grace would already be asleep, though it was still early.

But Evie was wide awake, sprawled on the bed opposite Maggie's, thumbing idly through a Sears, Roebuck catalog.

"You're in dutch," she said without looking up.

"Don't even start. Honestly, sometimes Da makes my teeth rattle."

Eva Grace turned to look at her. "Where were you anyway? I've heard him pacing and grumbling for the past half-hour."

Maggie hesitated. "At the square, listening to the music."

"This late?"

Maggie had no intention of telling her sister that she'd spent the evening with Jonathan Stuart. But she needn't have concerned herself. Eva Grace had already turned her back and was reaching for the lamp. "Can you change in the dark? I'm going to sleep."

"Sure," Maggie said, relieved Evie wasn't going to question her more. "Go ahead."

By the time she'd changed into her nightgown and slipped into bed, she was too pent up to sleep. She could tell by Eva Grace's breathing that she too was still awake.

There was something she wanted to ask her, but she couldn't bear it if her sister took to teasing her—or worse yet, asked too many awkward questions. Finally she couldn't stand it any longer.

"Evie?"

No answer.

"Don't pretend to be asleep. I know you're not."

There was a long sigh. "I'd *like* to be."

"Evie, promise not to make fun if I ask you something?"

Her sister made a sound under her breath that sounded like a growl. "I don't feel like talking, Maggie."

"You *never* feel like talking anymore. I'm beginning to wonder why you came home in the first place."

There was a long silence. Then, "All right. What's on your mind?"

"You're sure?"

"I said so, didn't I?"

There. That sounded more like the old Eva Grace.

"How do you—" Maggie swallowed, then tried again, "How do you know if you're...in love?"

Now she had her sister's attention. Eva Grace flipped over and propped herself up on her elbow. "*What?*"

She reached as if to light the lamp again, but Maggie stopped her. "Don't! Just tell me. What's it like?"

There wasn't enough moonlight that she could quite see her sister's eyes, but she sensed her stare.

"So you finally got yourself a beau. Who is he?" Eva Grace's tone was laced with a humorless edge.

"I'm not going to tell you a thing unless you answer my question," Maggie said, already wishing she'd kept quiet.

Evie was silent for a long moment, and then sank down onto her side. "Well...at first you think it's the most wonderful thing that's ever happened to you."

"At first?"

"In the beginning you feel flustered all the time. You can't concentrate on anything else but...him. And when you think about him, which is most of the time, you feel almost dizzy. You don't want to be with anyone else." She paused and Maggie thought she heard her voice catch. "He's your whole world."

"Is that how it was with you and Richard?"

A long silence followed Maggie's question.

"Evie?"

"Yes," her sister said so softly Maggie could barely hear her. "That's how it was."

Maggie hesitated but couldn't stop the question that was bothering her. "You said *at first.*"

"What?"

"You said that's how it is at first," Maggie prompted. "What about later?"

Eva Grace let out a long breath. "Everything changes, Maggie. The first craziness of being in love can't last forever."

Maggie thought about that. "But you and Richard still love each other."

Evie said nothing.

"Don't you?"

There was a long silence. Maggie leaned toward the other bed.

Even with the distance that separated them, she could feel her sister's tension in the moment before a wild sob exploded, followed by a storm of weeping.

She swung out of bed. This time Evie wasn't going to brush her off without an explanation.

"Evie?" She took her sister firmly by the shoulders. Without warning Evie collapsed against her, still weeping. Alarmed now, Maggie put her arms around her for support. "*Evie*—what's wrong?"

Eva Grace nearly choked on a strangled sob.

Frightened, Maggie wanted to go for their mother, but Eva Grace held on to her. "*Tell* me, Evie!"

"Oh, Maggie! I'm going to have a *baby!*"

Too stunned to say a word, Maggie held her sister close, her mind racing.

"But that's *wonderful!*" she finally managed. "Why did you wait so long to tell me? Do Mum and Da know?"

When Evie cried harder, Maggie came round to sit down on the bed beside her. "I thought you'd be happy, Evie. A baby—isn't that what you always wanted? A husband and a family? Here, let me light the lamp—"

"No!" Evie was obviously fighting for control, clutching at Maggie so she couldn't move. "I don't want the light. And you've got to promise me you won't tell Mum or Da about the baby!"

"But why *not?*"

In the deeply shadowed room, Maggie could just barely make out her sister's features. Something cold uncoiled itself as she saw the frantic look in her eyes.

"Why don't you want Mum and Da to know? They'll be overjoyed! You know how excited they were when Nell Frances had her first—"

"Keep your voice down!" Though little more than a whisper, her sister's tone was harsh. "It was different with Nell Frances," she went on, staring into the darkness of the room as if she were unwilling to meet Maggie's eyes.

Again Maggie felt the coldness of dread wash over her. "Different... how?"

Slowly, her sister lifted her head, finally meeting Maggie's gaze. "Because Nell Frances has a husband who doesn't beat her."

Maggie stared at her in horror. "Evie...no! Richard—"

"Richard is a monster."

Chapter Eleven

A Sister's Tears

Is there any warmer place to seek comfort
than in the consoling embrace of a sister?

Anonymous

⁓

The words her sister spoke were made even more terrible by the
angry hiss in her voice. For an instant Maggie was too shocked to
react. A part of her sensed what was coming, but she recoiled at
hearing it.

One of the difficulties in grasping what Eva Grace was telling her
had to do with the unexpected shift in their relationship. Evie was
the big sister who, before tonight, had always accepted that role. She
was the one who counseled Maggie and Nell Frances, listened to their
problems, and offered advice, even when she let it be known that
they'd brought their woes on themselves. There had also been times,
during truly grievous situations, when they had cried on Evie's shoulder, and she had always done her best to console them.

But now Eva Grace was the one who needed comforting. And

whatever she was about to hear, Maggie somehow knew her sister's plight was too dreadful to be fixed by a strong shoulder or a sympathetic word.

In acceptance of this awkward, but clearly necessary reversal of roles, she put an arm around her sister's shoulders. "Tell me, Evie," she said quietly. "Tell me everything."

How would she ever be able to live with the fact that her sister—the gentle-natured, oh-so-feminine Eva Grace who had never wanted anything more than to escape Skingle Creek, marry, and have a family—had been living a nightmare? And not for a brief time, but for most of her marriage—more than five years now.

"How have you managed to keep this to yourself all this time?" she asked after Evie finished her story.

"Who was I going to tell? I don't have any close friends in Lexington. Both you and Nell Frances had your own lives. And I couldn't tell Mum and Da. I just couldn't. You know how it would hurt them, not to mention what Da might do."

"Da's not able to do much of anything these days," Maggie said, her mind swarming as if under attack by bees. "But your pastor? A doctor? Surely you talked to *someone.*"

Eva Grace shook her head. "The pastor and Richard are friends," she said, bitterness edging her tone. "There's no way I could tell him what Richard is really like. Not that he'd believe me anyway. Everyone thinks Richard is the perfect husband. A regular saint."

She made a harsh sound in her throat that might have been a failed attempt at a laugh.

"When…he beats you, how—I mean, does he actually use his fists on you?"

Why had she asked that? The moment the question was out of her mouth, Maggie regretted it. She didn't want to know, not really. How would she ever rid herself of the image of Richard Barlow beating her gentle sister?

Eva Grace didn't look at her but sat hunched on the side of the bed, hugging her arms to herself. "Sometimes he uses his fists. Sometimes a belt."

"Oh Evie—" Maggie felt sick to her stomach.

As if she hadn't heard, Evie went on, her voice a flat, emotionless drone. "He's always careful where he hits me, of course. He never leaves a mark where it might show."

Maggie's mind spun with thoughts of fitting punishments for Richard, and she almost wished she could mete it out herself. She strengthened her grip on her sister's shoulder.

But Evie moved away, got up, and went to light the lamp on the table between their beds. She then turned her back to Maggie, slipped her nightgown off her shoulders, and stood immobile, saying nothing.

Nausea rose in Maggie, burning her throat, threatening to choke her. She struggled just to breathe as she sat staring at the evidence of what she'd just heard. Dark with ugly bruises, criss-crossed with deep red slashes, her sister's back looked as if someone had branded her in a fit of rage and brutality.

Maggie sat transfixed, stunned, and sick at heart.

Evie had called Richard a monster.

She was right.

Eva Grace rearranged her nightgown and turned toward Maggie, but she kept her gaze averted. Maggie stood, went to her sister, and gently pulled her close. "I'm so sorry, Evie," she choked out. "So terribly sorry."

A thought struck her. "Does Richard know about the baby?"

Evie slipped away from her and went to the window, where she stood, looking out into the night. "Oh yes. He knows. But it hasn't changed anything."

"You mean he's *still* beating you?"

Evie turned around. "I thought…at first…he might be different when he heard about the baby. And he was for a while. But then he started up again, worse than ever."

"How can he do this? *Why* does he do it?"

Evie shook her head. "He's always sorry afterward. He brings me flowers or some other gift and begs me to forgive him. And I always have. Until now."

She lifted her head, and the depth of sadness and hurt in her eyes broke Maggie's heart. She felt tears fill her own eyes, but they were scalding tears of anger and shame. Shame that she hadn't known what her sister was going through until now.

"Why did you wait so long to come home? Why didn't you leave him sooner?"

Evie went white, looking away. "I haven't really...*left* him, Maggie. I just had to get away for a few days to think."

"What do you mean, you haven't *left* him? Of course, you've left him! You can't possibly even *think* of going back to that—"

"He's my husband, Maggie. I'm going to have his child."

"He's a *madman!* You'll have your baby here!"

Evie raised a hand to warn her. "Keep your voice down!"

"Surely you don't intend to keep this from Mum and Da any longer? Evie, they have to know."

Maggie groped for the words that would convince her sister. "You can't go back to Richard. You could lose the baby, Evie. Could you live with that? Would you really take a chance on your baby being hurt? Or worse?"

For an instant, Evie looked confused. "It's Richard's baby too. I don't think he'd actually..."

Her words fell away.

"You just admitted that he's still beating you." Maggie didn't think she had it in her to be so harsh with her older sister, but she was suddenly afraid—afraid that Evie would actually weaken and go back to that—

"Evie—*think!* Even if the baby survives the beatings before it's born, what about after?"

"Oh, Maggie, Richard wouldn't hurt his own child! He's not *that* cruel!"

"He certainly has no compunction about hurting his own *wife,* does he? Are you really going to give him the benefit of the doubt? You'd actually risk your baby's life?"

"Well, what am I *supposed* to do?" Evie shot back, her eyes blazing. "How am I supposed to keep myself and a child? Do you have any idea what it's like for a woman who leaves her husband? And with a baby yet?"

Maggie had all she could do to keep from shaking her. "No, obviously I don't. But I *do* know that you have a family to take care of you and your baby. We won't let him hurt you again, Evie. You'll be safe here, you and the baby."

She stopped and caught her breath. "Evie, if you don't tell Mum and Da, I'm going to. And the only thing that will stop Da from going after Richard is if you stay here. But you've seen how it is with Da. He'd be no match for Richard, not with the shape he's in. You know I'm right."

Her heart ached when she saw that Evie was weeping again. Tears trailed slowly down her face as she stood there, looking for all the world like a wounded child.

"I loved him, Maggie. I thought it would stop if I could just love him enough..." Her voice broke.

"Evie, you can't stay with him," Maggie pleaded, her own voice trembling. "You wouldn't dare. He might *kill* you if you go back to him!"

As if deaf to Maggie, Evie went on, her words disjointed and erratic. "I didn't want to leave...I was afraid of what he'd do if he came after me...but the baby...I was frightened for the baby..."

"Of course, you were. And rightly so." Once again Maggie grasped her sister's shoulders and led her to bed, sitting down beside her and turning Evie's face toward her so she couldn't look away. "In the morning, we'll tell the folks. I'll help you."

"Da will have to go to work..."

Maggie pulled a face. "I forgot. All right. We'll go ahead and tell Mum though. And then we'll talk to Da when he comes home tomorrow evening. I'll be here all day tomorrow, so you won't have to face them alone. It will be all right, Evie. I know they vex us something fierce sometimes, but they love us more than everything, we both know that. Why, they'd be devastated entirely if they were to learn about this from someone besides you."

"They'll be devastated anyway," Evie said, her voice catching.

"Yes, they probably will be," Maggie agreed. "But not for long. You'll see. They're strong people, our folks. In no time, they'll be making plans for the baby."

Evie wiped a hand over her damp face. "You don't think Da will be angry with me?"

"Why would he be angry with *you*? He'll want to murder Richard, but he won't be angry with *you*."

Maggie got up and went to straighten her sister's bedclothes. "Come on now. You have to get some sleep. You can't go without rest. It's not good for the baby. And that's what you need to think about now—the baby."

Evie hesitated but finally gave in.

After Maggie extinguished the lamp, she leaned over her sister. Evie was still awake.

Patting the bed beside her, Evie said, "Stay with me, Maggie. Like when we were younger."

Maggie crawled into bed with her big sister and lay holding her until Evie fell into an exhausted sleep. Only then did she turn away to shed her own tears.

Chapter Twelve

Confrontation

Gone, gone, forever gone
Are the hopes I cherished.

Gerald Griffin

The next morning, Eva Grace told Maggie she'd changed her mind about how she intended to divulge her situation to their parents.

"Explaining it once will be hard enough," she said while they were dressing for breakfast. "I'm just going to wait until tonight and tell them both together. I can't go through that twice."

Maggie didn't like it, but she understood. Still, it was going to be a long day, being around her mother, trying to pretend that everything was all right.

"Ray will be here tonight, too, you know," she pointed out.

Evie's face clouded with uncertainty. "I can't possibly talk about this in front of Ray."

Fearful that her sister might yet change her mind, Maggie hurried to reassure her. "Actually, he might *not* be here. He and some of his friends usually get together on Saturday night. If you want, we'll wait until he's gone before talking with Mum and Da."

Her sister nodded. "But he has to know sooner or later."

"We'll let Da handle that." Maggie took her hand. "It's going to be all right. You'll see."

But the doubt in Evie's eyes plainly said that she didn't believe her, that she was afraid it would be anything *but* all right.

And if she were to be completely honest, Maggie had to admit that she shared the same fear.

As things turned out, they had no choice but to tell their mother before evening. Early Saturday afternoon, Maggie and Eva Grace were in the kitchen, baking a pie for supper. Ray had gone over to Tim Duggan's house to "hit a few balls." Their mother was in the front room, mending, so the house was quiet when they heard a knock on the door.

Maggie started to go, but stopped when she heard her mother's voice at the door.

"Richard! Why didn't you write that you were coming? Eva Grace—Richard is here!"

Evie went white. She was trembling, fear tightening her features.

"You don't have to see him," Maggie whispered, putting a restraining hand on her sister's arm. "You stay here. I'll talk to him."

"I *have* to see him, Maggie. Mum doesn't even know what's going on—"

"Well, she's going to know now. And you *don't* need to see Richard. Just stay right here."

Uneasiness rose in Maggie. What if he managed to talk Evie into going back with him? She had sensed her sister wavering throughout the morning, so locked up with her own thoughts that she scarcely spoke.

She couldn't let that happen. No matter what it took, she *couldn't* let Evie leave with Richard Barlow.

"Maggie, I can't just *hide* from him! I have to face him."

Maggie caught her by the shoulders. "Listen to me, Evie! You *don't* have to face him! He's given up any rights he ever had with you. I can handle Richard. You stay out of his sight."

She squeezed her sister's shoulders, took a steadying breath, and headed for the front room.

"Where's your sister?" her mother said when she entered. "Does she know Richard is here?"

He had the nerve to smile at her. One of his feigned brotherly smiles that virtually reeked of hypocrisy. "Hello, Maggie. It's good to see you again."

When Maggie said nothing but simply stood glaring at him, his smile faltered a little. "Well, I've come to collect my wife," he said, glancing back to Maggie's mother. "No doubt she'll be cross with me, but we really need to take the train back tonight. I have a board meeting at the church tomorrow afternoon."

Maggie's blood roared in her ears at his mention of the church. "Evie's not going anywhere with you."

"*Maggie!*" Her mother brought her hand to her throat, clearly shocked at this intolerable rudeness. "What's wrong with you?"

Something flared in Richard's eyes, but if she'd disturbed his icy composure, he showed no sign of it. He merely gave Maggie a long, speculative look before glancing toward the kitchen.

Before he could cross the room, Maggie blocked his way, darting in front of him. "I said, she's not going back with you."

He calmly lifted an eyebrow and touched a hand to his perfectly groomed blond hair. "Of course Eva Grace is going back with me. Now be a good girl and go and fetch your sister. Or I will."

"*No!*"

"Excuse me?"

"I said no. *You're* leaving, all right—and the sooner the better. But you're leaving *alone*. You've hurt Evie for the last time."

His fair skin flushed an angry red, and his voice turned hard as a stone. "I don't know what you're talking about, Maggie, but I am most assuredly not leaving here without my *wife!* Now let me pass, please."

Maggie didn't move.

"Maggie, what are you *doing?*" her mother choked out. "What's wrong with you?"

"Richard knows what's wrong, Mum." Maggie heard the tremor in her voice but ignored it. "Evie and I were going to tell you tonight. We'll have to explain later." She paused. "After Richard leaves."

But Richard had seen his chance to get past her. While her attention was diverted, he jostled her out of his way and started toward the kitchen.

He was a big man, but Maggie's anger had fired her with a strength she didn't know she had. She lunged sideways and, shoving hard at his shoulders, managed to push him back.

"*Don't* you touch me again!" he warned, nearly shouting now as he lifted a hand to warn her off.

"Or you'll do what, Richard?" Maggie shot back. "Beat me up the way you've been beating my sister? Not in *this* house you won't!"

She heard her mother gasp, saw Richard's eyes flare as he looked past her. Maggie half turned to see Eva Grace standing in the doorway, her face ashen, her hands knotted into fists at her sides.

"Stop it, Richard!" she choked out. "Leave Maggie alone."

He raked Evie's face with a murderous look that, had she not been so furious, might have frightened Maggie. As it was, her only thought was to keep Evie well away from him until she could get him out of the house.

She watched him struggle for control and grasp it, although his icy stare was unyielding. "Eva? What's going on here?"

Maggie saw the way her sister was shaking. Quickly she moved to slip a steadying arm around her shoulders.

She didn't miss the hatred in Richard's eyes as he looked first at her and then at Evie. He stood rigid in his anger, his hands knotted at his sides.

Maggie had never noticed before how large his hands were. She caught a momentary image of him using those hands to hurt Evie, and she had all she could do not to hurl herself at him.

"Evie, go back to the kitchen," she said.

But Evie didn't move. Instead, her tone suprisingly hard, she said, "Richard–I want you to leave."

"Why are you behaving this way, Eva?"

"You know why."

He smiled, a quick, emotionless slash that didn't fool Maggie for an instant.

As she watched, he made an unsuccessful attempt to curb his anger. "Apparently you've told Maggie that we're having difficulties. But I'm sure Maggie understands that all married couples have their problems."

"Richard, please. Just go."

Evie's voice had dropped to little more than a whisper, and Maggie felt her sway slightly. How long would she be able to resist Richard's clear intention of wearing her down?

She glanced across the room to see her mother hugging her arms to herself, her expression one of shock and bewilderment. Maggie hated the pain this was going to bring upon her parents, especially her mother. Ever the peacemaker, Mum was one to take everyone's problems on herself and try to solve them. But this horror that had come upon them now was more than a problem—and it wouldn't go away until Richard walked out of their lives.

And Maggie intended to make certain he did just that. Unfortunately, she had lost sight of the fact that Richard hadn't risen to his present level of success without more than his share of cunning and persuasiveness. In a mercurial change, his harshness gave way to a humble, conciliatory tone of voice. Just as quickly, his facial expression smoothed, his former belligerence replaced by a meekness that enraged Maggie even more than his earlier condescension.

"Eva, please," he said, his tone cajoling. "We need to talk alone. We can't work anything out here, in front of an audience." He shot a look at Maggie, and in that instant his pale-blue eyes glazed over with fury. But when his gaze shifted back to Eva Grace, the pleading penitent had returned.

Maggie held her breath. If Evie gave in to his performance—and Maggie was convinced that's what this was, a *performance*—he would win. Evie would go back to Lexington with him.

She could have moaned with relief when Eva Grace spoke up. "No, Richard. We're not going to talk. Not this time."

"Eva—"

"I said *no*, Richard. It's always this way. You're always sorry, and we talk, and you make promises and convince me it won't happen again. But you're *not* sorry, not really...and it *does* happen again. And every time it gets worse!"

"You're overwrought. You shouldn't do this. The baby—"

"The *baby*? Where was your concern for the baby when you punched me in the stomach the night of the Lockharts' dinner because I had been too *quiet* at the table?"

Maggie wanted to fly at him, pound him the way he had beaten her sister—repeatedly, savagely. Instead she could only stand and stare at him with revulsion and barely contained fury.

Her mother let out a strangled sound of anguish. "Eva Grace?"

Evie's eyes filled with tears. "I wanted to tell you, Mum. I was going to tell you today, truly I was. Maggie and I, we were both—"

But the shock in Kate MacAuley's eyes had already changed to something else, something Maggie had never seen in her mother before that moment as she lunged toward Richard.

"You've been *hitting* her? You hit your own wife when she's carrying your *child*? What kind of a man *are* you?"

So caught off guard was he by this unexpected explosion from Kate MacAuley that Richard actually stepped back. Maggie doubted that he'd ever thought his mother-in-law capable of anything more than a mild scolding. He plainly had never imagined her capable of the livid rage that flagged her face.

Maggie wouldn't have either. Something in her recoiled at the idea of her small, gentle-natured mother having to witness this ugliness.

She released Evie and went to restrain her mother, gripping her arm to hold her back.

Her mother's eyes burned with accusatory pain. "Why didn't you tell me, Maggie? One of you should have *told* me!"

"Mum—I didn't know until last night. We were going to tell you—both you and Da—tonight."

Her mother turned on Richard Barlow then, and Maggie thought she would never forget the look of black hatred and disgust that masked her usually placid features.

"*Leave my house!*" she ordered, her words heavy and threatening. "And don't you ever dare to come back. Matthew will kill you if you do, and I won't lift a finger to stop him! *Get out!*"

Maggie could actually see Richard measuring the strength of his mother-in-law's rage, fumbling to regain his control of the situation, debating whether he should defy her. She glanced at Eva Grace and realized that her sister was holding herself together by the slimmest of threads. Torn between her family and the father of her baby, she didn't know what to do.

"You can't be serious about this," Richard said to Evie in that hateful, supercilious tone Maggie had always disliked so much.

"*Go*, Richard!" was all Evie said. She sounded tired and riddled with sorrow, but her words were totally, uncompromisingly final.

"I'm not going to stand for this, Eva. You're having my child—"

"I'm having *my* child!" Evie's voice was like broken glass scraping bare skin. "I'll die before I ever let you near my baby! Now get out of here or Maggie will go for help. *Get out!*"

Maggie was so proud of her sister she almost shouted. Richard stood there, trying to stare Evie into submission, but she never wavered. She straightened her shoulders and met his gaze with a withering look, not even flinching at the ugly oath he hurled at her.

Finally he started for the door. Suddenly he stopped and turned back. "We're not finished," he warned, his tone menacing. "Don't you think for a moment this is over. That's my child you're carrying. Are you so simple-minded you actually believe any court will let you keep it? You left *me*, remember? You *deserted* me without any warning whatsoever. I can divorce you without lifting a finger, and you'll never see the child!"

And then he was gone.

One glance at Evie told Maggie she was about to fall over.

"Mum!" She motioned to her mother to go to Evie, then ran to slam the door behind Richard, throwing the lock with trembling hands.

When she turned back, her mother was gathering Evie in her arms and leading her to the sofa. Her sister was near collapse and weeping.

"Here, *alannah*, sit down. It's over now. It's over." Her mum went on crooning to Evie as if she were a child, helping her onto the sofa as she gestured for Maggie.

"You rest and then you can tell me everything. You and your sister must tell me what I should have known long before now."

She paused, drawing Eva Grace close. "And then you can tell us about the baby. I want to know about my new grandchild."

Maggie watched them, her heart swelling with love for her small, brave mother, even while it broke with sorrow for her disconsolate sister.

Chapter Thirteen

To Look Past This Night

I shall carry hope in my heart,
Though my heart lies in ruins,
For there are those
Whose love will bear me up.

Author unknown

Matthew MacAuley had once believed that the worst of the worries and frustrations that went along with raising three daughters were at an end once they were grown, especially with two of them wed and out of the house.

More fool, he.

He sat beside his eldest daughter on the sofa, awkwardly waiting for her to collect herself and go on with the unbelievable story she had just this evening leveled on him. When the first shock and initial storm of anger went roaring through him, he thought his head would explode. But once he'd heard the worst of it, he realized his heart would be destroyed before his head.

Not that his rage had cooled, not a bit. If Richard Barlow had been within sight, Matthew would not have thought twice about beating the blackguard senseless. He had all he could do to stay put while his daughter continued her story. More than anything else he wanted to flee the room and go crashing into the night where he could release the rage that threatened to crush him.

But the girl clearly had more to say, and he meant to hear it all, no matter how ugly it might be.

Kate sat at the other end of the sofa, pulling at her knuckles, her gaze traveling back and forth between himself and Eva Grace. Every time her eyes lighted upon him, she looked as if she expected him to do something. The same with Maggie, sitting on the footstool in front of the window, her chin locked in place, one hand kneading her skirt.

But what was he to do? He might have expected a marital quarrel or the like, but not something like this. Not something that reached into the dark cavern of his own past and made him want to retch.

As for his daughter, Eva Grace kept falling into fits of weeping. And when he so much as asked the girl a question, she looked as if she feared he might strike her.

What had he ever done to make his daughters fearful of him? He had never laid a hand on Kate or any one of the girls. Nor Ray either, for that matter, although it wasn't because the lad didn't test him often enough.

He was no Richard Barlow, after all. He would never touch one of his own in anger. He'd had enough of that madness as a boy from his own father.

With a defeated feeling that sank deep into his soul, he recognized that his girls had grown up thinking him hard-hearted. They couldn't know why he was the way he was, could never have understood that their father was in many ways two men, one who had grown up amid violence and was himself as volatile as a keg of dynamite, the other a man who found it impossible to open himself to anyone except his wife.

He had been a boy, and then a man, who guarded himself from

becoming close to anyone, from exposing whatever gentleness might be a part of his nature, and so had become hard and lived at a distance from everyone, even his children. Only with Kate could he be soft, even weak. He didn't intentionally hold himself apart from the ones he loved more than anything in the world. Matthew had simply lived within himself so long he knew no other way to be.

And so they all sat watching him now, obviously wondering what to expect. Even his wounded, battered daughter couldn't look at him. Father in heaven, he would die for any one of them! And his own daughter couldn't look him in the eye for fear of what she might see.

He swallowed down the taste of regret and a wrenching sadness. A moment more, and he reached for his daughter's hand and held it carefully in his. "What's the rest of it, lass?" he asked, careful to keep his voice soft. "There's more, isn't there?"

Finally, she looked at him through her red, swollen eyes. "I'm going to have a baby, Da."

Matthew felt the air go out of him. A rush of feelings came bearing down on him like a flood.

"Are you now?" he managed to choke out.

She nodded. "I'm sorry, Da."

"*Sorry?*" He stared at her, bewildered. "A baby is a wonderful thing, girl. Why would you be sorry?"

"Oh, not about the baby, Da! I'm glad for the baby. But for bringing all this down on you, this terrible thing and my shame. I'm so sorry, Da, but I didn't know what else to do except to come home."

Stunned, Matthew felt as though something inside of him was being ripped to pieces. He tried to speak, but could only squeeze his daughter's hand. Finally he found his voice. "Ah, no...no, Evie. You've brought nothing terrible to this house. Not now, not *ever*. And the only shame in any of this belongs to Richard Barlow." The man's name on his tongue tasted like a curse.

He pulled her close against him, lay a hand on her head, and stroked her hair. "Of course, you came home. You did exactly the right thing. As for what you've brought to us—you've brought us nothing but blessings, daughter. And now this—a new grandchild? What you've given us is a *gift*."

She collapsed against him, this daughter of his who was always so bright, so sure of herself, so lovely it seemed she could have the world if she wanted it. She melted into him, sobbing as if she were a little girl again.

"Oh, Daddy...Daddy..." Over and over she sobbed the name she had never called him before tonight.

Daddy.

And Matthew found himself grateful that she could call him that. "Da" was the name of the man who had raised her and been strong for her. But "Daddy"? Surely that was the name for a man whose shoulder she could cry on.

Matthew buried his face in his daughter's hair, hoping to transfer what strength there was in him to her delicate nature, to her suffering spirit, at the same time drawing comfort for his own pain from her need of him, her reliance on him. How strange a thing the human heart was, that even broken, it could still contain the sweetness of a daughter's love.

Later, Kate and Matthew talked for what seemed like half the night, until their shock and anger finally gave way to a sorrowful acceptance.

Kate felt a strange relief gradually settle over her, relief that no matter what her daughter had endured, she was now safe. Even so, she couldn't block out the thought of Eva Grace under the pounding hands of Richard Barlow. She had seen a fleeting image of his viciousness for herself this afternoon, the look of wild fury in his eyes when he turned on Eva Grace.

Kate shuddered, and Matthew strengthened his embrace even as he slept.

She sighed. This was the first time in months he had drawn back the curtain on his long withdrawal and opened up to her as he once had. She hated the thought that it had taken a tragedy—their daughter's tragedy—to bring him to the point where he could again show his need for her comfort.

He had talked in whispers, wept in her arms, and she in his, and when their sorrow finally gave way to exhaustion, peace had settled over them. It was then that he quietly confessed to her the ugly, violent thoughts toward Richard that had crowded his mind from the moment he learned of the man's perfidy.

"I've never been able to lose the memory of my father going after my mother in one of his rages, using his fists or a belt or whatever was handy to him. Oh, Kate, the thought of my own daughter as a victim of that sick savagery likes to tear me to pieces."

"You have to stop thinking about it, Matthew. Stop torturing yourself."

"But don't you see, Kate? This business with Eva Grace—when I heard, I could have gone after Barlow the same as I did with my da, that night I beat him off my mother. If I could have got my hands on that degenerate, I'd have murdered him! But that makes me no better man than Barlow or my father. The same thing is in me, that hellish, wicked rage that drives a man like Richard and my father. It's in me too, Kate."

"No! That's not true a bit, Matthew. Don't you *ever* think that way! Not for a moment. Do you actually believe I could live with you all these years and not know the kind of man you are?"

"Kate, do you doubt at all what I would have done to Richard had he been within my reach today? Do you, Kate?"

She ached for him. She had known, almost from the time they'd wed, that Matthew harbored a terror of the darkness he believed lurked inside him. It wasn't that she didn't recognize the truth, that he had a fiery temper and was often hard-pressed to restrain it. She'd seen evidence of it more than once, though it was never directed at her or the children. While he might grow impatient and irritable with any one of them at times, and though he could turn nearly livid with outrage about the injustices done to himself and the other miners and their families, he had never once became physical in his wrath.

Admittedly, his temper had shortened since the accident, but that was from the pain.

She knew about the bad blood between him and his father, who must have been a terrible, violent man—a tyrant with his own wife and sons. But Matthew had told her only what he couldn't keep locked inside himself any longer, that and no more. She knew there *was* more, but she didn't need to know what it was. Kate had seen enough evil to recognize it, and Matthew MacAuley was not an evil man. Nor was he a violent man, no matter what he believed of himself. In truth, her husband was a kind, even a gentle man, one whom she suspected had never known himself very well.

She reached up to touch his hair, kissed him lightly on the cheek, and lay enfolded in his arms, drawing strength and comfort from his warmth even as she wept quietly again for him, for herself, and for their first-born, broken daughter.

"Richard will try to take the baby."

"You don't know that, Evie."

The bedroom, as always, was colder than the rest of the house. But although Maggie and Eva Grace again tonight huddled in the same bed, it was more for comfort than warmth.

Exhausted from the turmoil of the day, Maggie fought to keep her eyes open and concentrate on what Evie was saying. She wanted to be a source of strength to her sister, but at the moment it was all she could do to stay awake.

"I know Richard. I know how he thinks. He'll try to take the baby, Maggie. He will."

A fresh blast of anger toward Richard roused Maggie from her drowsiness. "Well, even if he tries, it won't happen. Da won't *let* it happen."

"I don't know if even Da is a match for the likes of Richard. He's mean, Maggie. And he's clever. He's smart. And he's right about my leaving. I *did* run away. He can probably use that against me if he should decide he wants the baby."

Maggie refused to concede even the possibility that she might be right. The thought of Evie's baby in the hands of its father made her shudder.

"Listen, Evie, you can't think that way. Even if Richard tries to get custody, he can be stopped. We'll find a way. The only thing you need to concentrate on is staying well. You take care of yourself and the baby, and leave everything else to the rest of us."

A thought struck her. "I haven't even asked you when the baby's due! In all the confusion...I didn't think."

"I don't know exactly."

"You don't know?"

"I haven't seen a doctor yet." Evie's voice was strained. "I told you, our doctor is a friend of Richard's, and I was trying to keep the baby a secret until I decided what to do. But Richard noticed the weight I'd gained...the way my hands and feet would swell sometimes...and he figured it out."

Maggie thought for a moment. "The swelling—is that normal?"

"I suppose. I don't know."

"Well, there's no reason to put off seeing the doctor any longer."

Evie made a sound under her breath. "Dr. Woodbridge. Da's always claimed he's a quack."

"That's just Da. You know how he is." A thought struck Maggie. "Besides, you just might not have to go to Dr. Woodbridge after all. There's a *new* doctor on the outskirts of town. A *woman* doctor."

Evie's eyes widened. "A woman? Are you sure?"

"I haven't heard much about her, but I know where her office is. You have to see a doctor soon. You need to make sure..."

"That the baby is all right. I know."

Maggie chose her words carefully. "You did say Richard hit you in the stomach."

"But I've felt the baby move several times since then. She must be all right."

"She?"

"What?"

"You said 'she,'" Maggie pointed out. "You must think the baby is a girl."

Evie was silent for a long moment. "In truth I can't bear the thought of giving birth to a boy. I'm afraid he might grow up to be like Richard."

"Oh Evie!" Maggie reached for her sister's hand. "That won't happen! You'll be the one who raises your child, not Richard. Your baby will be just fine."

"I pray you're right, Maggie. But I'm so afraid…"

"Don't be." Maggie squeezed her hand. "You'll be a wonderful mother, and you're going to have a wonderful baby. But you do need to be finding out *when*."

"Maggie?"

"What?"

"Will you go with me to see the doctor? I don't want to go alone."

"I think Mum will want to be the one who goes with you, Evie."

Her sister sighed. "I'd rather it be you. Oh, I don't want to do this! Everyone in town is going to know what happened to me."

"That's not so. You don't have to tell anyone *anything*. It's nobody's business but yours."

"This is Skingle Creek, remember?" Evie said bitterly. "Everyone in town knows all there is to know about one another. There's no keeping any secrets around here."

"Well, even if a few people do know, they're not going to blame you for anything. They'll just be glad you're safe at home. And they'll be happy about the baby. Besides, since when are you all that concerned about what people think?"

Maggie stopped for a second. "Evie, I know right at this moment you can't look much further ahead than tonight. But you have a family, and you still have friends in Skingle Creek who will do everything they can to help you. You'll see."

When there was no reply from her sister, Maggie waited a few moments more. Hearing Evie's breathing deepen and grow steady,

Maggie turned onto her side, expecting to fall asleep in no time. Instead she spent another restless hour, unable to dismiss an encroaching fear of what might yet lie ahead for her sister. She had done her best to reassure Evie; she only wished she could reassure herself.

Chapter Fourteen

A Silent Suffering

They look up with their pale and sunken faces,
And their look is dread to see.

Elizabeth Barrett Browning

Jonathan knew he wouldn't have a chance to talk with Maggie until later in the day on Monday, but from the time she walked inside the building that morning he could tell something was wrong.

He caught only a glimpse of her as she walked by his office, gave him a quick wave, and went on. But the spring in her step was missing, and there was a rare droop to her shoulders, not to mention her distracted expression. He sensed she hadn't really seen him as she went by.

During lunch recess he went outside hoping to have a word with her, but Carolyn Ross was already in the school yard and came up to him as soon as he stepped out the door. He felt enough guilt about the day before that he couldn't bring himself to do anything but give her his full attention.

He'd behaved badly Sunday, and his conscience was still plagu-
ing him. The only thing Carolyn had asked of him, after all, was his
attendance at the recital for her music students, some of whom were
also his classroom students.

She had encouraged quite a few of the children to study music in
one form or another with her. Some merely learned to read the notes,
but others were actually playing instruments by now, thanks to the
donation of some used instruments from a music store in Lexington.
In addition, Ben Wallace, her pastor and Jonathan's, allowed the
students to practice on the church piano.

Jonathan found it somewhat curious that Carolyn had her own
piano at home but drew the line at letting the children come and
practice there. He would have thought that being childless, she might
welcome having youngsters around.

Of course, the lessons themselves meant a substantial sacrifice of
her time and effort. It was a generous thing to do, and he certainly
had no right to question her methods.

Yesterday, when he should have given her and the children his
undivided attention, he'd been hard-pressed to concentrate. Although
Carolyn had said nothing, Jonathan knew she must have noticed.

The truth was that the time he'd spent with Maggie on Friday
evening had left him preoccupied with thoughts of her. His attention
hadn't been on the recital or on Carolyn because he couldn't keep his
mind off Maggie.

What he should have done was to take Carolyn to lunch after
church, escort her to the recital, and perhaps suggest a drive or a
walk afterward. He *had* taken her to lunch, but he'd struggled to keep
his mind from wandering. Immediately after the recital he paid his
compliments to the students and made what must have seemed like
an unnecessarily hasty departure.

He was still berating himself for his conduct, which, if not altogether rude, had been at the least inconsiderate. Without question,
he needed to make up for his thoughtlessness. At the same time,
he couldn't help but steal a glance now and then at Maggie, and
when he did, there was no ignoring the shadows around her eyes and

the tight set of her mouth. The high color that usually characterized her complexion was considerably paler today; she looked unhappy. Unhappy and worried.

Unease crept over him, but he resigned himself to the fact that there would be no opportunity to find out what was troubling her until after dismissal.

In the meantime, he turned his full attention back to Carolyn.

"Are you well, Jonathan?"

He looked at her, not understanding. "Am I well? Why, yes. I'm fine. Why do you ask?"

Carolyn shrugged, still watching him closely. "I get the feeling you're anywhere else but here today. For that matter, you seemed awfully distant yesterday too."

Jonathan made a sincere effort to explain—without really explaining. "I'm sorry. I'll admit that I haven't been at my best lately. Too many things on my mind, I suppose."

She deepened his guilt with her reply.

"You do too much, Jonathan. You need to take better care of yourself. I hope you don't mind my bringing this up, but I know about your former illness. Shouldn't you be careful not to overdo?"

"Where on earth did you hear *that?*" Unreasonably irked, Jonathan spoke more sharply than he meant to. "That was over a decade ago, Carolyn. I'm perfectly fine now, and have been for years."

"I'm sorry. I didn't mean to pry. I was just concerned."

She glanced away, obviously stung. His conscience pricked, Jonathan touched her arm in a conciliatory gesture. "I know. I didn't mean to be short. But that was all so long ago I tend to forget about it. I suppose I thought everyone else had too. I really am sorry."

The smile she usually wore for him returned. "You're forgiven. By the way, you might not have realized it, but the children were ever so excited that you came to the recital."

"Oh, I enjoyed it! I really did. You do a fine job with them, you know. I saw quite a lot of improvement since last time."

"Why, thank you, Jonathan. I'm pleased that you noticed. I was wondering…"

She stopped. Jonathan waited. and then prompted, "Carolyn?"

She looked at him. "Well, I thought if—"

Whatever she'd been about to say was lost when a shriek sounded from the far end of the school yard. They both took off running. By the time they got there, Maggie was already on her knees beside little Huey Lazlo, who was lying face down beneath the big old hickory tree while some of the other children stood watching. His older sister stood nearby, staring at her brother with obvious fear.

Jonathan dropped to his heels. "What happened?" he asked Maggie. Carefully, he turned the boy onto his back. Huey was conscious, his eyes open, but he looked dazed.

"According to Selma, he climbed up in the tree at the beginning of recess," Maggie said. "Apparently he was just sitting there, watching the others play. When he started to come down, he fell."

Jonathan raised the boy's head a little, supporting him with his arm. "Huey? How do you feel?"

The boy offered nothing but a quiet, "All right." After quickly checking him over for any possible broken bones, Jonathan picked him up and carried him inside the building, laying him on the bench in his office.

"Do you need anything, Jonathan?"

He saw Carolyn turn a sharp look on Maggie, who seemed unaware of the other's scrutiny and the fact that she'd used Jonathan's given name.

In an effort to not show that the slip had pleased him, he shook his head, keeping his attention on the Lazlo boy as he dropped to one knee beside him. "You took quite a fall, young man," he said, helping Huey out of his sweater—much too thin for the autumn chill of the day.

"You seem to have torn your sweater in a couple of places when you fell, Huey. I'm afraid you may have a few scrapes or cuts. I'd better have a look."

Something flared in the boy's eyes. He clutched at his shirt before Jonathan could so much as undo a button.

Jonathan hesitated, then turned to glance at Maggie and Carolyn. "I wonder if you ladies would round up the children and take them inside? And then, Maggie, you can go on with your class. And, Carolyn, could you take my students for a while? I believe I'll stay here with Huey a few more minutes."

After the women left his office, Jonathan pushed the door closed and went back to Huey. "Do you think you can stand up, son?"

Huey nodded and climbed off the bench to face Jonathan, one small hand still clutching the collar of his faded blue shirt. Jonathan spied a blood spot in front, but when he moved to open the top button to see if perhaps the boy was hurt worse than he'd first thought, Huey twisted away.

"I won't hurt you, son. But I think you might have some scrapes that need to be cleaned. Just let me have a look."

Much to Jonathan's dismay, the boy's dark eyes took on a look of fear.

"Huey?"

When the boy didn't reply, but merely stood there, clinging to his shirt, Jonathan made no further move toward him. Still, he couldn't simply ignore the blood on his shirt.

Jonathan hesitated another moment, then made a decision. "Would you rather I have Miss MacAuley check you over, Huey?"

The boy didn't look at him, but shook his head.

"No? Well, then, it's up to you and me, it seems."

Jonathan sat down on the bench so he'd be at eye level with the boy. "Here, son. Let's have a look."

Finally, with obvious reluctance, the boy came to him. It took him only a moment to understand the reason for Huey's peculiar behavior. Upon opening the child's shirt enough to examine him, the first thing that caught Jonathan's attention wasn't what he had expected. Instead of a bad cut or scratch from the fall—though there were enough minor ones to explain the blood spot on the shirt—a map of ugly, dark bruises blotched the thin chest.

Huey never lifted his gaze from the floor. Slowly, carefully, Jonathan turned him around, pulling his shirt up enough to look at his back, only to find the same appalling sight.

He swallowed down the mix of sickness and anger rising in his throat. Then, trying to steady his hands, Jonathan turned the boy back to face him, holding him gently by his too-thin shoulders. "Who did this to you, Huey?"

The boy made no reply but simply stared at the floor.

"Huey? I need to know who hurt you." He paused. "It's all right to tell me, son."

The boy raised his head, his dark eyes still not quite meeting Jonathan's. "Nobody hurt me," he said in a small, choked voice. "I fall down a lot."

"You didn't do this falling down, Huey." The child jerked, and too late Jonathan realized that he'd raised his voice, startling the boy.

"Talk to me, son," he said, carefully lowering his voice to a near whisper. "Tell me who did this. Your father?"

A flash of fear again darted across the child's features, and he gave a vehement shake of his head. Then, in a slow, forlorn gesture that wrenched Jonathan's heart, the boy wiped the back of his hand over his eyes, obviously trying not to cry.

Finally Jonathan dropped his hands away and straightened, trying to think what to do. This wasn't the first time he'd dealt with a case of violence against a child. But it *was* the first time a child seemed so intent on keeping his silence once the mistreatment had been discovered.

"I'll be back in a moment, Huey," he said quietly, trying not to betray his own emotion. "Wait here for me."

He stepped outside his office, closing the door behind him and stood there, his heart pounding. Huey was Maggie's student, and therefore he was obligated to make her aware of the situation. And he would—but first he needed to collect his thoughts.

He had been suspicious of the Lazlo boy's home life ever since last year, and especially after his and Maggie's visit to the parents. But until now there had been no evidence of any physical mistreatment. How long had this child been suffering and hiding his pain without anyone knowing what he was going through?

That man—that awful man. How could a human being do this to a child? To his own *son*?

Jonathan had been through this before, so he recognized the familiar queasiness and anger rising up in him. Shaking, he stood with one hand behind him, still grasping the doorknob, and, still grasping the doorknob, stared out into the hallway.

Maggie's classroom was across from his office, her desk in direct view. At the moment she was seated and reading to her students. As if she sensed him watching her, she glanced up and met his gaze.

Jonathan crossed the hall and, managing a smile for the children, said, "Excuse me, Miss MacAuley. May I speak with you a moment?"

Maggie stood, putting a finger to her lips as a caution for the children to remain quiet, and stepped outside the room.

"Huey?" she asked. "Is he badly hurt?"

He passed a hand over the back of his neck. "Yes, he's hurt," Jonathan said, his voice tight. "But not from the fall."

She gave him a questioning look.

"He's been beaten. Badly. And over a long period of time, from the looks of it."

Maggie gave a low groan, her expression stricken.

"I'd like you to take a quick look at his sister. Check for bruising or any other marks on her arms and legs. They'll both have to be examined by Dr. Woodbridge, of course, but I'd like to know what you think before I leave with them. I'm hoping one or the other might talk to me once we're out of the building."

"Jonathan, have you heard anything about the new doctor just outside town? Dr. Woodbridge can be…somewhat gruff at times."

"I've heard that a lady doctor has set up practice, yes, but I'm not comfortable with taking any of the children out there until we know more about her."

"I think maybe that's who Eva Grace might want to see instead of—"

She stopped.

"What about Eva Grace? Is she ill?"

Maggie glanced away. "I'll tell you later."

Jonathan studied her. Just as he'd suspected, there *was* something wrong. And clearly it had to do with her older sister. He would have pressed her to explain, but there was no time.

"We'll talk later," he said. "For now, I'd like you to get Selma and take her down to the end of the hall. Just explain to her that Huey is hurt worse than we first thought. That will give you a chance to have a look at her, and she'll be more comfortable with you than with me. I can keep an eye on your students and Huey at the same time. Oh—and get her belongings together, would you, along with Huey's?" He paused. "They won't be going home tonight."

"Where will they stay?"

"Unfortunately, we've had to deal with this sort of thing before. Ben and Regina Wallace will keep them as long as necessary. I can't possibly send them home until we know what the situation is."

"I can't believe this is happening in Skingle Creek!" Maggie burst out. "How can one human being do this to another, to someone he's supposed to *love?*"

Jonathan knew Maggie had a heart for the children, and he also knew she had a tendency to take their pain upon herself. But the strength of her reaction to the situation still surprised him.

"There's no understanding it, Maggie. I know. I've dealt with it more than once over the years, and I still can't fathom what accounts for this sort of cruelty." His mind was spinning. There was so much to do when a situation like this came to light, and it had to be done quickly...and carefully.

"About dismissal. I'll have Carolyn take my class until then. Will you help her get the children on their way after the bell?"

She nodded.

He continued to tick off what needed to be done. "I'll have to stop by the deputy's office on the way back from the doctor's. The parents have to be notified that Huey and Selma won't be home tonight, and it needs to be done by someone in authority."

Her eyes widened. "That's going to frighten the children. Isn't there another way?"

Jonathan shook his head. "I have to report it as soon as possible. I can't simply take the children off somewhere without the parents knowing about it."

"They don't deserve to know," she said, anger sharpening her tone. "I still don't understand how something this horrible can go on here. This is a town of good people, Jonathan."

"For the most part, I'm sure you're right. But this sort of ugliness can happen anywhere. All it takes is a soul living in darkness, apart from God, and this—and even worse—can happen. And *does.*"

He reached to touch her arm, and then thought better of it. "You go on now and see to Selma. We'll do everything we can to take care of her and Huey."

Again she nodded and turned to go.

A few minutes later, after taking Selma back to class, Maggie reported to Jonathan what she'd found. "Nothing," she said. "I checked as closely as I could without alarming her. I didn't see any sign that she's been hurt in any way. I told her about Huey, but she wouldn't say a word. I think she's afraid."

Jonathan rubbed the back of his neck, where a headache was beginning to work its way up his skull. "Well, we'll see what the doctor has to say. I wish I knew for certain that Selma hasn't been mistreated. I'd leave her for now. I don't think either one of those children is going to tell me what's going on as long as they're together. But if I *don't* take her to the doctor, I won't know for sure that she's all right."

"Maybe you could talk with Mrs. Wallace and suggest she help Selma get ready for bed tonight," Maggie said quietly, watching him. "It might save the girl from having a doctor's examination."

As awkward as it was, Jonathan had to bring something else up.

"There are different kinds of ill-treatment, Maggie," he said quietly. "Some can't always be seen."

She didn't meet his gaze, but responded without hesitation. "I know about that, Jonathan. But Selma is more likely to confide in a woman than in Dr. Woodbridge. I'm afraid she might withdraw even more if she's subjected to…too intensive an examination."

It took him only a moment to see the wisdom of her words.

In the end, he decided to take Selma with him, but to forego the doctor's examination for the time being. "I'll be back as soon as I can, so you don't have to stay over too long. Check on my class once or twice, would you? Just to make sure Carolyn doesn't need any help. The older ones can get a bit feisty with her. They've been known to give her a difficult time because she's not a teacher."

"I'll take care of things until you get back. You know I will."

The thing was, he *did* know. He had always been able to count on Maggie, and he still could. In truth, he didn't know how he would manage without her.

What's more, he hoped he would never have to find out.

Chapter Fifteen

The Pain of Caring

I had a thought for no one's but your ears;
That you were beautiful, and that I strove
To love you in the old high way of love.

W.B. Yeats

By half past four, Huey had been seen by Dr. Woodbridge, who confirmed the appalling fact that just as Jonathan suspected, the boy had been the victim of numerous beatings for an extended period of time. Huey refused to break his silence.

From the doctor's office, Jonathan went in search of the deputy, leaving Huey in an adjoining room while he discussed the boy's condition with the peace officer. Afterward, he drove back to the school, collected Maggie and Selma, and took the children to the home of Ben and Regina Wallace.

From past experience, Jonathan knew the children would be well-cared for with affection by the pastor and his wife until more information could be collected about the Lazlos. When he tried to explain to Huey and his sister why this was something they had to do, he avoided making it sound like a permanent situation.

There was a heartbreaking moment when little Huey, obviously trying hard not to cry, tugged at Jonathan's arm, his dark eyes filled with unmistakable fear. "Please, Mr. Stuart, can't Sister and I stay with you instead of those other people?" He swiped a hand at the heavy shock of hair covering his eye. "Please?"

It was a question Jonathan had asked himself, and at first he'd been about to take them home. But he thought it important that Selma, especially, be under the care of a woman and Ben and Regina were well equipped to look after both children.

He dropped down and tried, gently, to explain this to Huey. Although the child appeared to accept the explanation, his shuttered gaze and lapse into silence tore at Jonathan's heart.

What Jonathan didn't mention was the fact that if it came to the point that the children had to be taken out of school temporarily, Regina Wallace would be at home full-time to look after them. They simply could not be left alone, not for a moment. Besides, Huey and his sister could only benefit from the love and kind attention Regina and Ben would offer. Their time spent with the Wallaces just might be the beginning of a healing process.

All the way to Ben and Regina's place, Jonathan silently fumed over his earlier exchange with the deputy sheriff. The more he thought about it, the more frustrated he became. The law officer hadn't been in the least encouraging about the children's future, explaining that although the boy might be removed from the home, it wasn't likely that his sister would be.

"Mr. Stuart, unless there's evidence that the little girl has been mistreated along with her brother, she'll have to go back to her folks. No matter how long Pastor Ben and his wife might be willing to let them stay there, we can't keep the girl away from her own parents indefinitely."

Jonathan couldn't believe what the man was saying. "You'd send her back into that place, knowing what's been going on with the boy? How can you possibly justify that?"

He saw the deputy bristle and regretted offending the man. But he couldn't simply stand by and say nothing when in all likelihood Selma would eventually be victimized as her brother had been.

"I don't have to justify it, sir," the deputy said. "All I do is enforce the law, and unless we find evidence to the contrary, we have to assume there's no reason to keep the girl away from her folks. And let me tell you something else. If the boy doesn't speak up and give us some proof that his pa was the one who's been beating him, we won't be able to keep *him* away from his parents for very long either."

Jonathan had all he could do not to shout at the man. "You've *seen* the proof," he said, ignoring the tremor in his voice. "The boy has been beaten repeatedly on his back and his abdomen. What else do you need?"

"It's proof *only* if he'll admit that the beatings were his pa's doing," the deputy rejoined with an annoying shrug. "You'd just better make sure the little fella is willing to talk. You said so far he hasn't told you a thing."

"Aren't you even going to arrest the father?"

"No, sir. I can't do that yet. We'll have to investigate first. The only thing I can do right now is go up there and let them know that the boy and his sister won't be coming home for a spell."

When they arrived at the Wallaces' house, Maggie and the children went with Regina while Jonathan talked with Ben. Ben was as outraged as Jonathan once he learned what the deputy had said. But he wasn't surprised. "We've been through this before, Jonathan. I don't like it any better than you do, but we both know it's the way things work."

"It seems that *things* don't work at all," Jonathan grumbled, "especially when it comes to our children."

Later, as he and Maggie were in the buggy and leaving the Wallaces' house, it started to rain. Jonathan hurried to get out and put the cover up. "I have to go back to the school and pick up my things," he said, stepping back inside. "Shall I take you home first?"

Maggie shook her head. "I need time to settle myself. I shouldn't go home this upset."

Jonathan made no move to drive away yet. Instead he turned toward her. "Maggie—what's wrong?"

She looked at him but made no reply.

"Maggie?"

"You have enough to deal with for the time being," she said. "You don't need anything else to fret about."

His mood gentled as he studied her. "If it concerns *you*," he said quietly, "I'm going to fret all the more not knowing what it is. When we get back to the school, why don't I make some coffee and we'll talk." He waited. "All right?"

She hesitated, but then nodded. Jonathan picked up the reins, clucked to the horse, and drove away.

Maggie sat watching Jonathan from the chair opposite his desk while he poured their coffee. She shouldn't be doing this. He was obviously still distraught over the Lazlo children. She had no right to burden him even more.

But she *needed* to talk to him. He was her only friend. He was a man who unfailingly invited the confidence of others, and she was certainly no exception. As a child and as his student, she had probably made a nuisance of herself, going to him with her questions and her problems. Most of her troubles back then had probably seemed trivial to him, but he had never once hinted that they might be unimportant. She had no doubt whatsoever that he still managed to make all his students feel special, as if anything that concerned them concerned *him*.

When a problem *was* critical, he always managed to ease the tension and the worry simply by listening and, when feasible, helping with a solution or at least offering a bit of advice.

Maggie knew for a fact that he would risk his own safety to protect a student. The night Billy Macken and Orrin Gaffney had attacked her and Kenny, for example. That night, though in poor health and physically frail, Jonathan had helped Da and Mr. Tallman rescue them.

More than once over the years, Maggie had wondered at the seeming unfairness of a man who loved children as Jonathan clearly did spending his life childless. What a father he would have been.

"It's Eva Grace, isn't it?" she heard him say.

Maggie looked up and nodded.

He came around and sat down on the corner of the desk. "You don't have to tell me anything you think she wouldn't want me to know."

"No, that's not it. If Evie would confide in anyone besides her own family, it would most likely be you. There's no one she's ever trusted more than you, Mr. Stuart...*Jonathan.*"

He smiled a little. "That's progress. You've called me Jonathan at least twice in one day. Now, tell me about Eva Grace."

Maggie sighed. "Evie left Richard—her husband—for good. She's not going back to him."

Sympathy crossed his face. "What happened?"

The room was growing shadowed, the late-afternoon gloom fading into an early twilight. Jonathan lit the lamp behind him before settling himself on the corner of the desk again. He took a sip of coffee.

"Richard was beating her," Maggie said tightly.

He held his cup suspended, and this time there was no mistaking the pain that crossed his features. "Oh Maggie," he murmured.

"She's going to have a baby," she blurted out. "And Richard knew it. And he still beat her."

He set his cup on the desk, shook his head slowly, and passed a hand over the back of his neck. "So she's come home to stay."

Maggie nodded. "Richard came to get her Saturday, but she stood up to him and refused to go."

"Good for her!"

"Yes, but she's so wounded...and sad. I've never seen Eva Grace like this. It's as if her whole world has fallen in on her."

"No doubt that's how she feels. Her trust...and her love...have been betrayed."

Maggie thought about that and realized he was right. In fact, she wasn't so sure but what Richard's betrayal might not have been as shattering as the beatings.

Jonathan leaned forward a little. "Nobody knew?"

Maggie shook her head. "She said there was no one in Lexington to tell. Apparently their only friends were *Richard's* friends. And she didn't want to worry the rest of us. Oh, Jonathan! She said it's been this way for *years!* I don't know how she lived with it all that time."

"Eva Grace was always a strong girl. She must have become an even stronger woman." He paused. "How did your parents take this? Are they all right?"

"They're hurt, of course. And worried. But they were wonderful when she told them."

He nodded. "Yes, they would be." Still leaning toward her, he lowered his voice even more. "But what about you, Maggie? How are *you?*"

She hadn't really had time to think about it. "Oh, I'm all right. I don't have much choice, do I? I have to be strong for Eva Grace. And for my folks. And now all this with Huey and Selma—" Maggie stopped.

"Huey and Selma will be taken care of," Jonathan said, although Maggie thought he didn't look as confident as he sounded.

He was looking at her in the strangest way, *studying* her, really.

"You've always been strong for everyone else, haven't you?" he observed quietly. "Even when you were a child. It seems to me that's one of the gifts God instilled in you."

Maggie didn't know how to answer. She didn't feel very strong at all. In fact, she felt as if she might burst into tears at any moment.

"The baby will help Eva Grace get on with her life, Maggie. And it will help Matthew and your mother as well." His dark eyes searched her face even more intently. "I predict Eva Grace's child will bless all of you more than you can imagine. Children have a way of bringing healing and *hope.*"

Maggie wasn't sure what came over her in that instant. Perhaps the kindness in his gaze, the hushed privacy of the room, and the deepening shadows of the day worked together to foster a closeness, an intimacy that at any other time would have seemed forbidden.

Whatever accounted for it, the words spilled out of her before she could stop them. "You should have children of your own, Jonathan. More than anyone I've ever known, you should have your own family!" Appalled by her outburst—so clearly out of place—Maggie watched for some sign of embarrassment, or even anger, on his part.

But if anything, only a trace of regret stole into his expression.

"I'm *sorry!*" She felt her face grow hot with humiliation. "I should *never* have said that. It's none of my business—"

To her relief, he merely waved off her apology and continued to look at her with what appeared to be a quiet affection.

Maggie had worked so hard to win his respect and wanted so much for him to see her as a mature woman. Now, because of her impulsive school girl outburst, she could scarcely meet his gaze.

"It's all right, Maggie," he said.

She raised her head to look at him and was relieved to see no trace of anger or reproach. "I really am so sorry," she said again.

He actually smiled a little. "I would have liked a family. I would have liked it very much. It simply didn't happen."

"It should have," she choked out.

Again came that peculiar look, that intense, searching scrutiny that had unnerved her before. "Well," he said, "one never knows. It could still happen." In an instant the look was gone, replaced by a light shrug and a smile. He eased off the desk. "We should get you home," he said with a glance out the window. "That rain has all the makings of a nasty evening."

He held out a hand to help her from her chair. They were close, his hand still holding hers, his gaze going over her face. His expression stilled, and neither made any effort to move away. For one breathless moment, Maggie thought he was going to kiss her. She was keenly aware of the warmth and the strength of the hand holding hers, and when she looked into his eyes she saw her own clash of emotions mirrored there.

Then something changed. His expression cleared and, releasing her hand, he stepped back.

Maggie blinked, trying to pretend nothing was any different, knowing that *everything* was different…unless she'd imagined what she'd seen in his eyes.

She retrieved her coat from the coat tree near the door. He held it for her as she slipped it on, but kept his distance. Somehow that made Maggie feel bereft, as if she'd stepped out of the warmth of the sun and into a cold and somber place.

Long after he dropped Maggie off at home, Jonathan sat in the darkness of his living room. He disliked himself intensely when he fell into these moods. Brooding was how he thought of it. And he'd been doing a lot of it lately. Mostly about Maggie, but after the shock of what he'd discovered about little Huey Lazlo today, his mood had grown even darker.

Still, he could not have been more grateful for people like Ben and Regina, people who could be counted on to step in when and where they were needed, people who cared more about others than they did about themselves. Thanks to them, Huey and his sister were removed, at least for now, from whatever wickedness resided in their home. But for how long? The deputy's words kept running through Jonathan's mind, and each time he remembered, the more disturbed he became. Clearly there was a good chance Selma would have to return home. And possibly Huey as well before too long a time.

He couldn't let that happen. He simply could not.

But how could he prevent it? He had no legal means of protecting those two children. If they *did* return home, he hadn't a thought of what he could do to make sure the abuse didn't continue with Huey or start up with his sister.

One thing was certain. He couldn't continue worrying like this. He thought he had settled this weakness in his nature between himself and the Lord a long time ago. No—not a "weakness." It was *sin,* and nothing else, to worry as if God could not be trusted, as if the Creator were incapable of caring for His created.

The times when he had seen things that were thought to be impossible become a reality were countless. And hadn't he been the beneficiary of divine compassion and power more than once? How many times when he had been unable to do anything in his own strength had he witnessed the Lord's power work yet another wonder? Wasn't he a great one for reminding his students to expend more energy praying over a troubling situation than fretting about it? Just what good was that advice if he failed to apply it to himself?

Newly convicted that he needed to heed his own counsel, Jonathan got to his knees beside the couch and spent a considerable length of time in petition for little Huey and Selma. When his thoughts turned to Maggie, he groaned aloud but stayed on his knees.

How was he going to live with this? He had been only a breath away from kissing her this evening!

He had been so careful to avoid the very type of situation he'd allowed this afternoon. Yet in an instant, overwhelmed by her closeness, her sadness, and her apparent trust in him, he had very nearly thrown all caution to the wind and acted on desire instead of reason and caution.

Her remark about his needing a family of his own had so moved him that he'd let down his guard. Sitting in the dimness of his office, alone with her, both of them still caught up in the emotions of the day and in her obvious distress about her sister, had made it more difficult than ever to observe the boundaries he'd set for himself.

What if he hadn't stopped when he did? He might have destroyed their entire relationship...whatever that relationship was. Maggie *trusted* him. He knew that only too well. She trusted him, even admired him—too much. From childhood, she had built him into something he wasn't. In her mind he was some kind of hero. Something more than an ordinary man.

He was no hero. He was pitifully ordinary. He knew his weaknesses, but he also knew he'd have a blazingly hard time convincing Maggie of them. Something inside him teased that he really didn't *want* her to know the worst about him, that he actually enjoyed her admiration and high regard.

He'd certainly done nothing to discourage it.

He was all too aware that if he were ever to give in to his feelings for her, the feelings that deepened daily, it might have devastating consequences for their friendship and their professional relationship as well. Was this the way it had to be? Always suppressing his feelings for her, never exploring hers for him—if she *had* any feelings for him, that is. Never daring to take that crucial step beyond friendship, forever keeping a safe distance from the woman she had become...the woman he was falling in love with.

Never to know what they might have together.

Was he really willing to live within those self-imposed restrictions indefinitely? *Could* he live that way?

Maggie was young and appealing. She was everything and more a young man could want in a sweetheart and a wife. Eventually, he would have to watch her fall in love, get married, and no doubt leave the school to make a home and have children. How could he bear it, losing her to another man—to another life—all the while knowing he had never made her aware of the true nature of his feelings for her?

What was the right thing in this? He knew in his heart that what he felt for Maggie was more than an older man's desire for a younger woman. No, it was far more than desire, although desire for her was a very real part of his feelings.

Humiliating as it was, he had to face the possibility that his feelings could be merely years of loneliness finally spilling over, crowding out common sense, tempting him, pressing him to want someone he *shouldn't* want. Had he finally grown so desperate to escape his solitary life that he had managed to convince himself that he might yet have a chance for a different kind of life—a life that included love and a family with someone who had been special to him and who had held him in the highest estimation for years?

Or could it possibly be within his reach...if only he wasn't too much the coward to pursue it?

He let out a long breath, impatient with himself. Why—*why*—

couldn't he have fallen in love like most normal men by now? With a woman like Carolyn Ross, for example. A woman closer to his own age, and one who invited his interest. How much easier his life would have been! He had no doubt but what Carolyn would make an excellent and devoted wife.

She might also smother me to death...

That was unfair. Perhaps because she'd had no children from her brief marriage, she was lonely too and simply compensated for that loneliness by trying to mother...*him.*

The uncharitable thought made him cringe with self-disgust.

He had to stop thinking. He was tormenting himself with all this introspection and speculation.

Jonathan shifted his weight a little from one side to the other but stayed on his knees, sighing so deeply a shudder coursed through his body. Then, with a deliberate act of will, he once again sought the only One whose counsel had never failed him, the One whose wisdom was the only wisdom in his life...the One who knew, and surely understood, more than any other, what loneliness could do to the human soul.

Chapter Sixteen

A Knock on the Door

Our deeds pursue us from afar,
And what we have been makes us what we are.

John Fletcher

Three days later, badly in need of something to divert his thoughts from the school, the Lazlo children, and Maggie MacAuley, Jonathan Stuart indulged in his favorite escape. Upon arriving home after school, he changed into some worn, comfortable clothes, fixed himself a cup of strong, black coffee, and went into the living room, where he put Enrico Caruso's recording of *Vesti la giubba* from *Pagliacci* on the Victor phonograph.

Over a year old now, the phonograph was Jonathan's pride and joy, albeit an uncharacteristic extravagance for him. It was the only thing he could remember ever buying on impulse. And what an impulse it had been! He smiled at the memory. He'd been visiting his father in Lexington during the summer before last, only to bring home the phonograph and a new flute along with it!

Although he'd never been inclined toward excessive spending, once the deed was done he absolutely forbade himself even the slightest exercise in guilt. At that time, he had been without a flute for years, ever since his elegant silver flute from his boyhood had been stolen. He decided that the purchase of a more modest replacement after a decade of going without could hardly be considered a luxury.

As for the phonograph, music was much more than a mere indulgence in his life. He thought it could best be described as the difference between living in a cathedral or living in a desert. Music was the cathedral of his being and without it, he suffered a genuine deprivation of the spirit. It was his companion in worship, a balm in sorrow, a comfort in solitude, and an agent of healing. He never enjoyed the emotional and spiritual experience it brought to him without breathing a prayer of thanks for what he believed to be the very voice of hope.

Sitting on the sofa, Jonathan propped his feet up on the table in front of him and eyed the mahogany box with its lacquered black horn and brass bell. He wondered if Maggie would enjoy this—just sitting quietly and listening. She was so full of life, so energetic and eager to be doing. Would she be bored by this perceived inactivity?

He had to smile a little at the thought of Maggie listening to opera. Somehow he couldn't quite picture that. What *did* she do in her spare time? More to the point, did she *have* any spare time? What with Eva Grace back home, a baby on the way, a teaching position, and whatever jobs she took charge of around the house, he thought it unlikely she would find much in the way of free time.

So much for diverting my thoughts from Maggie...

It was almost as difficult to avoid thinking of Huey and Selma. He hadn't heard a word from the deputy since taking the children to the Wallaces' on Monday. He saw them at school, of course, and they appeared to be much the same as usual. With Huey that meant somber, somewhat listless, and unhappy. But he thought he'd caught a glimpse of an uncommon lightness about Selma, the older of the two. Her usually dull gaze might have held just the faintest glimmer of enthusiasm during art today.

He was aware that Selma liked to draw, and he'd detected an above-average ability in the girl. He had tried to nurture that ability all along, but until today she'd shown little interest in experimenting with different colors or textures. Encouraged by this new spark of curiosity, Jonathan had given her a broader palette to work with, as well as a larger canvas.

Maggie's report on Huey had been less heartening. She told him the boy had been characteristically silent throughout the day, even somewhat sullen.

The good news from Regina was that Selma showed no signs of having been beaten. She seemed fairly certain that the girl had suffered no maltreatment at the hands of her father, but there was no way to make certain without subjecting the child to a doctor's thorough examination.

Jonathan fervently hoped that wouldn't be necessary.

Ben had stopped by yesterday evening to give an account of how the children were doing. "They're very protective of each other. We've seen that before with siblings who suffer violence on the part of a parent. They stick together. We tried to give them separate rooms, but the boy put up such a fuss we moved an extra bed into the room next to ours and kept the two together."

So far Jonathan had heard nothing from the deputy. He wasn't concerned about how long they had to stay with Ben and Regina. The Wallaces had kept children in their home for weeks at a time without complaint. But these two needed resolution as soon as possible. Decisions had to be made about their care and how to keep them a safe distance from their father.

Caruso was doing an admirable job with the *Pagliacci* aria, but for some reason Jonathan found the music neither soothing nor inspiring this evening. To the contrary, the weeping clown was beginning to get on his nerves.

He rose from the sofa to turn off the music, stopping when an insistent knock sounded at the front door. After taking time to set the phonograph arm in place, he went to the door. He half expected to see Ben standing on his porch. Instead, he opened the door to the hulking figure of Huey Lazlo's father, who loomed even larger than Jonathan remembered. He also looked angry enough to kill somebody.

The man was formidable. Jonathan knew better than to judge a person by his appearance, but Mr. Lazlo made it very difficult not to jump to conclusions. He was still in his mine clothing, which was filthy. Coal dust nearly concealed his face below the miner's cap and made him look even more dangerous than the first time Jonathan had met him. The eyes peering out from his blackened skin flickered with anger and malice, and his mighty fists were clenched, as if he were barely holding in check a pulsating rage that might explode at any second.

Jonathan took a step back. "Mr. Lazlo," he said, hoping his voice didn't sound nearly as unsteady to Lazlo as it did to him.

"I want my kids."

"Your children aren't here."

"Where are they?"

"In a safe place." Jonathan paused. "They're being well cared for."

"You got no right to take my kids."

Jonathan drew in a long breath. "And you have no right to hurt your son." The coldness of his tone surprised him.

The man was brutally muscled and unmistakably agitated. He thrust a leg forward as if to insinuate himself inside the door. Jonathan knew a hard shudder of fear. He must not let this man get past him and inside his house.

He did his best to block Lazlo's entrance by posting himself squarely in the doorway.

The other eyed him as if taking his measure. "I never hurt my boy. You can't keep him from me."

Anger roared through Jonathan, even though he knew he absolutely had to maintain control. "That has yet to be decided, Mr. Lazlo. Your son was beaten severely. He wears the bruises to prove it."

Lazlo's eyes flared. The heavy brows met, and the scar over his eye turned livid. "What'd he tell you?" His voice was guttural, an angry snarl.

It was on the tip of Jonathan's tongue to admit that Huey had told them nothing, but he thought better of it. "I can't discuss that with you."

"You took my boy and set that deputy on me, but I done nothing."

"Mr. Lazlo, you need to leave. Someone will be in touch with you once the situation is investigated."

Lazlo peered over Jonathan's shoulder, as if he expected to see his children. For an awful moment, Jonathan half expected the man to shove his way past him.

And then what would he do?

Waiting, he was surprised to see a look of uncertainty and confusion settle over Lazlo's brutish features. For a moment he actually looked bewildered, even distressed. In spite of himself, Jonathan felt a stab of uncertainty about the man.

But within the moment bitterness and rage pulled Lazlo's face into a swollen mask. "No one's got a right to keep my kids away from me," he said, his tone threatening. "You better not try."

They stood there, glaring at each other for what seemed an interminable time, Lazlo's eyes burning with anger, Jonathan doing his best to appear undaunted.

Finally Lazlo turned and stamped down the walk.

Shaken, Jonathan closed the door and leaned against it until his breath returned. He had been all too conscious of the fact that, at any point in the confrontation, Lazlo could have slammed one of those enormous fists into his face or alongside his head and destroyed him. So fierce had been the sensation of impending violence that he felt no real relief even with Lazlo gone. He was also chillingly aware that there was no guarantee the man wouldn't return, especially if the deputy delayed taking action on the children.

It struck him that he should have got a dog for himself when he'd first had the idea.

Chapter Seventeen

Larger Than Life

A man's a man for a' that.

Robert Burns

⁓

Maggie's reaction to the news that Burian Lazlo had come to his home last night gave Jonathan a jolt of surprise. He didn't like to upset her, of course, but he couldn't help but be pleased that she seemed so concerned for his welfare.

In fact, both Maggie and Carolyn seemed genuinely worried for him. He'd decided to tell them about Lazlo first thing this morning before school took up, mostly to put them on alert. It wasn't out of the question that Lazlo might show up at the school, and Jonathan wanted them to be watchful at all times.

He sat on the edge of his desk, facing both women as he continued. "I don't like doing this," he said, "but with Burian Lazlo coming to my house, until this situation is settled, I want to keep both the front and back doors of the school locked. I probably should have thought of it before."

"Perhaps the Lazlo children shouldn't even come to school for now," Carolyn said. "Wouldn't it be safer for them to stay in for a few days?"

"I thought about that," said Jonathan. "But this situation is hard enough on them as it is. Sitting around with little to do would make it even more difficult. I think they're better off in school. Besides, it's not likely that Lazlo will try anything here. Locking the doors is simply a precaution. It only makes sense to be safe."

"I wouldn't put anything past a man like that," Carolyn said, her tone sharp.

Jonathan shook his head. "There's something very strange about all this. I've dealt with similar situations before, but I don't remember ever having a case where one child was mistreated but not another in the same household. I'm sure it happens, but this is a first for me." He paused, thinking. "Even Lazlo himself doesn't seem typical. The man looks like a brute and mostly behaves like a bully, but there's something else about him. He seems...troubled. Perhaps confused. I can't quite put my finger on it, but he's different than I expected him to be."

Carolyn sighed. "Jonathan, you're always giving everyone the benefit of the doubt, but I don't see how you can in this case. This man deserves jail, not mercy."

"I'm not giving him the benefit of the doubt, Carolyn. And I'm not for a moment downplaying what he's done to Huey. I'm simply saying—" Jonathan broke off, feeling a sense of frustration. "I'm not sure *what* I'm saying."

Maggie had remained silent since her initial expression of concern. Jonathan glanced at her, wondering what she was thinking. But she volunteered nothing, so he went on.

"In any event, just be mindful of the locked doors. And keep a sharp eye out when you have the children on the playground." He stood then, indicating he had nothing more to say.

Carolyn left, going on to the office, but Maggie lingered a moment, watching him as if she had something to say.

"Maggie?"

Still she hesitated, her brows knitting in a frown. "I can't believe that man came to your home," she finally said. "Please be careful."

"I'm sure he won't come back. I believe I convinced him that I don't have the children."

"Still…"

"It will be all right, Maggie."

"Jonathan, what's going to happen to them?"

What indeed? He wished he knew the answer to her question and could put her mind at ease, but in truth he didn't know what to expect.

"I suppose we have to trust that everything will be settled for their best. But whatever is decided, it's probably not going to happen right away."

In an attempt to change the subject, he asked about Eva Grace.

"She's awfully quiet. Sad, of course. But I think she's relieved too, now that she's had it out with Richard." She paused. "If only he leaves her alone."

"You're worried that he won't?"

Her mouth tightened. "From what Evie told me, it wouldn't be like him to give up something that belongs to him. His wife, the baby…"

She didn't finish, but Jonathan understood. And he feared she might be right. A man who would beat his own wife—

He cringed. He'd been praying for Eva Grace ever since Maggie had told him of her situation. Clearly it would do well to pray even more.

"She's keeping busy," Maggie put in. "She's a great help to Mum, although I don't think she feels as well as she might. But she's making a game effort toward a fresh start. She's written to Nell Frances to tell her everything, and she's started sewing for the baby."

"Could I visit her one day soon, do you think? Or should I wait?"

"I think she'd like very much to see you, Mr.—"

She stopped and shot him a rueful grin. "Habit," she said.

"A good one to break," Jonathan said pointedly.

"There's the bell. I should get to my classroom."

Jonathan nodded. "Oh...Maggie? I don't suppose you'd know where I might find a dog?"

"A dog?"

"Yes, I've been thinking about getting one for some time now, but I don't know where to look."

"Oh, that'll be nice for you. We almost always had a dog at home." She smiled. "Sadie. She was a love. I'd think you might find one just about anywhere. They seem to be all over the place."

"But I wouldn't know a stray from a family pet."

"I'll ask Da. He should be able to help, working with most of the men from town."

"Good. I'd appreciate it."

"Are you wanting a dog for—" She stopped, apparently thinking better of what she'd been about to say. "Would you prefer a large dog or a small dog?"

Jonathan looked at her. "Something...substantial. Not one of those creatures that looks more like a rat than a dog. But smaller than a pony."

She laughed. "I'll be sure and tell Da your preference."

Was Jonathan getting a dog because he was afraid? Had Burian Lazlo frightened him by showing up at his house the night before? Maggie wondered. She could certainly understand if that were the case. The man had chilled her blood just by the way he'd stared at her during their visit to the Lazlos.

Somehow, though, she found it almost impossible to imagine Jonathan Stuart being frightened by *anything*.

Evie would have plenty to say about *that*. She could just hear her sister now, reminding her that their former teacher was "only a man." And she would be right to remind her. Maggie knew that at times, even now, she still had trouble seeing Jonathan Stuart as anything less than the paragon she'd made him out to be in her mind. In truth, she'd never quite been able to dispel her childhood image of him as *heroic,* as larger than life. Sometimes she thought she could stand at the top of Dredd's Mountain and look down on him, and he would still seem the tallest man she'd ever known.

But the truth was her admiration was more complicated than a case of hero worship. When she was with him and saw the gentleness and kindness looking at her in his dark, steady gaze, she knew she was seeing him through the eyes of a woman who had finally found the one man she had always been looking for, the one man she could belong to, the one...and only...man she could ever bring herself to love.

The one man she could never have.

The thought that he might actually be vulnerable enough to want a dog for *whatever* reason made him more real to her, possibly more accessible than she originally thought possible.

The Jonathan Stuart her childish heart had once thought could conquer the world had instead become a living, breathing, wonderfully endearing man who had conquered *her.*

So shaken was she by this unexpected recognition of the depth of her feelings that she had to brace herself against the doorframe of her classroom until her head cleared and her heart slowed enough to face her students.

She was so fond of reminding herself that she was no longer a schoolgirl. Why then couldn't she stop thinking...and behaving...like one?

Chapter Eighteen

Meeting Dr. Gordon

There is a time when trust is the only
Beacon to light our way.

Anonymous

～

Saturday morning Maggie and Eva Grace took the old farm wagon the family used for transportation and drove out of town, hoping to find the new doctor in.

Her office was in a small, white, clapboard house about two miles out, close to where the creek ended. The hills surrounding this part of the valley were a fiery blaze of color. Leading up to the building was a narrow gravel road, with the soil on either side dark and loamy. All things combined, the setting had the appearance of a colorful oil painting.

At one time this had been the home of Luanna Ransom, a widow who took in sewing and mending to keep herself and who was known for her unique quilts. Although the house had sat empty since her death more than a year ago, it now appeared that someone had recently given it a fresh coat of paint and topped the gravel road.

Maggie climbed down from the wagon, tied the horse to the rail in front, and went to help her sister.

Eva Grace rolled her eyes when she held out a hand to help her down. "I'm not crippled, Maggie."

"Cranky, though," Maggie said under her breath, standing aside to let Evie get down on her own.

On the porch, she put a hand to her sister's arm, saying, "Evie, you have to tell the doctor about your situation. I know it will be hard, but tell her...about the beatings. She needs to know everything for your sake *and* the baby's."

Evie's already taut features tightened still more. "I know," she said quietly, not looking at Maggie.

Beside the door hung a polished wooden shingle, letting them know that this was the office of Sally M. Gordon, M.D. When Maggie knocked, the door opened a crack on its own. She stuck her head in and saw a waiting room of sorts.

Entering, they looked around but saw no one. No doctor, no patients.

"Hello?" Maggie called, then again, "Hello! Is anyone here?"

The waiting area was a small, narrow room furnished with a long, painted bench and three or four wooden chairs with pads. A black coal stove squatted in the corner. The only window had been dressed with white ruffled curtains and a blind. The room was clean, orderly, and cheerful.

"Should we wait?" Eva Grace asked.

Just then the door to their left opened, and a tall woman about their mother's age appeared in a ticking apron. She topped Maggie by four or five inches at least, and Maggie was tall herself. The woman's fairly long, mostly gray hair appeared out of control, spiraling every which way with no pretense of style whatever.

Her eyes, a bright, startling blue, darted from Maggie to Eva Grace. "Yes?" she said, her gruff voice tempered by a faint smile.

"We're looking for Dr. Gordon," Maggie said.

"And you've found her. "

Maggie stared, and so did Eva Grace.

She wasn't sure what she'd expected—a more urbane, sophisticated type of woman perhaps. Possibly younger. This Dr. Gordon was quite ordinary, though not unattractive.

The blue eyes sparked a little. "I expect you're the one who wants to see me," the doctor said, her sharp gaze going over Eva Grace.

"I—yes."

Evie sounded...and looked...even more tense than she'd been when they entered.

"Well, come on back to the examining room, and let's see how you're doing. How far along are you?"

Evie seemed to have lost her voice. "I—I don't know."

Dr. Gordon looked from Maggie to Eva Grace. "You haven't seen a doctor?"

Evie hesitated. "No. Not yet."

"Well, let's get started then."

"While you're waiting," she said to Maggie, "why don't you take a piece of paper from that counter there and fill out the patient's full name and address, her age, and any information about previous illnesses or any particular health problems."

She held the door, gesturing for Evie to follow her. Maggie saw the apprehension in her sister's eyes. But the doctor put a firm hand on Eva Grace's shoulder and propelled her through the open door, closing it solidly behind them.

Maggie glanced at the "counter," a board that ran half the length of the room, ending at the door to the examining area. As the doctor had instructed, she took a sheet of blank paper to the chair beside the window and began to write.

This was altogether different from the way things had always been done at Dr. Woodbridge's office. She couldn't remember ever seeing *anyone* with paper and pencil there. For that matter, Dr. Woodbridge's waiting room was much smaller than this, dimly lighted, and had nowhere to sit and nothing to read.

It didn't take long to complete the information, but she waited

a good half hour or more before the door leading off the examining room opened. The doctor briskly crossed the room, pulled up
a chair next to her, and gave her a long, measuring look. "I want to
talk with you while Eva is getting dressed," she said. "You're sisters,
I understand."

"Is she all right?" Maggie asked.

The doctor's expression clouded. "Her baby will be born within
the next three months. Perhaps sooner." Her words were sharp and
direct.

Maggie caught her breath. "She's that far along?"

"Yes, and you should keep in mind that given what she's been
through, the baby might come early. Eva is living with you and your
parents?"

Maggie nodded. "She told you about her husband? That she's left
him...and why?"

"She should have left him years ago," the doctor said, her tone
hard. "Didn't anyone in the family know what he was doing to her?"

Instantly defensive, Maggie hurried to explain. "She didn't come
to visit all that often," Maggie said. "Richard"—her brother-in-law's
name left a bad taste in her mouth— "was always too busy. She never
breathed a word to any of us. We had no idea what was going on."

Dr. Gordon's tone softened a little. "Too many women keep their
silence in situations like this. Your sister is fortunate she has a family
who took her in. That's not always the case. More than one parent
will send a daughter right back to her poor excuse of a husband with
a firm admonition to obey him. Never mind that he treats her like
an animal."

"Our da would *never* have done that!"

Again the doctor regarded Maggie with a studying look. "Which
one of you is the oldest?"

"Evie is."

"Well, she obviously feels close to you, so you're probably going
to be the one who has to make sure she takes care of herself. Just so
you know, there are some things about her condition that already
concern me."

Maggie's heart clutched. She'd sensed for some time now that Evie wasn't well. She couldn't help but wonder if the numerous beatings might have damaged her sister—or the baby—in ways that couldn't be seen.

But apparently the doctor had another concern, one that *could* be seen.

"She's retaining a great deal of fluid. She mentioned that she gained a lot of weight fairly quickly."

Maggie nodded. "Even when she first came home, I thought she looked…puffy. Bloated. It was a shock. Evie's always been small and fairly slender."

"Well, we'd expect a normal weight gain, of course, with the pregnancy, but this isn't good weight. It's fluid, and that can cause some real difficulties. It can also be indicative of another condition, and I'm afraid that's what might be going on with your sister."

"What kind of condition?"

"Toxemia," she said, her lips thinning. "It can cause high blood pressure and the same kind of swelling and weight gain your sister is experiencing. It's a serious condition, and one that can turn worse without warning."

Dr. Gordon glanced back toward the waiting room door. "I don't mean to worry you, but your sister is obviously depressed. She wants the baby, but I'm not sure she's taking care of herself as she should. You need to watch her and make sure she follows my instructions."

She paused and her expression darkened. "And there's also the fact that she's been beaten. Now, Eva has been feeling life for several weeks—good, strong movement—so I'm hopeful for a perfectly healthy baby. At this point, I'm more concerned about your sister's condition than the baby's. I want you to be mindful that she isn't as well as I'd like her to be, and you need to do everything you can to see that she takes better care of herself."

The doctor went on giving Maggie instructions for Evie to follow: She was to have no salt, not even in cooking. She needed to elevate her feet several times during the day. She was to avoid any activity that might bring on exertion.

"Make sure she gets as much rest as possible. In fact, don't even bring her out here for checkups. I'll come to your house on a fairly regular basis so I can keep a close eye on any changes."

"You're frightening me," Maggie blurted.

Dr. Gordon stood up. "Don't be frightened. Just stay alert. Let me know right away if she experiences a noticeable weight gain over a brief period of time or if the fluid retention worsens. Watch for persistent headaches or sudden ones, and any double vision or nausea. I've explained all this to Eva, but I want you to be mindful of it as well. Make absolutely certain she rests most of the time."

"I'm a teacher, so I'm not home during the day. But I'll make our mother aware. We'll take good care of her."

The doctor surprised Maggie by patting her on the shoulder. "I know you will. Your sister's fortunate to have you." Her expression darkened. "Don't be surprised if that husband of hers shows up again."

"Evie made it clear that she wouldn't go back to him. She doesn't ever want to see him again."

The doctor's expression turned even harder. "Men who beat their wives aren't much interested in what their wives want or don't want. If he wants the child, or if he still harbors some deranged sense of affection for your sister, he'll be back. Don't let him anywhere near her if you can stop him."

"I understand," Maggie said, struggling with a wave of uneasiness.

Just then Eva Grace came into the waiting room. Maggie noticed that she was smiling. A good sign.

The doctor followed them to the door. "Eva—remember everything I've told you. It's extremely important that you follow the guidelines I gave you."

Eva Grace nodded and gave the doctor another weak smile. Although her sister exhibited no real enthusiasm for anything these days, Maggie sensed that Dr. Gordon had won her trust. Evie liked her, she could tell.

Come to think of it, so did she.

Chapter Nineteen

Mounting an Offense

Is not one's life itself an act of daring?

Francis Greenwood Peabody

⁓

By Saturday evening Jonathan had worked himself into exhaustion. Determined to stay busy, he'd launched an all-out assault on every room in the house, cleaning them from top to bottom. Constant activity seemed to be the only workable way to avoid those thoughts that had lately plagued him. All this when the reality was that his house didn't actually *need* to be cleaned. How much clutter could one man living alone—and seldom at home—create? The truth was that he had little else to keep him occupied to the point of distraction. And he needed distraction. So he cleaned. With a vengeance.

By five o'clock, he could see his reflection in almost every piece of furniture he owned and would have felt comfortable eating his dinner off the floor. Even the shed outside where he kept the buggy didn't escape his attention.

He washed up a bit and plopped down in the rocking chair

beside the fireplace, putting his feet up on the footstool. At least the energy he'd expended hadn't been entirely in vain. He'd managed to get his thoughts off the Lazlo children...and Maggie...for a few hours. Unfortunately, when he finally sat down to rest everything came rushing in on him again, especially his frustration and confusion about Maggie. Once again, his common sense pitched battle with his emotions.

This time he managed to take a good, long look at what he was doing to himself...aside from the fact that he was dangerously close to making a fool of himself, that is. He considered the very likely possibility, not for the first time, that loneliness had become more than a constant companion; it had actually become a predator, hounding him and gnawing at him until he'd fallen into the sorry and disgusting state of self-pity.

He had thought he was finished with that particular soul-eating sickness. The last time he'd nearly fallen prey to it had been years ago during his bout with heart failure. It had been all too easy during that period of his life, especially given his weakened physical condition, to live a self-defeating kind of existence, to allow the fragile state of his health and the equally treacherous state of his emotions to wear him down into a poor excuse of the man who had always professed faith in a power greater than himself.

But his health and his outlook on life had been restored in one miraculous event of healing, and for a long time afterward he lived in a state bordering on euphoria. No longer did he feel the need to avoid falling in love, have a family, plan for the future. He was a free man! Free to pursue what other men longed for and worked toward.

Then one day he woke up to the wrenching realization that years had passed, and in spite of his restored health and euphoric hopes, there was no "love of his life," no home, and no family on the horizon. Still, he adapted and made the best of life as it was. Over the years his students became his family and the school his home. He was a contented man.

Or so he had thought.

With Maggie's return to Skingle Creek had come a renewal of a special friendship, a familiar lightening of his spirit—and an end to his contentment. Once again he found himself longing for what he didn't have and perhaps could never have.

But this time he was finally coming to realize that there might be something he could do about it. In fact, he was fairly certain he knew a way to put a stop to this schoolboy fancifulness. He had to stop fooling himself that he might be falling in love with Maggie. She was too young for him by far. *She was!* Even if by some unimaginable chance she should come to care for him, he ought to do everything in his power to discourage her affection. He couldn't seriously expect her to tie herself down with a man so many years her senior. Especially when what might seem a blessing for him could eventually end up as a burden to her.

Although he had tried—and rarely failed—to trust completely in his God's power to keep him well, there were times...not often, but once in awhile, in the dead of night, when the tempter tested his faith...when he found himself filled with dread that his heart might weaken again, that his healing might not be permanent after all. During those times he told himself he must not even think of burdening a wife with an ailing husband. How could he consider loving her and at the same time be willing to impose upon her a situation so potentially unfair?

And now Maggie was in the picture. He stood to lose the gift of her friendship—possibly even her presence in his life—if he were to declare his affection for her and learn that it was unwelcomed. He couldn't risk it. He would rather have her as a friend and a part of his life than to lose her altogether.

Jonathan closed his eyes against the ache nagging at the back of his skull. If he must indeed set aside all thoughts of any relationship with Maggie other than friendship, perhaps there was a way to do so. He could start paying more attention to Carolyn Ross. As Ben Wallace continued to remind him, Carolyn held him in high regard, perhaps was even attracted to him. The age difference was minimal—three or four years at most—and they shared similar interests.

All right, he wasn't attracted to her. That didn't mean he *couldn't* be

attracted, did it? The woman had more than her share of appeal. Yet
he had never made any concerted effort to respond to her. Perhaps it
was time he did. Who knew but what Carolyn was the woman God
had intended for him all along, if he'd simply open his mind to the
possibility?

If he were really so convinced that Maggie *wasn't* that woman,
would it hurt to meet Carolyn halfway?

Tomorrow, he decided. Tomorrow after church he would invite her
to lunch. And this time he would be attentive. He would be mindful
of her obvious appeal and her indisputable charm rather than retreat-
ing from both. This time he would make a genuine effort to appreciate
her and take an interest in her.

He heard the clock in the hallway strike six and only then realized
that he'd been sitting here, woolgathering, for well over an hour.

So much for his resolve to stay busy.

He rose and started for the kitchen to put together something
for supper. But first he would tackle the shelves in the pantry. They
needed a good scrubbing and some rearrangement. And while he was
working he would think only of Carolyn.

Supper was over, and Maggie and Eva Grace were both in their
bedroom sewing—Eva Grace for the baby, and Maggie mending the
hem in her good black skirt.

"I'm still trying to get used to the idea that we have a woman
doctor right here in Skingle Creek," Maggie remarked. "Maybe now
more of the women around here will actually see a doctor instead of
having their babies without any help."

"Well, I certainly felt more comfortable with her than I would
have Dr. Woodbridge," Evie said. "Of course, I'd most likely be more
comfortable with just about anyone other than Dr. Woodbridge. I've
heard Da call him a quack so many times I can't think of him any
other way."

Maggie pulled a face. "I don't think Dr. Woodbridge is as bad as

Da lets on. But I wouldn't want a man doctor if I were having a baby either. And I think Dr. Gordon is going to be a really good addition to the town."

"She seems to know a lot about having babies. She has a certificate on the examining-room wall. She graduated from medical college, just like a man."

Maggie put down her needle and thread. "Plenty of women go to medical school these days. And I'd be willing to bet they're every bit as competent as their male colleagues."

Her sister stopped her own work to look at Maggie. "That's my little sister: still the bluestocking."

"Wrong word, Evie. A bluestocking is a woman who's absorbed with literary things. That doesn't exactly describe me."

Evie smiled. Maggie loved it when she could coax a smile from her sister these days. It wasn't easy.

"Since you seem to respect her so much, I hope that means you'll do exactly what she said you should." Maggie paused. "Do you know anything about this condition—this toxemia?" Maggie asked.

Her sister shook her head. "Never heard of it. And, yes, I plan to take care of myself just as she ordered." She gave Maggie a long, steady look. "I know you're worried about me, but you needn't be. I give you my word, I'll do everything I can to make sure my baby is healthy."

Relief swept over Maggie. *Thank you, Dr. Gordon!*

Evie picked up her sewing again. "Maggie?"

"Hmm?"

"The night I told you about Richard...you asked me what it was like to be in love, how a person could tell if she was?"

Maggie looked at her sister but said nothing.

"You never told me who he is."

"No, I suppose I didn't," Maggie said, trying to keep her tone casual.

"That was my fault. I was so preoccupied with my own problems, I never really gave you a chance." She stopped. "Who is he, Maggie?"

Maggie ducked her head over her sewing again, willing herself not to blush.

"It's Mr. Stuart, isn't it?"

Maggie's head came up with a jerk. "Why in the world would you think that?"

Evie studied her long and hard. "I thought so."

"I'm not going to talk about it."

Evie gave an annoying shrug. "That's up to you. I just thought you might *want* to talk about it. It's hard when you care about someone, isn't it, not to tell everybody you know?"

Surprised at her sister's perception, Maggie paused for a moment and then sighed. She swallowed against the dryness of her mouth and asked, "How did you know?"

Evie was smiling again...*really* smiling at her now. "It might have something to do with the way your whole face lights up when you say his name. Or the way you turn red when anyone else says it." She went back to her sewing for a moment. "Is he—does he have feelings for you? Do you know?"

Maggie shook her head. Hard. "Of course not! To him I'm just Maggie. A little girl. A former student. A teacher at his school."

Her sister's eyes went over her, glinting with a rare flash of humor. "Mr. Stuart is a very smart man, Maggie. I doubt if he still sees you as a little girl. You're actually kind of attractive, now that you're all grown up."

"Oh, well, thank you very much," Maggie muttered.

"I'm teasing. You won't win any ugly contests, how's that?" Evie was quiet for another moment. "He's a lot older than you, you know."

"Almost sixteen years."

"That much?"

"Yes, *that much*. And I couldn't care less."

"Don't get all uppity with me. It's not so hard to understand, even if you are a lot younger."

Maggie looked at her. "You don't think it's strange?"

"Why would I? Good grief, Maggie! Every girl in school was in love with Jonathan Stuart at one time or another. But seriously, are you sure he's not interested?"

Again Maggie shook her head. "Well, I don't actually know. Sometimes the way he looks at me…but I have to be imagining it. Why would a man like Jonathan Stuart be interested in me?"

Evie's hands stilled again, and she fixed an intense, searching look on Maggie. "Honestly? Maybe because you've grown up to be an attractive young woman who's intelligent and funny and just plain nice. Maybe because he sees your heart, Maggie, and likes what he sees."

Maggie had to blink back tears at this completely unexpected and uncharacteristic praise from her older sister. "Even if he did care about me—and I'm sure he doesn't—but even if he did, he wouldn't do anything about it," she said glumly. "He's so noble. I was his student, and now I'm a teacher in the same school. He'd probably consider it improper to show any interest in me. You remember what he's like."

"But you *are* in love with him?" Evie asked, her tone gentle.

Maggie paused again, and this time she almost choked on the unshed tears lodged in her throat. "Yes, I am. I know it's absolutely hopeless, but I'm afraid I am." She waited, wondering if she should tell her the rest. "There's this woman—the secretary at the school, Carolyn Ross—"

"What about her?"

"Well, she's a widow. And she's *extremely* attractive. Very feminine. Knows just how to dress, never a hair out of place. And she's probably in her mid-thirties at least—a good ten years older than I am, I'm sure. She's crackers over Jonathan. You can't miss it. She's set her cap for him, you can tell. And they do have a lot in common—she's musical, just like he is, and smart and…and *mature.*"

Even the thought of Carolyn Ross made Maggie feel miserable. "It makes me sick to admit it, but she's probably perfect for him. With her around, there's no way he's going to be attracted to me."

Evie was looking at her with a strange expression.

"What?" Maggie said.

"I'm just thinking about what we can do to make *you* look a little more...mature."

"Oh, Evie—honestly!"

Again her sister turned that same narrow-eyed expression on her. "You're giving up too easily. You love the man? Then do something about it."

"Like what?"

"Tomorrow we'll experiment. I have an idea for your hair."

"There's nothing that can be done with my hair! It's ugly and stubborn and I've hated it all my life! And don't forget the way you and Nell Frances used to make fun of it. You thought it was ugly, too."

"Now you're being childish. We never thought your hair was ugly. Not a bit. We were your older sisters, for goodness sake. Teasing is what older sisters do. We'll make a nice tidy twist for you. I have a pretty alabaster comb you can use to hold it in place. Getting your hair away from your face will bring out your eyes. They're enormous, you know. You ought to make the most of them. It will show off your cheekbones, too. You have amazing cheekbones."

Maggie put a hand to her face. "I do?"

Evie shook her head. 'Have you ever looked at yourself, Maggie? Really *looked?*"

Maggie pulled a face. "Then...you don't *disapprove* of the way I feel about Mr.—about Jonathan."

"Why would I disapprove?" A look of pain in Evie's eyes belied her casual tone of voice. "Do you have any idea what I'd give if I'd fallen for a good man like Jonathan Stuart instead of Richard? Of course, I don't disapprove. And you need to ignore anyone else who *does* disapprove—and that includes our parents. If he's the man you want, then fight for him."

Fight for him? The thought had never occurred to Maggie. She had assumed all along that her thoughts, her feelings, were so elusive as to be nothing more than a dream.

But sometimes you have to fight even for a dream, don't you?

She had fought for her other dreams, hadn't she? She had fought against her father's stubbornness when she set her mind to go to college, even though, with Jonathan Stuart's help, she'd won numerous scholarships. Da had been dead set against her leaving home for "the city." And she had fought him again—and her mother as well—when she went away to Chicago. Neither of them had wanted her to leave. She would never have gone to college, never have had the experience of working at Hull House, never have become a teacher, had she not fought for her dreams.

But how in the world could she fight for Jonathan Stuart? She didn't even know where to begin.

"We need a plan," Evie was saying. "We'll have to give this some thought. But we'll start with your hair."

Something about Evie's businesslike approach to the matter made Maggie want to laugh. She didn't though. To the contrary, she decided that for a change she might not give her big sister any argument.

Besides, this was the first time she'd seen any real enthusiasm or liveliness in Evie since she'd come home. Maybe this was just what she needed. Something to keep her occupied while she wasn't allowed to do much else. A project.

Yes...*she* would be Evie's project.

It might not help her situation with Jonathan Stuart in the least, but if it helped her sister even a little, it would be worthwhile.

Chapter Twenty

A Painful Encounter

Yet we, for all that praise, could find
Nothing but darkness overhead.

W.B. Yeats

~

Maggie was walking home with her parents after church on Sunday when Jonathan passed by in his buggy with Carolyn Ross seated beside him. They were laughing about something and looked like any other happy couple riding home from Sunday services.

Maggie might have pretended not to see them had her parents, in front of her, not waved. Da even called out to them.

Somehow Maggie forced a smile and a lift of her hand even while the pain in her heart threatened to crush her. She looked away, blinking against the tears that scalded her eyes. Not since she was ten years old and had the breath knocked out of her by a fall from a hay wagon had she taken such a blow.

Yes, she saw them together every day at school. But that was different entirely. Today they were really...*together*. Like a couple.

Had it been only last night that Evie had persuaded her to fight for him? And she had nearly convinced herself to do just that, believing she might actually have a chance.

Foolish! Oh, how could she have ever been so foolish as to think he might care for her, that he might ever look at her the way he looked at Carolyn Ross.

Da slowed his pace a bit and glanced over his shoulder. "Was that the school secretary with Jonathan Stuart?"

"Yea, that was Mrs. Ross," Maggie said, hoping her parents wouldn't detect the hurt in her voice.

Da nodded. " Looks like they're a bit cozy," he said to Mum, who smiled in agreement.

"Wouldn't it be nice if he finally found someone after all these years?" she said, turning to look at Maggie.

Maggie didn't answer; instead she pretended to be absorbed in the front window of Hubbard's Cupboard.

A memory flashed through her mind, sharpening still more the knife that had lodged in her heart. This wasn't the first time she'd recalled the evening spent with Jonathan at the diner—the feelings she had experienced sitting across from him, listening to him, watching his face, basking in the smile and the attention that, at least for that evening, had seemed entirely for her.

What she had seen today had tarnished that special memory— spoiled it, replacing it with something painful instead of something to treasure. Bitterness burned her throat. She was suddenly angry with herself—and with him. That night had meant everything to her, but it almost certainly had meant nothing to him.

She was even angrier with Carolyn for being just what Maggie had told Eva Grace she was only the night before: perfect for Jonathan.

Everything Maggie was *not!*

She had never known real jealousy until now. There had been the schoolgirl piques, of course, when the prettiest girl in the room had set her sights on Kenny Tallman, or when Eva Grace captured all the compliments at the Harvest Festival, leaving Maggie to feel like the ugly duckling scurrying around in her shadow. But never had she experienced real heartbreak, when someone she cared for couldn't see her because of someone else.

As a child, she'd occasionally been admonished at home for wanting what one of her sisters had. She had also sat through many a Sunday school lesson that expounded on the sin of jealousy. In fact, Jonathan himself had taught principles in the classroom around the very same subject, totally unsuspecting, of course, that he might eventually be the cause of some silly female's broken heart.

A silly female. That's exactly how she was acting. She had to stop this. If Jonathan wanted to keep company with Carolyn Ross, he had every right to do just that.

It's none of my business whom he squires about town. I'm not going to end up as an emotional shipwreck over a man who thinks I'm still twelve years old with freckles and pigtails. It doesn't matter. He's far too old for me anyway. Carolyn Ross is just right for him. She's an older woman...they're perfect for each other.

Maggie suddenly felt sick...sick of herself. If anyone could have read her thoughts, she would have died of humiliation. Had she always had it in her to be this hateful, this nasty-minded?

An old, discomfiting memory inserted itself into her self-disgust: Jonathan standing in front of the class when she had been just a small girl—it must have been not long after he first arrived in Skingle Creek—teaching about love. Genuine love. God's kind of love.

"Love always puts the other person first, always wants what's best for the other. A heart that holds love doesn't have room for jealousy or a mean spirit or selfishness. Love doesn't take or keep. It gives...and keeps on giving."

He had taught that same lesson of love, built around St. Paul's message to the Corinthians, time and time again, every year, to every class, as if it might be the most important lesson he would ever teach them. "A heart that holds love doesn't have room for jealousy."

If I loved him...really loved him, I'd want what's best for him. Even if what's best for him is Carolyn Ross.

Her heart still aching, she started praying at that moment, knowing all the while that as soon as she reached home, she needed to go directly to her knees and continue praying until God's words...and Jonathan's...had once again taken hold of her heart and shaken this awful pettiness out of her.

Jonathan had to make a concentrated act of will to keep the promise he'd made to himself just the day before: that he was going to make a genuine effort to appreciate Carolyn, that he would take an interest in her and be attentive to her. In short, he'd had every intention of talking himself into becoming attracted to her.

She had seemed so pleased when he invited her to lunch after church that he almost felt guilty. They drove out of town a few miles to a country inn called Holly Hill House, a small, friendly looking place decorated in spruce, white, and red colors. It was a bit too frilly for Jonathan's taste, but he had treated Ben and Regina Wallace to supper here a few times, and Regina had taken to it right away. Thinking that its appeal might be mostly to women, he nevertheless found the food good and the scenery inspiring. And just as he'd hoped, Carolyn enjoyed it immensely.

During their meal he tried gamely to draw her out, prompting her to talk about herself so that he might get to know her better. He listened closely, or at least attempted to, doing his best to take in every detail, every nuance of what she had to say. He smiled when he knew he should, making small sounds of agreement and understanding in the proper places.

And the entire time he felt like a total fraud.

This was so wrong. He should never have gone through with this, taking Carolyn to lunch, behaving as if he really wanted to be with her...when all the while he couldn't stop thinking of Maggie.

Deception was a trait he despised, an attribute he wouldn't have thought to be part of his character. But here he sat, deceiving a perfectly fine woman with each phony word of encouragement, each compliment, each smile.

Carolyn deserved better than this. He had no right to ask her to lunch in the first place, much less treat her as if she were special to him. She was a good person, an excellent secretary, a dependable helper. No doubt she would make a loyal friend. But she was *not* special to him. And she never would be, not in the way a woman *should* be special if there's to be more than friendship.

From the moment he'd seen Maggie walking along the boardwalk with her parents, her cheeks flagged with color from the brisk air, her pretty blue coat open at the throat, her cloud of fiery hair glazed by the noonday sun, he'd wanted nothing else but to get Carolyn home as quickly and decently as possible and go in search of Maggie.

The way she had looked at him in that one instant, when their eyes met…had he imagined it or had it been pain that darkened her gaze?

A thought teetered at the fringes of his mind, but it was too unlikely to seriously consider. Still…was it possible that seeing him with Carolyn had been responsible for that wounded gaze? Could it be that she cared enough for him to be *jealous?*

"Where are you, Jonathan?"

"What?"

Carolyn was watching him closely, and he realized with a start how far from her his thoughts had strayed. The exact thing he'd meant to avoid.

"I'm sorry. Bad habit of mine, I'm afraid."

"That's all right. I know you must have a lot on your mind. But it's good for you to relax now and then, you know."

As he watched her take a bite of cherry pie, he realized that he'd been toying with his own dessert—a slice of applesauce cake. He proceeded to make a show of finishing it off.

"I know the Lazlo children are a real burden for you," Carolyn went on. "Has there been any news about their situation?"

He shook his head, choosing to let her believe the children were the reason for his silence since he could hardly tell her what he'd *really* been thinking. At least this was a subject he could discuss without feeling deceitful. "There's been no word at all. I just hope for the children's sake that this doesn't drag on too long."

"Well, you've done everything you can. The rest is up to the authorities. And the Wallaces *did* say that the children are welcome to stay there as long as necessary."

"Yes, but I don't believe that Lazlo will leave them there indefinitely."

"You don't know that. Perhaps he's not all that eager to have them back. The way he's treated them, I wonder if he wouldn't just as soon be shut of them for good."

Jonathan didn't think that was the case and said so. "Remember, he's already come looking for them at my house." He shook his head. "No, I'm convinced he'll make a fight for them at some point, and I think it will be soon."

"Well, for now you need to stop worrying yourself about it. It may turn out better than you think. So...what shall we do after lunch?"

He knew he was being touchy, but he found himself irritated by the way she dismissed the subject of the children, much as she might have brushed off an annoying bug. Nor did he want to do anything after lunch. Not with Carolyn, at any rate.

He cleared his throat. "I'm afraid I don't have the entire afternoon free. In fact, we probably should be getting on our way. I still have some things I need to do."

Her face fell. Stung by his conscience, Jonathan moved to make amends. "We'll have to do this again soon," he said. "It's especially nice out here in the winter, when we have snow."

"Well, I hope I don't have to wait until it snows to spend time with you again." Her tone was teasing, but her expression was intense.

"Of course not," he said, digging his fingers into the palms of his hands under the table. "But I really should check on Huey and Selma yet today. You're more than welcome to come with me if you like."

She considered the idea, but not for long. "No, they'd probably be more comfortable if you go alone. I'll see them at school tomorrow. But so will you. Why go today?"

"I keep hoping Huey will eventually open up to me. Selma too, for that matter. Selma does seem to be responding a little, but I can't get more than a few words out of the boy, not when I see him at school, and not even when I visit them at Ben and Regina's."

He paused, nodding to a couple from town who recognized him and were smiling in his direction. "Deputy Akin is pressing me to get more information," he went on, " but the only place I'm going to get it is from the children. And I've had absolutely no success with that. In fact, Huey simply won't talk to me at all other than a routine 'good morning' or 'goodbye.' Maggie says he doesn't participate in class, and he stays to himself at recess and lunch as well. I'm at my wit's end with him."

He stopped. "By any chance, does he respond to you?"

"Never. I've tried talking to him, but the boy shrinks away from me. He's such a skittish child."

Jonathan shook his head. "I don't know what to make of him. Even in the worst of situations, I've never had a child completely refuse to communicate with me. Selma doesn't have much to say either. She always seems such an unhappy little girl, but at least she'll smile now and then. And she does occasionally speak up in class."

He got up then and went to help Carolyn with her chair and her wrap, resisting the urge to hurry her along as they left. He owed her at least the courtesy of patience, especially since he seemed to have disappointed her in every other respect.

Before they drove away, he felt compelled to apologize for his preoccupation. She patted his hand and smiled. "You need never apologize to me for being the man you are, Jonathan. I imagine I understand more than you realize."

Her remark left him puzzled, wondering just what, exactly, she understood that he didn't.

Chapter Twenty-One

Figaro

Hail, guest, we ask not what thou art;
If friend, we greet thee, hand and heart;
If stranger, such no longer be;
If foe, our love shall conquer thee.

Old Welsh Door Verse

After dropping Carolyn off at her house, Jonathan made the decision to stop at home before going on to the Wallaces'. He could visit the children later in the afternoon…if he went at all.

He was in a strange mood. Irritated with himself and increasingly puzzled by what he *thought* he had seen in Maggie's expression that morning, he felt a need to withdraw for a while, to be alone, to think. Yet he was unwilling to fall into the same brooding, introspective mood he'd been in the day before. He finally realized that he didn't actually want to think; he wanted to escape. Perhaps what he needed was something entirely different, something to take his mind away from Maggie, from Carolyn, from the Lazlo children. Something that might even lighten his spirits.

He went to the closet off the living room and retrieved his flute. He put on a recording of the first act of *The Barber of Seville,* wound the phonograph, and began playing along with the music. The patter song in which Figaro, the town's barber and local busybody, dances onto the scene was a foolish, lighthearted number. Jonathan would often accompany the recording with his flute, resetting the phonograph's arm time and time again. The music invariably gave him a lift.

When he first heard the unfamiliar sound, he passed it off as his imagination. Something on the recording, perhaps. The next time he heard it, he stopped and lifted the arm to inspect the needle. He played through the aria again, but, hearing nothing amiss, went on to the "little voice" aria before returning to Figaro's number. Jonathan was definitely feeling better now—lighter, almost carefree.

And then he heard it again. Louder this time. Finally he realized the sound wasn't coming from the phonograph after all, but from outside. From the back of the house.

He set the arm back in place and stood listening.

Nothing but silence.

After waiting another moment and hearing nothing, he started the music again and began to play.

There it was again. An eerie, moaning sound…like howling.

And it was closer this time.

Jonathan stopped the music and put the flute down on the chair. In spite of the fact that it was the middle of the afternoon, an icy finger touched his spine. It wasn't unheard of for a coyote or even a wolf to wander in from the hills looking for food, although they usually showed up only at night.

He went to look out the side window of the living room, but seeing nothing, he started down the hall toward the kitchen. He had no more than stepped inside the room when something hit the door, followed by a blood-chilling howl.

Jonathan stopped dead. He didn't keep a gun and had no means of protection in the house. Whatever was out there sounded huge and vicious.

The back door was solid. It had no glass in it so he couldn't see out. And he couldn't see the porch from the window at the sink.

The next howl was more demanding—and again accompanied by a *thump* against the back door.

He was safe, of course, so long as he stayed inside. No coyote or wolf was going to beat the door down and come crashing into the room. He would simply wait until whatever it was gave up and went away.

Sooner than later, he hoped.

He couldn't stop himself from going over to the door and putting his ear against it. The exact instant he did, the creature, whatever it was, hit the door hard.

And then it barked. And barked again. A loud bass, commanding bark that seemed intent on evoking some sort of response.

So it wasn't a coyote or a wolf. It was a dog.

Jonathan might have been relieved had the bark not sounded like that of a very *large* dog.

Unexpectedly the barking stopped, giving way to a series of whimpers and wails. Heartbreaking sounds. Sounds guaranteed to gain attention, perhaps even to open doors.

Jonathan looked around. He spied a stew kettle he'd washed and dried the night before but hadn't put away. He tested it for weight and sturdiness. Then, with weapon in hand, he went back to the door.

He hesitated, but the creature was still whimpering pathetically and so after a long, steadying breath, Jonathan cracked the door open ever so slightly to peek out.

The creature hit him full on, knocking him off balance and toppling him onto his backside as it shoved its way through the door. The next thing Jonathan knew he was eyeball-to-eyeball with a bedraggled beast lapping at his face with a tongue that had to be at least a foot long. A solid, pewter-gray boulder had settled itself on his chest and was holding him down with one enormous paw that looked to be the size of a dinner plate.

The creature was a demon in a bristly coat, a slobbering one at that—and it smelled as if it had just spent the last six months hiding at the bottom of a privy.

Jonathan squawked and shoved, trying to roll away. *"Ugh! Get... off...me!"*

Again he shoved as hard as he could, and this time he managed to dislodge the ugly beast. He scrambled to his feet before it could flatten him again and bent to pick up the stew kettle he'd dropped upon collision. He had never hit an animal before and hoped he wouldn't have to start now, but just in case...

With the cooking pot firmly in hand, he stood, poised, taking the dog's measure. It wasn't quite the size of a calf, but it didn't miss it by much. The gray, somewhat wavy coat was spotted in several places with dried mud and tangled with burrs. It had a fairly long muzzle and small ears—one ear pricked up, the other loppy, giving it a roguish appearance. Open-mouthed with that over-sized tongue in full display, it looked eager to renew its assault on Jonathan's face.

"I have news for you, you filthy beast. You're the one who needs a bath. You are one dirty dog."

It cocked its head and grinned at him.

There was no sign of a chain or collar, and upon closer inspection, Jonathan could see that in spite of its hefty frame, its ribs were visible.

It tilted its head a little more, its expression unmistakably expectant.

"Yes, I can see that you need a good meal. But the kitchen's closed for the day. I'm afraid you'll have to go catch yourself a pig or something. Much as I hate to tell you this, your visit is over."

Jonathan opened the door wide and waited. His unwelcome visitor merely sat and stared at him. *This might not be easy,* Jonathan decided. "Look—when I said I wanted a dog, I meant something...*dog-sized.* You're not exactly what I had in mind."

It whimpered. It lowered its head with a woeful look and actually *whimpered.*

"Now, listen to me! You can't stay here, and that's all there is to it."

The great head came up, and for the first time Jonathan saw that the beast had a look of intelligence about it. In fact, there was something...*knowing* in those dark eyes. Something that appeared ancient and almost wise.

It was watching him carefully, closely.

"No! Absolutely not."

It would almost certainly eat enough for two normal-sized dogs. Worse yet, he had been around dogs enough to suspect that this one wasn't even fully grown as yet. He couldn't be sure, of course, but something about the uneven consistency of the coat, the one loppy ear, and the overall frisky look to the creature shouted *puppy*.

Slowly, the dog brought its front legs closer together, then crossed its feet, one over the other. The head lifted, and the tongue disappeared. And suddenly it looked noble. Proud. *Mature*.

Trying to ignore the stench, Jonthan moved a little closer to study it better. The dog got to its feet. Jonathan ran a hand over its back, and the creature trembled. He dropped his hand to its side, and after the slightest hesitation, the dog leaned into him slightly, as if seeking closeness, and began to nuzzle his fingers.

Jonathan dropped to his heels, continuing to stroke the animal—his head, his back. The dog met his gaze straight on, never wavering.

Unusual, that. Most dogs would have glanced away after a few seconds.

He straightened. "I can't possibly keep you. You're a horse masquerading as a dog. You're just too...big."

The dog stared at Jonathan. Slowly, it started toward the open door. It looked back once, its expression sorrowful. Disappointed, even disillusioned. Then it headed toward the door again.

Until Jonathan said "Wait."

❧•❧

The late afternoon found Jonathan on his knees in the kitchen. It was too chilly outdoors for giving a dog a bath. Or was the dog giving him a bath? By the time he finished, they both had a proper washing.

"Don't shake," he warned the animal as he reached for both towels he'd set aside. "Just stand there. No! I said *don't*—"

The dog shook. Hard and happily. Vigorously, in fact. Jonathan looked down over himself, his soaked shirt and splattered trousers. In that split second, the dog yanked the towel out of his hands and went running across the kitchen with it. The large pup made a dash for the upstairs. Up he went, Jonathan right behind him.

They made two full circles of the house, first and second floors, before Jonathan was able to grab a handful of snout and throw the towel over his eyes to slow him down.

He finished drying him in the kitchen and removed the remaining burrs he'd missed on the first try. With the dog curiously looking on, he emptied the washtub off the side of the back porch and turned it over to dry out.

When he came back inside, his damp visitor was resting his head on the counter beside the sink, greedily munching on the last apple in the fruit bowl.

"Dogs don't eat apples, you numbskull."

While the dog devoured the rest of the apple, including the core, Jonathan fried up three eggs and a handful of sausage, dumping the mix into an old piece of stonewear. As he placed the bowl on the rag rug in front of the sink, the four-legged giant looked up at him with something akin to a swoon before setting about noisily devouring the entire serving in three or four gulps.

Watching him, Jonathan decided that the bath and thorough brushing had worked a wonder. The beast was almost handsome. *Almost.*

With his tail wagging furiously in a circle, the animal came to lie as close to Jonathan as he could manage. Jonathan knelt down to rub the dog's head, and immediately the ornery creature kicked over on his back for a belly-rub.

"Where did you come from, I wonder? Not from around here, I'm thinking." The dog sighed. Jonathan kept on rubbing. "From the looks of you, you've been on the road for a while, haven't you? Most likely for a long time."

The dog rolled to his side and began to nibble—lightly—at Jonathan's fingers.

Now Jonathan sighed. It seemed that instead of finding himself a dog, a dog had found *him*.

"Well," he said, rescuing his fingers, "looks like you're home now."

Later, he dug an old quilt out of the storage trunk and fashioned it into a snug bed beside his own. Just before he fell asleep, Jonathan leaned over for another look at his new friend. The dog looked back at him with a grin, obviously pleased with himself and life in general.

Figaro, Jonathan decided. "Your name is *Figaro*."

Beside him, the dog made a low sound of approval in his throat, turned over, and began to snore.

Chapter Twenty-Two

Figaro Goes to School

No one appreciates the very special genius
Of your conversation as the dog does.

Christopher Morley

⁓

Maggie nursed her hurt feelings alone all week. She couldn't bring herself to tell even her sister about seeing Jonathan and Carolyn together. For the most part, she thought she did a credible job of acting normal.

So as not to arouse Evie's curiosity, she agreed to let her style her hair, putting it in a twist one day, a top knot another, and once a sleek chignon, which stayed put a whole hour before escaping and falling apart.

She noticed Jonathan looking at her with a questioning expression more than once. But naturally he didn't ask what was going on, and she didn't offer an explanation.

No doubt if *Carolyn* had changed her hairstyle more than once in the same week, he would have had something to say about it.

He *had* taken her aside once or twice to tell her about his new dog. Maggie was genuinely glad for him; she couldn't help but delight in his obvious excitement. He was like a schoolboy in his enthusiasm every time he mentioned Figaro. She wished she could share more in his happiness, but she kept her distance as much as possible now, talking to him only when a school-related matter required it.

She actually thought she'd seen a hint of disappointment in his eyes once or twice when she'd avoided him, but that wasn't likely. Probably just wishful thinking on her part.

When Friday came around, though, she finally did get to meet the dog that was responsible for his high spirits. And five minutes with Figaro was all it took to win her over.

Jonathan decided it was time for Figaro to go to school.

He hated leaving him alone every day. The dog carried on like a spoiled toddler every time Jonathan left the house without him. For four straight days now he'd come home to find evidence of yet another bout of mischief: an overturned lamp in the living room; a plundered garbage receptacle in the kitchen; a pair of curtains yanked from the rod, their ruffles shredded; and—the dog's favorite annoyance—newspapers strewn from one end of the house to the other.

There was also the fact that he had to leave school every noon hour to rush home and let Figaro out to do his business. It had taken only a day or two for the dog to pick up on the routine; indeed, he mastered it so quickly that Jonathan suspected he'd had previous training.

While he had yet to have an accident in the house, Figaro could hardly be expected to control himself for the entire day. The solution was simply to take the dog to school, and Jonathan didn't really see a problem with doing just that. Figaro could be a terror when left alone; he was still as rambunctious as most pups, even when Jonathan was with him to curtail his mischief. But when he sensed that his master meant business, he toed the mark surprisingly well.

Besides, there might just be a side benefit to having him on the school grounds: If someone *should* be up to no good, they were likely to think twice before going up against something the size of Figaro, who could look—and sound—dangerously fierce when it pleased his fancy.

Jonathan wasn't sure what the school board might say about a dog on the premises, but since Ben Wallace—his closest friend—was the board president, he thought he could talk himself out of trouble if it came to that.

So on Friday morning, with Figaro perched proudly on the seat next to him, he drove away from the house. Having his dog at his side gave him the brightest morning he'd had all week.

Maggie's behavior continued to trouble him on a daily basis. She'd been polite, but definitely chilly all week. Jonathan sensed that she was deliberately avoiding him, keeping her distance except for the times when she found it necessary to bring something to his attention. Even then, she was patently obvious in her rush to get away.

He felt he'd somehow offended her. He still hadn't been able to forget the way she'd looked at him last Sunday when he and Carolyn had passed by in the buggy. If he thought for a moment that might be the cause of her strange behavior, he would try to explain the incident. But if he were wrong—well, then she'd *really* be offended by his presumption.

"And what on earth is going on with her hair?"

Figaro looked at him and gave a small chuff in reply.

Jonathan had fallen into the habit of talking to the dog as if he expected an answer. He sighed. Another sign that he spent too much time alone.

As for Maggie's hair, he couldn't imagine why she'd want to change it. He loved it just as it was: its fullness, its deep, fiery color. He found it fascinating in all its untamed glory.

He pulled up in back of the schoolhouse as he always did, in hopes of not causing too much of a stir when the children got their first look at Figaro. Unfortunately, he wasn't quick enough to stop the mischievous dog from leaping from the buggy and plowing around the side of the building at top speed, dragging his leash behind him.

The dog had seen the children on the way in—and they had seen him.

By the time Jonathan made it around to the front, Figaro had also seen Maggie. Standing on his hind legs, he had her pinned against the front of the building, one big paw on each shoulder, flashing his widest grin as the children looked on, pointing and laughing.

"*Figaro! Down!*"

The dog turned to look at him, then back to Maggie, who was, Jonathan saw with relief, laughing.

"I said *down!*" Jonathan ordered.

Again the big hound looked his way—and again chose Maggie over obedience to his master.

Master? What a joke!

"I'm sorry, Maggie!" Jonathan hurried over to her and hauled Figaro down by his collar. "Figaro—*sit!*"

He grabbed the leash and turned back to Maggie. "Did he hurt you?"

"Goodness, no!" she said, still laughing. "What a big ox he is! But he's *so* cute!"

Jonathan looked at his dog. *Cute?* Figaro had finally dropped to his haunches and sat, tongue lolling, eyes bright, watching Maggie adoringly. "Cute" might pertain to a beagle or a kitten. Definitely not to an escapee from the Black Forest.

Maggie was watching Figaro with a wide smile, and the dog did his best to escape Jonathan's firm hold on the leash by scooting toward her, an inch at a time.

"I see you, you big lummox. Now behave!" Jonathan demanded, giving the leash a tug.

By this time they were surrounded by children, and, finding himself the center of attention, Figaro could no longer bear to sit quietly, not even with Maggie as an incentive. With a pitiful whimper, he strained at the leash.

Jonathan thought for a moment and decided to let him get

acquainted with the children. Unsnapping the leash, he stood watching as every child in the schoolyard went charging after the great hound, squealing and shouting. Figaro ran in circles, leaped in the air, reversed himself, and led them all on a wild chase down to the gate.

Both dog and followers seemed to have completely lost their wits as they ran and tumbled and hopped and screeched.

"Jonathan—look," Maggie said, her voice low.

His gaze traveled the direction of hers...to Huey Lazlo standing off by himself near the gate. The boy had caught Figaro's attention. The two now squared off, eyeing each other, one taking the other's measure. They scarcely moved for a few seconds more until Figaro made a playful lunge at the boy, and then another. Huey chuckled. That was all the encouragement the dog needed. He charged him, butting him to the ground.

Jonathan started to move, but Maggie put a restraining hand to his arm. "Wait," she said.

Figaro was giving the boy the same kind of eager face washing he'd inflicted on Jonathan the day of his arrival.

And Huey was laughing! Giggling, actually. On his back, his feet pedaling in the air, while Figaro nuzzled and lapped his face.

Until this moment, Jonathan didn't think he had ever seen Huey smile. Now a great explosion of laughter was bubbling up from the boy, and it was one of the sweetest sounds he had heard in all his years of teaching.

Dear Lord, that clown of a dog doesn't look remotely like a divine messenger, but I'm beginning to believe he just might have been heaven-sent.

When he turned to look at Maggie, there were tears in her eyes.

"I love your dog, Jonathan," she said, her eyes locking with his. The hitch in her voice sounded throatier than usual as she repeated herself. "I really do love that dog."

Her words set his blood to humming. She might as well have said she loved *him,* so dizzying were her words and the way she was looking at him.

He noticed that her hair was done up in some kind of a fancy twist today, and again he wondered what was going on. But he hadn't the nerve to ask, certainly not with the cold-shoulder she'd been giving him all week.

She had already turned away, as if she were about to go inside.

"Maggie…" he ventured, all the while knowing that the time was all wrong for this, yet feeling as if he couldn't let it go on any longer. "Are you angry with me? Have I done something?"

She looked at him, but Jonathan couldn't read her expression. "I'm not angry with you, Jonathan," she said quietly. Her gaze went to Figaro and Huey Lazlo. "But even if I were, I'd still love your dog."

With that she went inside before Jonathan could stop her.

Chapter Twenty-Three

Through a Sister's Eyes

The way to love anything is to
Realize that it might be lost.

Gilbert Keith Chesterton

Because of Dr. Gordon's orders, Evie was almost entirely confined to the house. She couldn't go to church, couldn't go visiting, couldn't do much of anything except stay inside and rest.

On Sunday afternoon, hoping to help make the time pass more quickly for her sister, Maggie hurried through the kitchen cleanup and then went to challenge Evie to a game of checkers in the front room.

The house was quiet. Mum had actually given in to take a nap while Da went outside to rake leaves. Ray was still out at cousin Jeff's farm, where he would be spending all his weekends now.

Maggie had been surprised when her father gave his consent to the Taggarts' proposal that Ray work for them on weekends, staying at the farm until Sunday evening. Cousin Jeff's original idea had been for Ray to live with them full-time. Apparently Jeff was finding it hard to keep up the farm in addition to working at the lumber mill and needed help. Da wouldn't agree to a full-time arrangement, but he did finally compromise and allow Ray to work on weekends.

So now Ray left for the Taggarts on Friday right after school and didn't come home until late on Sunday. Maggie was almost certain Da had mixed emotions about this. With his health being what it was, he could have used Ray's help himself, especially on weekends when there was no school. But she suspected that her father's own love for farm life had entered into his decision. He of all people would understand Ray's affinity for working the land.

Besides, Jeff was paying Ray a fair wage for the few hours he put in, and no doubt Da was hoping that having some money of his own in his pockets would dampen any lingering thoughts her brother still had about going into the mines.

She figured it had been a wise move on her father's part. Surely there couldn't be much choice for a boy between working below ground in a dark, dank coal mine and working outdoors, unconfined, and far enough away from town that the air was fresh and free of coal dust.

"You've been awfully quiet," Evie remarked.

Her sister was lying on her side on the floor, balancing herself on one elbow. Maggie thought she didn't look any too comfortable, but Evie insisted she was fine.

"Is something wrong?" she asked Maggie as she considered her next move.

"No," Maggie said. "What would be wrong?"

Her sister looked up. "I don't know. That's why I asked."

Maggie kept her eyes on the checkerboard, saying nothing.

"Maggie?

She still didn't look at Evie, but finally answered. "I haven't wanted to talk about it, but I suppose I might just as well tell you." She sighed, then went on. "Last Sunday after church Jonathan passed us on the way home. Carolyn Ross was in the buggy with him, and they were obviously having a grand old time together."

She could feel Evie's eyes on her. Finally she looked up. "Don't look at me like that."

Evie lifted one eyebrow. "Like *what?*"

"Like you feel sorry for me."

"I *don't* feel sorry for you. I'm sorry you were hurt, that's all."

"I'm not hurt. I'm just glad I finally realized how foolish I've been. I don't know why I ever thought he'd be interested in me. Not with a woman like Carolyn around. And besides, he really is too old for me. If I think so, I'm sure he does. Now, can we talk about something else? I really don't want to think about this anymore."

Maggie turned her attention back to the checkerboard, but she could still feel Evie's gaze on her. "It's your play," she reminded her sister.

Evie jumped one of Maggie's pieces and then another. "Well, I suppose it's good that you found out how things are now, rather than later," she said. "And I expect you're right, after all."

"Right about what?"

"About Mr. Stuart being too old for you. You're probably better off holding out for someone more your own age."

"I'm not holding out for anything," Maggie snapped. "I absolutely won't marry a miner, I can tell you that. And just try to find a man in Skingle Creek who *isn't* a miner. I probably won't marry anyone."

What she left unsaid was that she wouldn't marry anyone if she couldn't have Jonathan Stuart.

"Whatever happened to Kenny Tallman anyway? Everyone thought the two of you would get married after you graduated."

"He's off in a jungle somewhere," Maggie said.

Evie made a face. "I always thought he was a little strange." She started to make a move, then stopped, pushing herself up as she tried to see out the front window. "Who's Da talking to?"

"What?"

"Someone's out there with him."

"Probably Mr. Quigley."

Just then they heard feet stamping on the porch and the door flew open to admit Da—and Jonathan Stuart.

Maggie clambered to her feet, at the last minute remembering to give Eva Grace a hand up from the floor.

"Brought you some company, Eva Grace," Da said. "I expect you'll be glad to see this gentleman."

Jonathan gave Maggie a quick smile, but when she glanced away he went directly to Evie, taking both her hands in his. "Eva Grace, it's so good to see you! I hope it's all right that I came by without letting you know first."

"Oh, of course it is, Mr. Stuart. I'm glad to see you too."

A faint blush stained Evie's cheeks. Maggie could tell this was awkward for her sister. It was only natural that it would be, given the fact that she hadn't seen Jonathan Stuart for years. Indeed, Evie had had little contact with anyone but family since leaving Richard, and with her condition being so obvious now, she would likely be easily flustered.

But with characteristic tact, Jonathan managed to ease the moment. "Who's winning?" he asked, releasing Evie's hands and gesturing to the checkerboard on the floor.

Evie smiled now, though she stood with her hands clasped in front of her, as if to minimize her condition. "I think we're taking turns today, although Maggie usually gets the best of me."

Maggie busied herself with picking up the game pieces so she wouldn't have to look Jonathan in the eye. The pain of seeing him and Carolyn together last Sunday still lingered.

"Kate's having herself a bit of a nap," said Da. "I'll call her–"

"You'll do no such thing," Jonathan told him. "I can't stay. I came by only to say hello to Eva Grace." He paused. "And to see if Maggie would like to come with me to visit the Lazlo children."

Maggie whipped around to find him watching her. Surprised by the unexpected invitation, she didn't quite know what to say. In truth, she'd been wanting to visit the children. There was little if any time during school to speak privately with either of them. Yet she was reluctant to be alone with Jonathan, knowing it would be difficult.

Everything seemed different now that he and Carolyn were a couple. Even at school, she sometimes found herself feeling young and inept and gauche. It seemed that every time she turned around she saw Carolyn going in or coming out of his office, and the woman invariably had a cat-caught-the-mouse smile on her face.

Still, he was merely offering her a ride to visit the children. That was all.

But did she really want to be with him so much that she'd tag along like a pup on a rope, just to keep him company? Even knowing what she did about him and Carolyn?

"Yes," she said impulsively. "I'd like to go. I'll just go and put up some bread for tomorrow so Mum won't have to do it. You can let me know when you're ready to leave."

Without waiting, Maggie escaped to the kitchen. At the same time she heard Da take his leave. "Well then, Jonathan, while you and Eva Grace have your visit, I'll be tending to the rest of those leaves. The way the sky looks, we'll be getting some rain later this evening."

In the kitchen Maggie stood at the sink and took in some long, steadying breaths, already wishing she'd refused to go. She'd scarcely been able to face him when he walked in today. How was she going to handle being alone with him? She should have told him no. Maybe she still would. She could just tell him she'd changed her mind...or she wasn't feeling well.

Or she could tell him to go collect Carolyn and take her instead.

Even as she fought to quiet her emotions, she was remembering the way he'd looked at her only a moment before...as if he were confused by her behavior...or even hurt.

Well, if he was hurt, Carolyn would be only too glad to patch up his feelings.

Now she was being *really* childish.

She wished she had somewhere to go to get her own wounds healed. Then she remembered she *did* have somewhere to go...and Someone who cared enough to heal her wounds. She could hardly get on her knees this minute, though, lest someone walk in.

That was all she needed: Jonathan, seeing her on her knees, praying for an end to this silly infatuation that was turning her into the village idiot.

It was doubtful that she'd ever know what Eva Grace and Jonathan had talked about during their visit. Whatever it was, they were together long enough that Maggie had the bread put up and the counter sponged off before Evie appeared in the kitchen.

Maggie saw right away that there was something different about her.

It was ever so subtle, but unmistakable no less. Something about her eyes. The combination of sadness and apprehension that had been present ever since Evie had come home seemed finally to have given way to something else: the faint glimmer of confidence that had once marked her sister's bearing, along with a hint of something new. The care-worn expression of a woman bowed by uncertainty and dread of the future had lifted ever so slightly to reveal a look of purpose. Her expression had brightened just enough that Maggie thought she could detect a glimmer of hope.

For the first time in a long time, Eva Grace was her big sister again.

"If you can bring yourself to come out of hiding," she told Maggie with a quirk of a smile, "Mr. Stuart is ready to go. He said to take your time though. He went outside to talk to Da."

"I'm not hiding," Maggie snapped. "Besides, he didn't come to see me. He came to see you."

"Actually," Evie said quietly, her gaze traveling down the front of her dress, "he came to pray for me...and my baby."

She looked at Maggie. "I can't think of any other man I've ever known—not even Da—who could have done that without embarrassing me, given the situation I'm in. I'd almost forgotten how remarkable he is." She paused. "No wonder you fell in love with him."

"Evie!" Maggie grabbed her by the arm. "Keep your voice down! And I'm *not* in love with him! That foolishness is over."

Her sister turned a look on her that made Maggie feel cornered. "I can't believe you haven't seen it before now. Maggie—Jonathan Stuart is in love with you."

Maggie stared at her. "Why in the world would you ever say something like that to me? This isn't anything to tease me about, Evie!"

"I'm not teasing," her sister said evenly. "I saw it the minute he looked at you—the minute he walked into the room. And the way he watched you when *you* left the room."

Maggie stood mute, her mind spinning, her heart racing.

"You're wrong…"

Evie shook her head. "No, I'm *not* wrong. I know what I saw. And what's more, I saw the way you looked at *him* when you didn't think anyone was watching. It seems to me that it's about time you and Jonathan Stuart faced the truth."

She gave Maggie one more long look. "For now, though, you'd best go and wash the bread dough off your face and powder your nose. I do wish we'd worked on your hair earlier, but apparently it's fine the way it is. *He* seems to like the way you look just as you are."

Maggie didn't move. She wanted to protest what her sister seemed so sure of, wanted to convince her she was wrong.

But what if she wasn't wrong?

"Maggie—" Evie pointed a finger at the door. "*Go!*"

Maggie went.

Chapter Twenty-Four

For the Love of Maggie

May God be praised for woman...

W.B. Yeats

⁓

Outside, Jonathan couldn't help but note how tired Matthew MacAuley looked. Jonathan was certain his face was more deeply lined than it had been the last time he'd seen him. He suspected that was pain etched across those broad Irish features.

According to Maggie, her father lived with almost constant misery, and had ever since the mine cave-in last year. Matthew never talked about it. He wouldn't. Not even to his own children, apparently. Maggie had indicated that she knew the little she did only because her mother had confided in her.

Jonathan hated seeing Maggie's father in such a wretched condition. Matthew had once been the strongest, most physically powerful man he'd ever known. But little by little he was becoming a veritable shadow of himself. His lameness seemed more pronounced each time

Jonathan saw him, and his clothes hung loosely on his once brawny frame.

As much as Jonathan was worried about his friend, he knew it had to be even harder for Matthew's family. His concern prompted a question that he knew might prove inflammatory, but he felt the need to ask it anyway.

"Have you heard about the new doctor in town?" he ventured carefully.

"The lady doctor, you mean," said Matthew, leaning heavily on the rake. "As a matter of fact Eva Grace saw her last week. She liked the woman."

"Good." Jonathan hesitated, groping for just the right words. "What about you, Matthew? You've said all along that Dr. Woodbridge has been no help to you. Have you thought about making an appointment with Dr. Gordon?"

Had he suggested a trip to the gallows the other couldn't have looked more shocked. "A *woman?*"

Clearly this wasn't going to go well.

"She's a graduate of medical college, and according to Ben Wallace, she's been in practice for some years now. And," Jonathan pointed out, "she's the only other doctor besides Lebreen Woodbridge within traveling distance."

Matthew continued to stare at him as if he'd lost his senses altogether. "I'll not be going to any woman doctor, I don't care how long she's been in practice." His mouth tightened even more. "And how did such a fine *physician* end up in a coal town like Skingle Creek, I can't help but wonder."

Jonathan had noticed before how Matthew's Irish brogue thickened with even the slightest aggravation. He probably shouldn't pursue the subject, but he wasn't inclined to back down just yet.

"I'm curious, Matthew. Why *wouldn't* you see a woman doctor?"

He knew the reason, of course.

Matthew's heavy eyebrows came up sharply. "Would *you?*"

Jonathan wanted to be fair, so he asked himself the same thing.

He supposed it would depend on the type of ailment he had. And its location.

"I believe I would, yes. In fact, I'm certain I would if I needed help."

"Well, that's fine for you then, Jonathan. As for me, I'll stay on with Doc Woodbridge. Even if he is a quack."

"Lebreen Woodbridge is no quack, Matthew," Jonathan said more sternly than he'd intended. "But I'll admit that he doesn't seem to have helped you."

"Well, he's not that much of a doctor. Never has been."

"There—that's my point. If you have no faith in Dr. Woodbridge, then why won't you consider Dr. Gordon?"

Still leaning on the rake, Matthew straightened a little. Jonathan didn't miss the way he winced with the effort.

"Jonathan, there's no man in town I respect more than you. I hope you know that. But to be straight with you, this is my business. Don't worry yourself about it."

Heat rushed to Jonathan's face. "I apologize if I'm out of line, Matthew. The only reason I raised the subject is because we're friends, and it bothers me to see you in pain."

"You live with what you've been given," the other said with a shrug.

Matthew's tone was too mild to be safe. Jonathan had learned that his Irish friend was often a good case in point for the adage about the calm before the storm. He was definitely not a man to press too hard. Yet he was reluctant to give up.

"I still wish you'd consider the idea."

"You're a good man, Jonathan," Matthew said, unexpectedly cracking a grin. "But I'd wager that if it came down to it, you wouldn't be all that quick to drop your drawers for a lady doctor."

"Modesty is a small price to pay if there's any chance she might be able to help you."

Still grinning, Matthew shook his head. "You're the smartest fella I ever knew, Jonathan, but even you can sometimes be a bit foolish."

Knowing himself to be defeated, Jonathan sighed. "You're as

smart a man as I am, Matthew, but *you* can sometimes be a bit thick-headed."

"And haven't I heard that before from Kate?" His expression turned sly. "So, then, got yourself a lady friend, have you?"

Jonathan frowned at the abrupt change in subject. "What?"

Matthew made no reply but simply watched him, clearly waiting for some sort of response.

Then Jonathan remembered. "You mean Carolyn Ross? Oh, no—it's nothing like that. We're just...friends."

"Ah, now. No need to be embarrassed. Kate and myself, we were pleased to see you with a lady companion for a change."

"No, Matthew, really. You've got the wrong idea altogether. There's nothing between Carolyn and me."

If he only knew the "companion" I really want, he just might toss me out of his yard here and now.

Matthew looked disappointed. "Well, that's too bad, man. I thought perhaps you'd finally found someone."

If he only knew, Jonathan thought again.

And if he *did* know? Would it mean an end of their friendship? How would a man like Matthew MacAuley take to the idea of the town schoolteacher courting his daughter? Assuming Maggie would allow it, of course.

Jonathan didn't like to think about the answer. And yet, depending on Maggie's response to the question he intended to ask her this evening...if he didn't lose his nerve...he might *have* to think about it. And sooner rather than later.

He was relieved when Maggie walked out, buttoning her coat. Everything else, for the moment at least, was forgotten.

Kate stepped out onto the porch just as Maggie and Jonathan drove away. She watched them for a moment, and then came out into the yard.

Matthew leaned his weight on the rake.

"Eva Grace told me Jonathan was here. Why didn't you wake me?" she asked.

"I figured you needed the rest. Besides, Jonathan said not to. He came to visit with Eva Grace for a bit."

"That was good of him. She's always admired him so." She yawned and shook her head a little. "Where are he and Maggie off to?"

"He asked her to go along with him to look in on those Lazlo children. They're staying at Pastor Wallace's place, you know."

She nodded. "Poor things. What are they going to do about that father of theirs, do you think?"

"Hard telling. Jonathan's more than a little troubled about that situation."

Her gaze went to the pile of leaves he'd raked. "Matthew, why didn't you leave that for Ray? He'll be home soon."

"It's going to rain. He won't be able to get to them for another day or more. Besides, I'm almost finished."

"Are you sure we've done the right thing, letting him stay out at Jeff and Martha's every weekend? You could use his help here."

He shook his head. "This is good for him, Kate. I had my taste of farm life. I want the boy to have his. Indeed, I'm grateful to Jeff for asking."

"But it makes that much more work for you. If you'd asked, I'm sure Maggie would have stayed home instead of going off with Jonathan. She's always good to help out."

Matthew saw Jonathan's buggy turn off at the fork in the road.

"Matthew?"

He looked back to his wife. "Have you seen them together, Jonathan and our Maggie?"

Kate glanced toward the road and then back to him. "Of course I've seen them together. Why?"

"No, I mean, have you seen how they *are* when they're together, the way they look at each other?"

She stared at him. "Maggie and Jonathan Stuart? What are you saying?"

Matthew thought perhaps he should have kept his silence, at least for now. He might be mistaken. He'd seen it for himself only today, after all.

"*Matthew?*"

Too late. She'd not be leaving it alone now. "He claims there's nothing between him and that school secretary, you know. And I believe him. Especially after seeing the way he is with our girl."

Her eyes widened. "Surely not—" She broke off. "Jonathan Stuart isn't the kind of man to dally with a girl Maggie's age."

"Did I say anything about dallying, woman? The man is smitten with the girl, is what I meant. And furthermore, she's in the same fix over him."

Kate brought a hand to her mouth, her eyes boring into his. "Are you sure, Matthew?"

"Not entirely. But it's what I'm thinking."

"But Jonathan—he's so much older than Maggie." She paused. "*How* much, do you think?"

Matthew shrugged. "He was her schoolteacher after all. Hadn't he just come to town when she started school?"

"Yes, but he was quite a young man at the time."

Kate was obviously calculating things, that clever mind of hers no doubt breezing right by his own, which was usually the case.

"Well," she finally said, "he's certainly not too old to take a wife and have a family yet. And he *is* a fine-featured man."

"Oh, is he now? I wouldn't have thought a grandmother like yourself would be noticing a man's features."

She gave him a look. "I'm a very *young* grandmother, as it happens."

"Now that's the truth," he said, his gaze going over her until her face turned red. "So, what then—are you saying you'd have no problem with it, if I'm right?" he challenged her.

"I don't know whether I would or not," she finally said. "But it's hardly unusual for a young woman to marry a man several years her senior. We've both seen it done, and with a good enough outcome."

"The lass is little more than a child."

Kate drew back, looking at him as if he'd lost his wits entirely.

"Maggie is twenty-four years old. When I was her age, I had two babes already."

Matthew brought his chin up. "Not by an older man, you didn't."

She studied him for a moment. "That's true. My man was still a green *gorsoon* who didn't know enough to hold a babe right side up or dandy her on his knee without dropping her on her head."

She was goading him, and he was enjoying it. Things had not been this light between them for a long time. "I wasn't *that* bad."

She smiled at him and put a hand on his arm. "No, you weren't. And I haven't had time yet to think about this business with our Maggie and Jonathan Stuart. But I will say that the girl has always been older than her years. And I can't remember when she hasn't had a good strong grip on herself. If you're right about this, it just might be that the Lord in his wisdom has brought it about because it's best for both of them."

"You *are* saying you wouldn't object."

His wife never ceased to amaze him. Matthew had been expecting her to be riled. Instead she sounded like the voice of reason itself.

"I'm saying let's not be jumping to any conclusions, but instead wait and see if you know what you're talking about."

Matthew frowned at her, which of course she ignored entirely. "Well, I believe I usually do."

"Usually," she said. "Not always. As for Jonathan and Maggie—well, he's a good man, there's that. The best there is, except for yourself."

He lifted an eyebrow. "Softening me up now, are you?"

"As if I could."

"And we both know you can."

She moved to take the rake from him, leaning it against the tree. "You've done enough for today. Come on inside now!" she ordered him. "You shouldn't stay out here in this damp cold. It'll only make your back worse. I'll go and make us some fresh coffee."

Matthew stood watching her as she breezed up the steps to the porch. With her straight back and slender waist she still looked like a young girl herself.

His mood threatened to sour. Heaven knew Kate deserved better than she'd gotten with him. He wasn't much good for anything these days, thanks to the stubborn pain. Sometimes it was like a buzzard eating away at his bones. He was so weary most of the time it was all he could do to drag one foot after the other. And when he took the medicine Woodbridge had given him, his mind seemed to turn to mush.

It wasn't fair to Kate, not at all. But to save him, he didn't know what to do about it.

He almost wished he had the nerve to take Jonathan up on his suggestion about seeing that woman doctor. If he thought there was the slightest chance...

He curled his lip. He wasn't *that* bad off yet.

Deliberately he turned his thoughts away from himself and back to Maggie and Jonathan. Perhaps Kate was right about them. The girl had always seemed older, that was true enough. But she had always been headstrong and willful as well. Maybe the good Lord *had,* as Kate said, brought this about for the good of both of them.

He wanted his daughter to have a good husband—a good man. And Jonathan needed a good wife, which Matthew was convinced Maggie would be—to the right man. All the same, he didn't know that he would make it easy on them, if it came down to it. He'd put Jonathan through his paces, even if he was a mature man and not some young dandy out for a lark. It was a father's job, after all, to take a fella's measure when he came looking to make a man's daughter his wife.

Matthew's thoughts turned somber, even grim, as it occurred to him what a poor job he'd made of it when he took the measure of Richard Barlow. Friend or no, he wouldn't go too easy on Jonathan. He had no intention of failing his youngest daughter as miserably as he had his eldest.

Chapter Twenty-Five

The Wind Harp

The sounds are in the grass and the trees and the bushes,
And they make a kind of music that's carried on the wind.
But only a few can hear the music of the wind harp.

Maggie MacAuley

For most of the way to the Wallace home on Grant Street, the only sound was the soft pounding of the horse's hooves and the light patter of rain on top of the buggy. At first Jonathan had tried to make light conversation, but he soon gave it up. He didn't remember Maggie having "moods," but if this wasn't a mood he didn't know what to call it.

She hadn't been rude—merely quiet. Uncharacteristically quiet. So quiet that a genuine tension had arisen between them. So quiet that he was reluctant to attempt any means of breaking through the silence. He had asked a few questions about nothing important, and she'd answered each one with an equally superficial reply.

He was actually relieved when they pulled up in front of Ben and

Regina's. Perhaps the company of the Wallaces and the children would help to dispel the chasm that seemed to have opened up between them.

He sensed the same relief in Maggie, who wasted no time whatsoever in getting out of the buggy.

This visit was mostly the same as all the others he'd paid since the children had gone to stay with Ben and Regina. Huey did seem somewhat livelier than usual, but he still maintained the same familiar, frustrating distance from Jonathan and Maggie. He seemed especially shy of Maggie, even though she was his classroom teacher. Jonathan had noticed this before; it was one of the things about the child that puzzled him most. The boy was around Maggie all day. By now he should have become far more at ease with her. Indeed, he couldn't think of another child from school—at least among the younger ones—who didn't adore her. Most of the students had quickly become attached to "Miss Maggie." Even during recess time, she could hardly get a minute to herself because of the way they swarmed around her.

But Huey still avoided her. Jonathan had noticed this from the beginning of the fall term, and couldn't think for the life of him what accounted for the child's peculiar behavior. On the other hand, Huey's older sister, Selma, always an exceedingly shy, quiet child, seemed to blossom under the slightest bit of attention from Maggie or himself.

One bright spot in the evening was a noticeable difference in Selma. They hadn't been there long, all of them sitting in the living room, when the girl, holding a piece of paper, walked up to Jonathan and, in a near whisper, said, "I made you a picture after school, Mr. Stuart. Miss Regina said you were coming to visit."

She thrust it at Jonathan before immediately scurrying off to the opposite corner of the room, where she and Huey had been playing Chinese checkers.

This was the first time the girl had ever shown any initiative with

Jonathan, and he was inordinately pleased by the gesture. He studied the drawing carefully, smiling at what he saw. It was clearly a picture of himself—with *very* large eyeglasses—along with Maggie at his side, a rather wild-looking "mane" of copper-colored hair dwarfing her face. On Jonathan's other side was Selma, holding his hand. And then there was Huey.

Here, Jonathan managed to maintain his smile only with a deliberate effort. Of all the figures, Huey appeared the most realistically drawn. Thin and small, he was holding onto Selma's hand. Dark hair fell over one eye, but large tears could be seen tracking down his face.

Beside him, Maggie caught a quick breath, and Jonathan knew she had noticed Huey's tears too.

Managing to keep his smile intact, he quietly called Selma over to him. Her pale skin was flushed and somewhat splotched as she approached. Her eyes never left Jonathan's face.

"May I keep this, Selma?" he asked.

She favored him with a shy smile and a nod, then immediately ducked her head and looked down at the floor. But Jonathan reached out and with his index finger gently lifted her chin so she would meet her eyes. "This is an *excellent* drawing, Selma. I think if you work hard you might one day become a true artist."

The child's face flamed, but her smile was almost ecstatic.

"I'm going to find a frame for this when I get home and mount it on my wall," Jonathan told her, intending to do just that.

Even the smallest sign of progress with these two gave him hope.

He glanced across the room at Huey. He was surprised to find the boy watching him in return, his eyes intent, his expression one of longing, a sorrowful set to his features.

It struck Jonathan in that moment that here was a child starved for affection yet for some reason unable to respond to it when it was offered.

Out of the corner of his eye, he saw that Maggie too had seen something in Huey's face that caught her off guard. He knew she was puzzled—and possibly hurt—by the way the child continued to cut himself off from her. He also knew that she had tried every means she could think of to win him over, all in vain.

After what Jonathan had seen tonight, he was convinced the boy's withdrawal had absolutely nothing to do with Maggie, nothing to do with himself either, for that matter, but most likely had everything to do with the kind of life the child had been forced to live.

Huey was simply afraid to accept affection—and was even more wary of giving it. As for the tears in Selma's drawing, had she merely sensed her younger brother's pain? Or had she witnessed the cause of it?

Jonathan was resolved to find out what went on in that dilapidated house on the Hill that would move a ten-year-old child to paint tears on a drawing of her little brother.

On the way home, Jonathan again ventured an attempt at conversation. Thinking Maggie might need to talk about Huey, he first brought up the subject of Selma's drawing.

"The way she depicted Huey made *me* want to weep too," Maggie acknowledged. "I wish I could find a way to win that boy's trust. He breaks my heart."

"You do realize, I hope, that his lack of response has nothing to do with you."

She gave a long sigh. "Well I'd hate it if something about me puts him off. But if that's not it, then what accounts for his behavior?"

"He's really not much different with me, you know. He simply doesn't communicate with any of us. Except perhaps for Ben and Regina. Ben told me he's seeing faint signs of progress where both children are concerned. Especially with Regina."

"Oh, goodness, who *wouldn't* warm toward Mrs. Wallace? She's wonderful!"

Jonathan smiled. "They're an exceptional couple, aren't they? If anyone can help those children, they will."

The dusk of evening was quickly drawing in on them. The rain was light, with only a breeze driving it, not the high wind that so often marked these October rains in the mountains. Jonathan had closed the buggy's flaps before they drove away from the Wallaces', and with that and a lap robe for each of them, it was almost cozy inside the well-crafted little vehicle.

"Are you warm enough?" he asked, glancing over at Maggie.

She nodded slightly.

Jonathan was trying to detect her mood. He sensed that her earlier remoteness had passed, but now she seemed pensive, perhaps even sad. He wondered if her state of mind was altogether due to Huey or if something else had upset her.

"You're troubled," he noted carefully. "Is it Huey?"

She seemed unwilling to look at him, keeping her gaze straight ahead. "No, not really. Oh, Huey's a part of it. But I honestly don't believe I'm the reason—not the *only* reason at least—that he's so hard to reach." She stopped. "Actually," she said, her voice low, "it's just... the rain."

Jonathan looked at her. "The rain?"

She nodded. "I know it sounds foolish, but sometimes...when it rains like this in the evening, and it's cold and gloomy and quiet, it makes me feel sad."

Her hands were folded on top of the lap robe, her fingers laced tightly together.

After a moment, she went on. "Da says I'm the most Irish of us all. He says I have the dark in me."

What kind of a thing was that for a man to say to his daughter?

"What does that mean?" he asked.

She turned and he was relieved to see a faint smile curve her lips. "That's just Da's way of describing the melancholy. It's nothing bad, really. Some folks are just affected by the weather, the change in seasons, even the time of day—"

Again she stopped and turned her gaze back to the road.

"I still don't understand," Jonathan prompted.

"It's the wind harp," she said, her voice even lower than before and strangely dreamy. "I'm one of the ones who hear it. Like Da—he hears it too."

This was a side of her Jonathan had never seen, and he was intensely curious. "The wind harp?"

"Some say it's the sound of Ireland's sorrows," she said, her voice low. "A common grief."

To his surprise, she seemed to brighten a little. "Have you ever noticed the little wind boxes Mum makes—the ones in the windows?"

"No, I don't think I have."

"They're musical. Mum strings them like you might a harp and stands them upright or lays them flat on the windowsill. When the wind comes through the window and blows over them, they make music. It's a sad sound, but lovely too."

"A kind of Aeolian harp," Jonathan stated.

"I don't know about that, not being musical. It's an old legend, you see. Supposedly the Irish who are forced to leave their land take their sorrows with them wherever they go. And sometimes the sound of their troubles...all the terrible things that have happened to the country and its people...are carried on the wind. The sounds are in the grass and the trees and the bushes, and they make a kind of music. But not everyone can hear it."

By now her voice was little more than a whisper.

"Da says that you feel it more than you hear it, that you don't hear it at all with your ears, but in your soul."

Caught up in the magic of her words, Jonathan looked over at her. "And you're one of the special ones who can hear it," he said quietly.

Still smiling a little, she said, "Sometimes I do. Not always."

"I'm not surprised," he said quietly. "I've always known you were special."

Out of the corner of his eye, he saw her turn to look at him, but he said nothing more. They drove along in silence, his senses filled to overflowing with her presence.

Finally, though, unwilling to let her close herself off from him again, he decided to broach the subject that had been nagging at him all week. "Maggie...I know I asked you this before, but I need to ask you again. Are you angry with me?"

Again she fixed her gaze on him. "Why would I be angry with you?"

Where were the words he needed? Why was it that so much of the time when he was with her, he became totally inarticulate?

"I thought perhaps...last Sunday, you might have misunderstood—" He stopped. "Never mind," he said, wishing he hadn't asked.

"You mean about you and Mrs. Ross," she said.

He nodded, embarrassed that he had evidently been so transparent. "I—if that's the problem, I want to explain..."

He didn't finish. Besides the fact that he didn't quite know where he was going with this—to his ears, he sounded like a bumbling fool.

He glanced over at her to find her watching him, her eyes enormous in the last fading light of the day. "I wasn't angry, Jonathan," she said softly. "I'm sorry if you thought I was." She paused and he heard a catch in her breath. "I was...jealous."

Jonathan's hold on the reins loosened. Surely he had heard her wrong.

They crossed the covered bridge over the creek, the horse's hooves pounding the wooden planks, the buggy wheels creaking. Just ahead, several yards off to their right stood a massive old oak tree, its branches hanging heavy with the rain. Instinct...or impulse.. compelled Jonathan to turn off.

Before he could question his own intentions, he drove the buggy beneath the sheltering arms of the oak and came to a halt.

Chapter Twenty-Six

When Love finally Speaks

I love thee to the depth and breadth and height
My soul can reach.

Elizabeth Barrett Browning

~~~

With the canopy of the tree limbs, the rain was now little more than a soft patter on the roof of the buggy. The wind had weakened until it made only a soft whispering as it ruffled the oak's few remaining leaves. Maggie was vaguely aware of the lapping of the creek, the horse puffing and thumping his hooves once, then again. But nothing else, nothing but the sound of her own breathing...and the drumming of her accelerated heartbeat.

Jonathan sat looking straight ahead, across the field and at the hills beyond, too veiled in rain and mist to be clearly seen.

He sat that way for a long time before finally turning to her, his dark gaze searching, probing, as if what he was about to say depended on what he saw in her eyes.

"Maggie," he said at last. "Tell me what you mean. I need to know."

She had always loved his voice. It invariably made her think of warm honey and butter...smooth and soothing and comforting. When she was a child, just the sound of his voice could calm her and reassure her. As a teen, and still today, only a few words from him would make her heart leap and set something deep inside her to singing. But at the moment his voice was rough, and his words came slowly and fitfully as if with a terrible effort.

"Maggie, look at me."

Slowly she turned toward him.

"*Tell* me, Maggie. What did you mean about being jealous?"

She simply could not hold his gaze. She felt as if he could read her very soul. "You seemed so...happy." Her voice sounded as if it were rising from a deep well. "I suppose I just wanted to be in her place. I wanted it to be me with you and not Carolyn Ross."

Humiliated, she finally forced herself to look directly at him. But *his* eyes were closed now, his features drawn.

She had embarrassed him...and herself.

He opened his eyes, but Maggie found it impossible to read what she saw there.

"Carolyn Ross isn't important to me, Maggie. The truth is—" his voice caught, "the truth is, I did a terrible thing that day. I was with Carolyn...because I was trying to get you out of my mind." He shook his head. "It didn't work. The entire time I was with her, all I could think about was you."

Maggie stared at him in amazement. He was watching her with that same seeking, questioning intensity that had been there only a moment ago, and she knew she should say something in response to the incredible statement he'd just made. But he had taken her breath away, and apparently her wits as well.

"Jonathan..." she finally whispered.

He reached to press a finger to her lips, then dropped his hand away. "It's all right. You don't have to say anything. But if I keep this to myself any longer…I'll explode. I know all the reasons I shouldn't be telling you this—believe me, I've reminded myself of every one of them more times than I can count—but it seems that I'm not strong enough to keep my silence."

Maggie's mind skidded past reason and went falling into a place where she couldn't think but could only feel.

His eyes seemed to be drawing her into himself. He wasn't touching her, had made no move to touch her, and yet with the strength of his gaze, he was holding her.

"Unless you stop me, I'm going to say this before I lose my nerve altogether. I've tried…I have tried so hard, for so long, not…to care for you. But I have feelings for you, Maggie. The kind of feelings some would say I *shouldn't* have. Given my age and yours, the fact that you were my student, that I'm your supervisor at the school—it's questionable, even from my perspective, whether I should voice those feelings."

He drew a long, shuddering breath. "I've prayed about this. You've no idea how much I've prayed about it. More than once I thought I sensed an urgency to just come right out and tell you how I feel, but I kept putting it off…for so many reasons. And then you said what you did…and now I can't *not* tell you, in case there's a chance you do care for me."

His words drifted off, and Maggie could *feel* him reaching…struggling.

Just say it, Jonathan, her mind pleaded. *Tell me Evie was right, that she really did see what she thought she saw when you looked at me. Tell me I'm not crazy for believing in the impossible. Tell me!*

As she watched, he seemed to go very still, as if he weren't even breathing.

He looked away once and then swung his gaze back to her.

And in that moment Maggie realized what he needed her to do, what she *had* to do if he was ever to say what her heart was begging him to say.

He was so close…so close she had only to lift her hand and touch it to his lean, tightly drawn face. He turned toward her touch and caught her hand in his, lacing his fingers gently through hers.

His eyes darkened even more, his gaze so impossibly tender it melted her heart.

"You know, don't you?" he asked, his voice even softer than before. "You already know that I love you."

"I was afraid to hope…" Maggie felt as though she were winding her way out of a fog.

He brought her hand to his lips, his eyes all the while holding her. "Oh, Maggie…I do…I do love you."

Unexpectedly, Maggie felt tears burning her eyes. "But I've loved you longer, Jonathan," she said softly. "I've loved you forever."

"*Maggie.*"

He spoke her name with incredulity and wonder—and overwhelming gratitude.

She loved him!

"Are you sure, Maggie? Are you absolutely sure?"

"Oh, Jonathan! Have you really never seen it? Every time I look at you, every time I'm with you or even think about you I feel as though I might as well be waving a banner with '*I love Jonathan Stuart!*' painted all over it!"

"I didn't think it was possible."

He moved closer, reached for her—and saw her startled reaction in time to draw back. "Maggie, I'm sorry…"

But she smiled and shook her head. "No, don't be sorry. I'm…just realizing that everything is changing. You're not Mr. Stuart anymore. I have to learn how…to *be* with you."

Jonathan's arms were aching, his heart thudding, but he kept his distance. "Just be *Maggie,*" he said. "You don't have to be anything other than yourself."

So many years he had known her, yet he had so many questions to ask her, so much to find out about her so he could *really* know her.

She was everything familiar and dear and beloved...and yet she was changed and even a little frightening in her newness. And she was looking at him as if there was something she needed to see in him, something she was expecting from him.

"Jonathan," she whispered, freeing her hand from his to trace the lines of his face, his jaw, his chin, his eyes...all the while looking at him as if she were seeing him for the first time.

He held his breath, clenched his hands to still their trembling... and to keep from drawing her to him.

Finally, unable to bear her touch any longer without crushing her in his arms, he caught both her hands in his and held them, gently but securely. "I'm going to take you home now," he said," because I can't be alone with you like this. Not without speaking to Matthew. I have to tell him...what's happened. I won't ask you to marry me until he knows."

Her eyes were brimming. "You want to marry me?"

Did he want to go on living? "If I didn't want to marry you, Maggie, I would never have said the things I did."

"I wish you'd ask me now," she said quietly.

Taken aback, Jonathan swallowed against what felt like a musket ball lodged in his throat. "I hope that means that when I *do* ask, you'll say yes," he said.

Unexpectedly she gave him an impish smile. "You'll have to ask before you know the answer to that now, won't you?"

Studying her, the piquant features, the amazing eyes, the cheekbones sharp enough to pierce a man's heart, Jonathan held her by her forearms—closer than before, but not too close. He bent his head, and she sighed, raising her face to his, expectantly, it seemed.

But he knew what he had to do and what he could not do—not yet anyway. This was Maggie, *his* Maggie. God had brought them this far, had brought them together, had blessed his life with a miracle for the second time. God had entrusted Maggie to him, and in no way would he betray that trust...or hers.

So with all the self-restraint he possessed, he touched his lips to her forehead for a moment, and only a moment. Then he put her gently away from him.

"It's too late to talk to your father tonight," he said, his voice hoarse and not overly steady. "But soon. One night this week, I'll come to the house—"

"Jonathan, I don't want to wait. But you shouldn't try to talk to Da on a work night. He's always so tired...and hurting...after work all day. He goes to bed really early, too.

"I need to wait until next *weekend?*"

She might just as well have asked him to wait a month or more.

"I'm afraid so. It's for the best, really it is. You don't want to surprise Da with something like this when he's dead tired." She paused. "And he *will* be surprised."

Jonathan passed a hand over his forehead. "All right," he said reluctantly. "Whatever you think. I want his blessing." He paused. "Do you think he'll give it?"

"I'm twenty-four years old, Jonathan. I don't need my father's permission to marry you."

"And I'm thirty-nine—soon to be forty—my love, but I *want* your father's permission. And his blessing." He squeezed her hands. "I want everything to be right for us, Maggie. Right with your parents and right with God. This is important to me. I think it's important for *us.*"

She searched his eyes before nodding her agreement. "Whatever you want."

Again Jonathan had all he could do not to touch her. Setting his gaze straight ahead, he flicked the reins, and drove away.

Chapter Twenty-Seven

A Different World

A man in love sees all things as new.

Anonymous

~

Jonathan, along with Figaro, arrived at school early Monday morning. Despite the comfortable familiarity of his surroundings, he felt as though he'd stepped into a whole new world. Everything had changed. He had changed; life had changed. He couldn't remember ever being this lighthearted, this happy. He thought his heart might be in danger of bursting.

He took Figaro into the office with him and sat down at his desk. Right away the dog came and plopped down in his place, which he'd claimed almost upon sight last Friday: underneath the desk, with his hind quarters sprawled just so toward the wall in order to lay his head on Jonathan's feet. Here was where he would stay while Jonathan was in class next door.

As long as Jonathan was in the office with him, though, every time he got up from his chair, Figaro would lift his head for a look, then, reassured of his master's whereabouts, return to his nap. Jonathan estimated that in the course of a twenty-four hour day, the dog slept a minimum of twenty.

A dog's life, indeed.

He realized that, temporarily, the great hound would be a real distraction for the children, but he was optimistic that it wouldn't take long before the students accepted the animal as easily as Figaro had accepted *them* as a central part of his life.

When Maggie breezed in fifteen minutes later, the children were still in the school yard. She stopped in the doorway, and Figaro very nearly knocked Jonathan out of his chair getting to her. With his tail beating the air in a circular motion, he plopped down at her feet, tongue lolling as she stooped to rub his ears.

Jonathan stood, unable to take his eyes off her. She quite literally took his breath away. Her cheeks were flushed from the cold morning air, and her hair was in a heavy braid. When she looked across the dog's head and smiled at him—a smile that appeared to be *just* for him—he could hardly manage a civil "Good morning."

This was going to be more difficult than he'd realized. Seeing her here every day, keeping a professional demeanor at all times, which included not grinning like his idiot dog every time he caught a glimpse of her, well, it wasn't going to be easy. In fact, it was almost certain to complicate his life. At least until they were married.

Until they were married!

Six more days before he could speak with Matthew. He almost groaned. Instead, he called Figaro back to the desk, and walked halfway across the room. "How are you?" he asked, keeping his voice down.

Still smiling, she glanced over her shoulder, then turned back and said, "I'm wonderful. And you?"

"Surprisingly well, considering I spent an almost entirely sleepless night."

Her smile grew even brighter. "So did I!"

He couldn't stop staring. And he was pleased to note she seemed to be suffering the same affliction.

"It's almost November," she said, enthusiasm dancing in her eyes as she pulled off her knit cap.

His eyes followed the movement. "So it is."

"We'll have to start working on the Thanksgiving Day program soon."

"Yes, I expect we will, won't we?"

"I already have some ideas," she said.

"Excellent. We can't start too soon. We should get together and discuss your thoughts."

"Oh, that would be good," she said agreeably. "Perhaps in a few days?"

"I'd say so. The sooner the better."

She was actually sparkling.

"By the way," he said. "I like your hair better that way."

She put a hand to her head. "You don't think it's childish? It's just a braid."

"I like braids. What was going on last week, by the way? Every time I saw you, you had a different hair style."

She grinned at him. "Eva Grace was trying to make me look older."

That stopped him. "Any special reason?"

"I'll tell you all about it one day," she said, giving him a sly look. "Right now I need to round up the children."

He went to the window and watched her as she hurried outside into the school yard, her braid swinging back and forth.

He sighed. It was just as he'd thought. This wasn't going to be easy.

He turned around just as Carolyn walked into his office. "Jonathan."

It took a moment to find his tongue. "Good morning, Carolyn."

She was studying him with that sharp look of hers, as though she was trying to read his mind.

"I looked for you after church yesterday," she said, clearly expecting some sort of explanation.

"Oh...yes," he said, fingering his tie. "I had to leave right after the service. I had...some things to do."

She continued to regard him with that speculative expression that never failed to make him uncomfortable. "Well," she said, "I was going to ask you if you'd like to escort me to the cake social next Saturday night. Since I missed you yesterday, I'll ask you now."

He had never been any good at dissembling. He usually ended up a stammering fool if he even tried. The rare occasion when he found himself in such a situation was when he was trying to avoid hurting someone's feelings.

A situation much like this one.

"I...can't really say for sure right now. Let me get back to you on that, all right?"

She nodded, even smiled. But he hadn't missed the faint flush that stained her cheeks. He'd made things awkward and perhaps embarrassed her.

That couldn't happen again. He would have to talk with her. And soon. As soon as he spoke with Matthew, as soon as he and Maggie could be openly...engaged.

Engaged.

He was going to marry Maggie. He repeated it to himself half a dozen times or more, testing the way it sounded in his head.

It was still playing through his mind when he walked into the classroom and called what seemed to be an unusually rowdy group to order.

At noon Jonathan ate about half of the lunch he'd packed. Food seemed so unimportant, he felt as if he could go for days without even getting hungry. He then took Figaro outside, knowing the children would be hoping for a few minutes of playtime with the dog before afternoon classes.

Maggie was nowhere to be seen. She usually ate her lunch at her desk and read for a few minutes while the children were outside. To his relief, Carolyn had also stayed in. This wasn't the place to initiate a conversation of any sort, much less the kind of conversation he knew he needed to have with her.

He sat down on the top step, watching the children. It was cold, but an invigorating cold with no bitter wind accompanying it. The three or four small groups that usually dotted the school yard had merged together as soon as they spotted Figaro. They all vied for his attention, but Jonathan was keenly interested to see that the dog seemed to have latched onto Huey Lazlo as a special friend.

The boy was sitting on the ground, leaning against the same hickory tree from which he had fallen three weeks past, apparently carrying on a discussion with Figaro. The big dog rested on his haunches directly in front of Huey, looking unusually solemn as he took in whatever the boy was saying.

Jonathan smiled at the sight. Perhaps…just perhaps Figaro would be able to do what no one else, himself included, had been able to accomplish: break past the isolating wall the boy had built around himself.

A movement in the woods across the road caught his eye and he watched. One had to be constantly on the lookout for a wild boar or even a bear in this area. It wasn't unusual for either to pay an unwelcome visit to the town. The school was close to the woods and out just far enough that they were never entirely safe from wild animals.

When he saw nothing after a few minutes, he went and rang the bell to call the children in. He noticed that for once Huey Lazlo wasn't trudging along by himself toward the building. Figaro loped along at his side, his tail circling happily, as they made their way up the school yard.

Jonathan decided that this new relationship could be a good thing. A very good thing indeed.

Chapter Twenty-Eight

A Visit from Dr. Gordon

Remember to show hospitality.
There are some who, by so doing,
Have entertained angels without knowing it.

Hebrews 13:1-2 NEB

⟿

Maggie told no one what had transpired between her and Jonathan—except Eva Grace. She had to tell *someone*, had to give vent to at least a measure of her new joy or her heart would surely burst. Besides, she'd already confided her feelings about Jonathan to her sister, not to mention the fact that Evie claimed to have seen how things were before Maggie figured it out.

Evie seemed genuinely happy for her, but Maggie couldn't help but feel awkward, even a little guilty, that her own happiness was coming at a time when her sister's life had fallen apart. Evie tried her best not to inflict her pain on anyone else in the family, but there wasn't a one of them unaffected by her sadness. Maggie only hoped that Jonathan was right, that the baby really would make a difference for her sister.

After school Monday afternoon, she was working in the kitchen with Evie and her mother when a commotion sounded outside. The three of them headed for the front room to look out the window.

Dr. Gordon was just pulling up in a sturdy black buggy. Two of the neighborhood dogs had circled her, barking and growling and generally making themselves obnoxious. The doctor quickly dispatched them all with the shake of a fist and a loud shout before climbing down and starting for the house.

Maggie opened the door for her and made the introduction to her mother, who clearly found the lady doctor interesting, to say the least. Kate MacAuley had probably never been rude a day in her life, but she couldn't stop staring at Dr. Gordon.

Just as Maggie remembered her, the physician was tall, with an ample figure and strong features. Her fairly long gray hair was in disarray, with no hint of styling. She carried a scarred medical case and wore what looked to be a man's work jacket, unbuttoned to reveal a faded ticking apron.

"I'm sorry to come by so late," she said, "but this is the first chance I've had all week." Without being asked, she tossed her coat over the back of Da's rocking chair, and then turned to Eva Grace.

As Maggie watched, the doctor's piercing blue gaze took in Evie's appearance in one sweep. She didn't seem particularly pleased with what she saw.

"Let's go to the bedroom so I can have a look at you," the doctor said, dismissing both Maggie and her mother with a look as she followed Evie out of the room.

As soon as they were out of the room, her mother turned to Maggie. "She's all business, isn't she?" she said, her voice low.

Maggie nodded. "Yes, she's very…professional."

"Well, so long as she takes good care of your sister, I don't care about her manners. I hope they don't finish before your father gets home though. I'd like him to meet the doctor. He's been curious about her."

"Evie's been wishing he'd *see* the doctor. She has as little faith in Dr. Woodbridge as Da does."

"She surely knows your father well enough not to think he'd let a woman doctor touch him," Mum said with a wry look.

"Oh, yes. We talked about that. Still, you never know."

"If the two of you think there's any hope of such a thing, you might just as well forget it. That's as likely to happen as the chickens laying goose eggs."

Maggie had to smile. She knew her mother was right. It was too bad though. Da clearly needed more help than Dr. Woodbridge could provide. In fact, he seemed to be getting worse all the time.

It was another half hour or more when Dr. Gordon finally walked into the kitchen where Maggie and her mother had just sat down to have a cup of coffee.

"I thought I'd talk with you while Eva is getting dressed," the doctor said. At Mum's insistence, she accepted a cup of coffee and sat down. "You may have noticed the swelling in Eva's hands and ankles. It's more noticeable now than when I saw her last week. She told me she's eliminated all salt from her diet, and she's elevating her legs several times a day." It seemed more question than statement.

"I'm not cooking with any salt at all now," Maggie's mother said, returning to her chair after getting the doctor's coffee. "And as far as I can tell, Evie is doing everything you've told her to do. Isn't it helping?"

The physician shook her head. "Some swelling is natural at this stage, of course. But not this much. I've explained to her that she needs to stay off her feet as much as possible. Most of the time, in fact. Other than that, and totally eliminating her salt intake, there's little else she can do. She did say that she's not having any headaches or dizziness, which is good. But be sure to let me know right away if that changes. I'm still concerned about toxemia."

Maggie knew she was going to have to reassure her mother as soon as possible, but she also wanted to ask the doctor about the Lazlo children. When Dr. Gordon got up to leave, she followed her out.

The mine whistle had already blown, so Da would be home soon. But little Huey and his sister had been much on Maggie's mind all day, and she trusted this woman's expertise. It couldn't hurt to ask for any advice she might be willing to give.

As they walked down the front yard to the buggy, she wished she'd grabbed a sweater. Darkness was drawing in, and the evening air was cold and still damp from the previous day's rain.

She hugged her arms to herself as they reached the buggy. "Dr. Gordon, I wanted to ask your opinion about two of the students at our school. Can you spare me another moment?"

The doctor nodded, her demeanor still brisk but interested.

Maggie explained about Huey and Selma: the obvious beatings Huey had suffered; his refusal to confide in anyone; his prolonged silences and detachment from his classmates; and the futility of her own efforts—and Jonathan's—to extract any information about the abuse from either the boy or his sister.

"Huey's sister apparently shows no sign of mistreatment. And though she seems to be a naturally shy girl—she's very quiet and reserved—she finally seems to be warming more and more to the Wallaces, and, to some extent, to Jon—to Mr. Stuart, her teacher."

She went on to explain her fear that if Huey didn't open up and confide in someone about what was going on at home, both he and his sister were likely to be sent back and the beatings might well start up again.

"We're at our wits' end, not knowing what we can do to protect them."

The doctor didn't reply right away, but stood watching the procession of miners now coming up the road, the lamps on their caps lighting the way. When she finally turned back to Maggie, she said,

"Without having seen either child, I can't possibly give you a medical opinion. But based on experience and what you've told me, I *would* caution you to do everything possible to keep those children from being returned to the home situation."

She paused. "If you want, I'll be glad to have a look at them myself. I'm not questioning your company doctor, understand, but I'd need to see the boy and his sister before I could say anything more." Again she stopped, then added, "It's curious that the girl hasn't been mistreated also. What do you know about the mother?"

"The mother? Nothing, really. We don't actually know anything about either parent. I met the mother. She seemed—I'm not sure how to put it—perhaps not exactly feeble-minded, but...slow, almost certainly. She was very peculiar."

"Mentally impaired in some way?" the doctor prompted.

Maggie nodded. "Yes. There's definitely something wrong there."

"And the father?"

Maggie couldn't stop a shudder. "He frightened me a little."

"You suspect a mental problem there too?"

Maggie thought about the question and shook her head. "No. He's just a very rough type of person."

"Well, as I said, if you decide you'd like me to see the children, I'd be glad to."

"Thank you. Let me talk with Mr. Stuart and see what he thinks."

"I've heard a lot of good things about this Mr. Stuart. He's the principal at the school?"

Maggie tried not to beam. "Yes. And he teaches too. In fact, he was my teacher the entire time I was growing up."

"Well, he's certainly held in high regard around here."

Still smiling, Maggie saw that her da was nearing home now. She waved to him, then turned to the doctor. "My father," she said.

Dr. Gordon was watching him closely. "That's a bad limp. What caused it?"

Maggie watched him approach. He appeared to be practically dragging his leg as he came closer.

"He was injured in the cave-in last year," she said. "His knee was shattered, and he broke his back. Da never says anything much, but my mother told me he's never without pain."

"That's a hard way to live," the doctor said, still watching Maggie's father as he walked up to them.

Maggie introduced them, and Da touched his fingers to his cap, saying a quick hello. He was covered with coal dust, of course—his clothes, his hands, his face. His eyes, green like Maggie's own, were the only bright spots to be seen behind the black grime that masked his skin.

He was polite, but wasted no time in taking his leave. Maggie watched him go around to the side of the house, where he would enter directly into the washroom. For as long as she could remember, her father had never stopped to make an appearance in the kitchen or any other part of the house until he'd shed his dusty mine clothes and had his bath. She suspected he observed this ritual as much out of respect for her mother as for any personal dislike of the coal dust that was an integral part of a miner's life.

"Does he wear a brace?"

Maggie turned back to the doctor. "A brace?"

"Yes, for his back or his leg."

"I...don't really know. I don't think so. Why? Would that help him?"

"It might. By now some arthritis has probably set in as well. These days there's help for that too. Well," she said, "you have a nice family, Miss MacAuley. And I can see that you're taking good care of your sister. Keep it up. Now I really have to go. I still have one more call to make."

Maggie thanked her again, then started for the house. She wished she had the nerve to mention to Da what the doctor had said about a brace—and the arthritis. But she knew her mother was right. It would be pointless to even bring it up.

Still…if she could find a way to get around his stubbornness, she wasn't beyond venturing a suggestion. Da was used to the women in his family not minding their own business.

Chapter Twenty-Nine

A Secret Revealed

Why is it effects are greater than their causes...
And the most deceived be she who least suspects?

Oliver St. John Gogarty

Finally the longest week Jonathan could remember was nearing an end. Two days more, and he would speak with Matthew MacAuley. It might just as well be two *months* more, so slowly did the hours pass.

On Thursday Jonathan combined his class with Maggie's so that she could take Selma Lazlo out to see Dr. Gordon. Somehow Maggie had gotten it into her head that this new doctor might be able to provide insight into the Lazlo children's situation—insight that had so far eluded everyone else.

Jonathan had serious doubts this would be the case, but then he hadn't met this Dr. Gordon, had not as yet had a chance to discover for himself what it was about the woman that inspired such confidence in Maggie. Certainly for the children's sake, he was willing to give it a try.

Earlier he had tried to coax Huey into going along with his sister and Maggie, even offering to send Figaro with them, but the boy was adamant in his refusal. Finally, seeing that the child was becoming distraught, he gave up the effort, cautioning Maggie not to press the boy.

She had planned to take the MacAuley's farm wagon, but Jonathan insisted that she use his buggy. "It's too cold for the two of you in that wagon. You'll both take a chill. At least you can put the top up on the buggy and close the flaps."

As soon as they drove away, he went back inside the school building to face the daunting task of capturing the interest and attention of a room full of energetic, high-spirited youngsters of all ages.

Times like these made him wish the school budget would allow for a third teacher.

He had thought about asking Carolyn to take his class so he could go along with Maggie and Selma, but at the moment he wasn't comfortable asking any favors of her.

He absolutely must talk with her sometime today. As yet he hadn't given her his reply about the cake social, and he was beginning to feel guilty for putting her off. Not only that, but it wasn't right to keep it from her any longer that he was seeing someone else.

He wished he knew how to deal with the situation delicately. Of course, he had no intention of telling Carolyn about Maggie until after he spoke with Matthew and then everything could be out in the open. The last thing he needed was for Matthew to learn about his and Maggie's...understanding...from someone else.

If anything would get him off on the wrong foot with Maggie's father, that would do it.

Maggie agreed with Dr. Gordon's opinion that she should probably see Selma alone. Given the girl's excessive shyness, the doctor explained, and also because she was in daily contact with Maggie at the school, no doubt it would be wise to keep things as private as possible for her.

"I'm not going to examine her—just talk with her. I promise that I'll call you in at once if she asks for you or if I see that she's uncomfortable with me. But let's try it my way first, all right?"

"What exactly do you plan to do?" Maggie asked.

"I'm just going to try to win her confidence and put her at ease. You said she likes to draw, didn't you? I'll have her draw some pictures for me, perhaps let her play with a couple of dolls I keep on hand for children. She'll be fine."

Even though Maggie trusted the doctor's judgment, it wasn't easy to watch Selma follow her into the examining room alone. The child's reluctance couldn't have been more obvious as she continued to glance back at Maggie with almost every step.

Jonathan had almost forgotten why he'd fought so hard to convince the school board to add an extra room and an extra teacher. It took no more than half an hour alone with thirty-nine energetic, high-spirited youngsters from the ages of six to sixteen to refresh his memory.

He was accustomed to dealing with the various age divisions all together in one room, of course; he'd had to teach that way for years. But it had never been easy—and certainly not ideal. It made for much greater distraction in terms of noise and activity—and mischief.

Some things, he noted, never changed. The younger students still tried to show off and imitate the older ones. The older students still reveled in teasing the younger ones. From year to year, there was always a young Timmy Neal who had to go to the outhouse at the most inconvenient times. And seldom was there a year without an Annabeth O'Toole, who could capture the attention of every male in the room, right down to the six-year-olds, by tossing her mane of golden hair and flirting with her china-doll blue eyes when she thought the teacher wasn't looking.

He could also recall almost yearly duos like the seven-year-old

Dottie Russell and her nemesis, Sissie Miller, who had only to look each other to ignite their ongoing feud.

But where, when he needed them, were this year's Maggie MacAuley and Kenny Tallman?

Well, there was Maggie's brother, Ray. Fourteen now and never a scholar, Ray preferred the outdoors to a schoolroom anytime, no matter how inclement the weather happened to be. Still, despite the boy's indifference to his studies, he could be helpful and was usually dependable when the situation required it.

This situation required it. "Ray, take the first- and second-grade boys over to the other side of the room and have them write their spelling words for you, please. Then have each one spell them orally."

And by all means, Ray…take your time.

Maggie was getting concerned when an hour passed and the doctor still hadn't appeared. She had looked through the out-of-season *Sears, Roebuck* catalog, leafed randomly through an almanac, and chatted with another lady who was waiting to keep her appointment.

By the time Dr. Gordon finally opened the door to the waiting room and gestured that she should come in, Maggie was wringing her hands and struggling to keep her worry in check.

"We'll talk in my office," said the doctor, showing Maggie in. "I gave Selma some coloring pages to amuse her. She'll be fine in the examining room until we've finished."

The doctor sat down, folded her hands on top of the desk, and without any hesitation said, "I believe I can reassure you on one point: Selma has not been physically harmed in any way."

Maggie let herself slump a little with relief.

"I'm fairly certain, however, that there's been a kind of emotional abandonment going on with the girl—and that can be almost as injurious as physical mistreatment. As for her younger brother—and I realize I'm simply confirming what you already know—he has definitely suffered continual beatings."

For a moment the physician's professional composure slipped a fraction but she quickly recovered. "Selma is, I believe, a very confused child. Unless I'm mistaken, and I don't believe I am, she's been raised in the midst of conflict and cruelty on one hand and an unconscionable indifference on the other. Her emotions and her loyalties are clearly at odds. I think her pattern of defense has been to withdraw from her parents and her surroundings whenever she can. She makes herself as...*unnoticeable*...as possible, except with her younger brother."

The doctor glanced up. "Are you following me?"

"I think so," Maggie said. "Did Selma talk about Huey at all?"

The doctor sighed. "Yes, she did. She's been led to believe that her brother is 'bad.' A 'bad boy.' That's why he has to be 'punished' so often. But since she loves her little brother and tries in her own way to defend him and take care of him, her sense of what's true and what isn't is often confused. And there's also the fact that she feels guilty about his taking all the punishment."

Maggie had to struggle with her own confusion. Yet the more the doctor explained, the more it made sense.

"How—I hope it's all right for me to ask you—but how do you know all this?"

The doctor's lips curved in a faint smile. "I learned a great deal about Selma and her family by studying the drawings she made for me. And the way she interacted with a doll. Later, when I asked her some questions, she opened up enough to give me a good idea of what's been going on."

She paused, leaning back a little in her chair. "It's somewhat ironic. I came to Skingle Creek to get away from this sort of thing, only to be confronted with it again almost as soon as I arrived."

"I don't understand."

"In my previous practice, I worked a lot with children," Dr. Gordon said. "Especially troubled ones. It's what I set out to do when I graduated from medical college, and I spent several years of my practice concentrating on children. But eventually I got weary of all the pain: the physical pain brought on by mistreatment, the emotional pain, the parents who should never have had children, the almost totally ineffectual programs available for helping them *or* the children. It was eating me alive. I had to get away from it."

"But why Skingle Creek?"

The doctor shrugged. "No special reason. There are always missionary organizations looking to place physicians in areas where doctors are either scarce or nonexistent. This is where I ended up."

"That's more or less how Jonathan—Mr. Stuart—came here too. I have a feeling the town will eventually be as grateful for you as we've always been for him."

Dr. Gordon smiled. "Thank you. I hope you're right, especially considering how highly regarded your Mr. Stuart seems to be around here."

She leaned forward. "Getting back to Selma, I'd suggest you encourage her affinity for drawing and painting. This is a definite outlet for her and may very well help in the healing process. But something has to be done about those parents."

"Oh, I know! That awful man needs to be behind bars, and the sooner the better!"

The doctor's eyebrows lifted. "Miss MacAuley—Maggie—" she said quietly, looking directly into Maggie's eyes. "It's not the father who's abusing the boy. It's the mother."

Chapter Thirty

Truth in the Shadows

The Lord God judges "crime" above,
But not as man has weighed it.

Mary Kelly

~

By the time Maggie arrived back at the school with Selma, she was strained to the point of snapping. Somehow she managed to put a normal face on things with Selma, mostly by listening to the girl's childish praise for "the doctor." Whether Dr. Sally Gordon realized it or not, she had a new admirer.

Actually, she had *two*. Maggie had been silently thanking God all the way back to school for this woman who, she was more and more coming to believe, had been heaven-sent. But she was also somewhat stunned from learning that it was the children's *mother* who had beaten little Huey, not the father. It was beyond the reaches of her imagination to fathom how a mother—or a father—could commit such heinous acts of violence on her or his own child. But whether she could comprehend the situation or not, shock and fury had combined, igniting a fierce resolve to somehow free both children from that deranged woman's clutches.

And the father—wasn't he just as bad? The little information Selma had divulged about the man seemed to indicate that he had done nothing—*nothing*—to protect his own children from his wife's madness!

No. No, that wasn't quite true. According to Dr. Gordon, the father had apparently tried, when the beatings first began, to stop her—only to have her turn her demented rage on him. Eventually he had backed away, abandoned his own son, and left the small, defenseless Huey to suffer one attack after another.

It seemed that Huey's father wasn't a child beater—he was a coward. In Selma's words, he "went away" during those times when his wife turned her rage on Huey. *Probably to the local tavern,* Maggie thought bitterly. He simply left the house as if he had no son and no daughter who needed his protection.

As Maggie drove around to the back of the schoolhouse and tethered the horse, she felt not just physically ill, but sick at heart as well. Everything in her was crying out for Jonathan. She had to talk to him. He would help her make sure the children were kept safe. He would know what to do.

He always did.

Jonathan took one look at Maggie's face when she brought Selma to the classroom door and knew immediately that something was terribly wrong. She was absolutely ashen, her eyes enormous and riveted on him. Even when Selma came the rest of the way into the classroom and sat down at her desk, Maggie didn't leave, but merely stood there, as if waiting for Jonathan to come to her.

Thinking fast, he put Ethna Duggan, his oldest student, in charge of the class and went to the door.

"Jonathan—"

He took her by the arm and led her across the hall to his office.

"What is it? What's happened?" he asked once they were inside the room.

Naturally, when Figaro caught sight of Maggie, he stumbled out from under the desk, bumping his head in his haste to reach her. The dog seemed to give Maggie at least a moment of comfort, but Jonathan finally had to get more stern than usual with him, so he could hear what Maggie had to say. He sentenced him to his place underneath the desk, where the big hound lay pouting, watching every move Maggie made.

"I don't know where to start. Oh, Jonathan—we have to do something. We can't let them send those children back to those people. We can't!"

"Maggie, that's not going to happen. Sit down now and tell me what's wrong."

"No, I can't sit down. I'm too upset. What do you mean that's not going to happen? How can you know that?"

"I know because Ben Wallace was just here a few minutes ago. I didn't realize he'd written to a friend of his, another pastor in Ashland, where the Lazlos lived before they moved here."

As he spoke, Jonathan led her to the chair across from his desk and finally convinced her to sit down. "Ben just received a reply from him yesterday," he continued, sitting on the edge of the desk. "Apparently, at Ben's request, the other pastor made some inquiries and found out that Lazlo had been fired from his job at a mine just outside of Ashland. It seems that he'd been drinking on the job—so much so that some of the other miners complained. Miners have to depend on each other, as I'm sure you realize. They won't stand for having a man they can't trust on the job with them. It's too dangerous."

He ran a hand across the back of his neck, mindful of the beginning of a headache. "Ben's friend also wrote that Lazlo's wife had set fire to the house more than once. Apparently Lazlo usually caught them in time and put them out. Do you remember his hands? The scars on them? I thought they might be burn scars. It appears now that they probably are.

"Anyway," he went on, "the day Lazlo lost his job, his wife started another fire. This one burned the house down. Word had it that they all just barely escaped."

Maggie looked sick.

He leaned forward. "Don't you see now, Maggie? This information about the mother and the evidence of Huey's beatings—well, that's enough to keep the children away from them. In fact, Ben was taking the letter to the deputy sheriff as soon as left here, to insist that they arrest Mr. Lazlo. Obviously something will have to be done about his wife too. In any case, Huey and Selma won't be going back to their parents. Huey's had his last beating from his father."

Unexpectedly Maggie moaned and buried her head in her hands.

"What is it? Maggie—is it Selma? Don't tell me we were wrong about her not being beaten. There was no sign—"

She raised her face to look at him. Tears were spilling over from her eyes, and Jonathan reached to take her hands in his. But she drew back, again shaking her head. "The children, Jonathan—"

He glanced across the hall. She was right, but he had to clench his fists to keep from touching her...from comforting her.

He sighed. "Tell me what the doctor had to say about Selma."

His mind went spinning with her first few words.

"Jonathan, it's the *mother* they need to arrest! Maybe...the father too, I don't know. But definitely their mother."

Chapter Thirty-One

Light Out of Darkness

I refuse to believe that there is anything or anywhere so dark
That God cannot bring light to it.

Jonathan Stuart

❧

Anxious to learn what transpired with the deputy sheriff, Jonathan had made Ben promise to come by the school yet this afternoon. Since there was no telling just how late Ben might be, he charged Maggie's brother, Ray, and his friend, Tim Quigley—the two biggest boys in school—with walking the Lazlo children to the Wallaces' place.

As soon as Maggie learned that he was staying late, she also refused to leave. "I have to know, Jonathan. I can't simply go home and forget about this. I need to know what's going to happen to those children."

He could see the strain and tension of the day gripping her and saw the agitation simmering in her, just a step away from boiling over. "All right," he said, trying for a soothing tone. "We'll both stay. I'm sure Ben won't be all that late. In fact, I'm surprised he hasn't already come by. Of course, he may have had other things he needed to do first. I can't think it would take too long for the deputy to slap some sort of a restraining order on the Lazlos. Or he may just go ahead with an arrest—"

"But he won't know to arrest the *mother*, Jonathan! Pastor Wallace didn't know about her, so the deputy won't either. What if they don't do anything about the mother?"

His head was throbbing viciously now. "They'll have to do *something*, it seems to me. With her history of setting fires, and with what Dr. Gordon was able to learn—"

Clearly, she wasn't convinced.

"Maggie, look at me." He waited until she met his gaze. "This is going to be all right. It *is.*"

Finally she drew a long, shaky breath and nodded.

"What a huge relief it will be when it *is* finally over," Jonathan said, attempting to lighten both their moods. "Not only will we be able to have some peace of mind about Huey and Selma, but perhaps we can get back to more cheerful matters."

She looked at him, a faint smile finally softening her features. "I'm so thankful for you, Jonathan," she said softly. "You can't imagine."

"Oh, I expect I can," he said dryly. "Just ask the Lord how many times a day I thank Him for *you.*"

It was past six now and nearly dark. Figaro had been lying directly in front of Maggie, his head resting on her feet. She apparently didn't mind; in fact, she seemed to have fallen in love with the big lug. And it was disgustingly obvious that the dog was smitten with *her.*

Just then Figaro's head came up, and he gave a low growl. Jonathan went to look out the window. There was just enough light to see Ben Wallace getting out of his buggy.

"It's only Pastor Ben, Figaro," he said. "Not the bogeyman."

Jonathan studied his friend closely as he stepped into the office. Although the pastor's hair had turned almost totally white years ago, Ben wasn't much more than fifty, if that. At the moment he looked older than Jonathan could remember ever seeing him. The few lines in his face seemed to have deepened over the past few hours, and his mouth was thin and tightly set.

Jonathan tensed, bracing himself for whatever he was about to hear.

"What's wrong?" he asked.

Ben looked from him to Maggie. "The children—they're with Regina?"

Jonathan nodded. "What is it, Ben?" He moved to give him the chair behind his desk, but the other made a dismissing gesture with his hand, remaining where he was.

His friend eased his shoulders a little and rubbed his neck. "Well... they've arrested Lazlo. He's already in jail."

"So they decided he's also guilty," Jonathan said, expelling a sigh. "I couldn't agree more."

Ben Wallace frowned. "What do you mean he's also guilty? Of course he's guilty. He shot his wife."

Jonathan put a hand on the desk to steady himself. In the same instant, Maggie scrambled to her feet.

"Lazlo...shot his wife?" Jonathan repeated, his mind struggling to grasp what Ben had said.

Ben nodded. "She was dead by the time the deputy and I got there. Not before she tried to burn the house down though."

He stopped, then went on to explain. "According to Lazlo, the woman set fire to a mattress, but he managed to put it out. Then she tore into him, started screaming about the schoolhouse, that she was going to burn it down and everyone in it. Lazlo had a gun. I don't know where he got it—from somewhere in the house, apparently. He claims she tried to get the gun away from him, and it went off in the scuffle. I don't know what to believe. Neither does the deputy. But she's dead, and he's locked up. He turned himself over without putting up an argument."

He shook his head. "Now I have to go and tell the children. What an awful thing for them to hear."

"I'll go with you, Ben," Jonathan said, his mind still reeling.

Again the pastor shook his head as if to clear it. "No. No, that's not necessary. I have to deal with taking bad news to folks all the time, Jonathan. Though it's always harder when there are children involved."

"Ben—"

"No, I mean it now. You and Maggie here must be as weary as I am. You see her home, and then go get some rest yourself. I'll handle this."

Jonathan knew his friend well enough not to try to change his mind. "All right. But first you need to hear the rest of the story. There's more to this than you know." He explained what Dr. Gordon had learned from Selma about the children's mother, Lazlo's abandonment of his son to the violence, and all the rest.

When he had finished, Ben was holding his head between his hands, pressing his temples as if to squeeze away a vicious pain. "Unbelievable," he said, his voice low. "There is no imagining what those two youngsters have lived through."

He lifted his head, dropping his hands away. "It's a terrible thing to say, I know. God forgive me, but I can't help but wonder if things won't be better for the children without them."

Maggie spoke for the first time. "It's not such a terrible thing to say, Pastor Wallace. Those people hurt their children in the most unthinkable ways."

The pastor nodded. "It's probably too soon to bring this up, Jonathan, but Regina and I have already talked about it. We couldn't know how all this would end up, of course, but we decided, if it came down to it and the children needed a home—ours is open to them. We've grown more than a little fond of both of them. We always wanted children, you know, but it never happened. We'd raise Huey and Selma as our own, if they were agreeable, even adopt them if the law allows. Will you vouch for us if it comes to that?"

Jonathan went to his friend and gripped his hand. "You know you don't have to ask. Any child would be greatly blessed to belong to you and Regina."

"You're a good friend, Jonathan. Thank you. Now I need to get home. I wouldn't want this to get out and have Regina or the children hear it before I can tell them myself."

He shook Jonathan's hand and turned to go. He stopped just before he reached the door. "Jonathan, do you remember the night—it was around Christmas of last year, I believe—after church services one evening, when we were talking about darkness and light? Do you recall what you said?"

Jonathan tried to think, but nothing came to his mind. "I'm afraid not."

"You said you didn't believe that there was anything or anywhere so dark that God couldn't bring light to it."

It came back to Jonathan now and he nodded.

"Let's pray He does just that with this awful thing that's happened. For Huey and Selma's sake, let's pray that God will banish the darkness those children have lived in most of their lives and give them a new beginning, one that's absolutely flooded with His light."

"It seems to me He's already begun to do just that, Ben," Jonathan said, taking Maggie's hand in his own as he watched his friend and pastor open the door and walk out into the night.

Chapter Thirty-Two

In Search of a Blessing

He's heart-sick with a longing sweet
To make her happy as she's fair.

Coventry Patmore

⁓

On Saturday evening, Jonathan waited until six-thirty before making his appearance at the MacAuley residence. He intended to arrive late enough that the family would have finished their dinner, but early enough that he wouldn't have to rush through his conversation with Matthew. Although at the moment, rushing through it didn't sound like a half-bad idea.

He walked from his house to Maggie's, leaving the buggy behind. It was a nice if somewhat cold evening, and walking had a way of ordering his thoughts, which he badly needed to do.

It had also occurred to him that he might need the walk even more once his meeting with Matthew MacAuley ended.

Even through his gloves, he was aware that his hands were clammy. By the time he started up the stone walkway to the house, perspiration

had broken out on his forehead as well, and his knees felt treacher-
ously unstable.

So this was what it was like to be a *suitor.* Clammy hands, runaway
heartbeat, and a fire in his middle lapping away at his stomach.

He had known he'd be nervous. But he hadn't expected to be *this*
nervous. Why was he in such a state anyway? He and Matthew had
been friends for years, beginning with that awful time when Maggie
was still a child and she and Kenny Tallman were being bullied by
Orrin Gaffney and Billy Macken, two of their classmates.

Over the years, Jonathan had come to hold Maggie's father in high
regard. Matthew could be a hard man in many ways, but he was a
good man, one with an uncompromising integrity and an unshakable
moral code. Indeed, Jonathan had been pleased when he realized
Matthew liked him, even respected him. Although in the beginning
the friendship had been somewhat guarded, eventually they'd become
comfortable with each other, and a high level of trust had been estab-
lished.

That was all well and good, but would any of it make a whit of
difference once Matthew learned that his "friend" wanted to court…to
marry…his daughter?

On the porch, he hesitated a moment before knocking. He hoped
that Maggie had alerted her father to the fact that he was coming to
visit this evening. He doubted that this was the sort of surprise a man
like Matthew would appreciate. It would be good if he'd had some
warning, so he wouldn't be caught off guard.

*Coward. The truth is you're counting on Maggie to bank the dragon's
fire so you won't get too badly burned.*

This wasn't going exactly as Jonathan had hoped. Matthew seemed
more interested in talking about dogs or President Roosevelt than
anything *he* might have to say.

The women had almost immediately disappeared to another room
after he arrived, most likely the kitchen, since he could smell the rich

aroma of fresh coffee. Any other time he might have felt comfortable enough to ask for a cup. "Comfortable," however, was not a word he would associate with this particular visit.

Upon his arrival, Maggie had stayed in the front room only long enough to offer a soft hello, accompanied by a look in her eyes that wasn't far from raw fear, before scurrying out of the room behind Eva Grace and their mother.

Clearly there was to be no help from that quarter.

As for Matthew, he looked completely relaxed, even a little drowsy. Jonathan reminded himself that the man had just put in a full day's work in a coal mine; it was a wonder he could stay awake at all. All the more reason to get on with why he'd come—if he could somehow deter Matthew from the subject of dogs and President Roosevelt's age.

"Youngest president we've ever had, isn't he? What is he now—forty-five, forty-six?"

"Somewhere around there, I believe. Matthew, if—"

"Aye, well, let's hope he doesn't end up at the end of a bullet like McKinley did. Seems as though there's some who don't want him in office for the next time around. Myself, I think he's done a decent enough job since he took over."

"I agree. And I feel sure he'll win the election." Jonathan hurried on before Matthew could dip any deeper into politics. "Matthew, I know I'm intruding on your evening, and I'm sure you're tired, so I should get right to the point as to why I wanted to stop by tonight."

Maggie's father shoved his bad leg out in front of him and leaned back contentedly in the massive rocking chair, which looked to have been built especially for a man of Matthew's considerable size. He said nothing by way of encouragement, but merely sat watching Jonathan with an intent expression. Jonathan noted that his earlier drowsiness seemed to have disappeared.

He drew a long breath. How many times today had he rehearsed this? And still he didn't know where to begin.

"So then, what's this about, Jonathan?"

One more deep breath. "Actually, Matthew…it's about Maggie."

Matthew frowned. "What about Maggie? Is there a problem?"

"No! Well, I don't think it's a problem. I hope it won't be…"

Jonathan had always considered himself passably articulate. He was a teacher, after all, accustomed to making himself understood. How was it then that over the past hour he had managed to lose the ability to form a single coherent sentence?

Did falling in love automatically make a man a bumbling fool?

"Are you all right, Jonathan?" Matthew asked. "You don't seem yourself tonight."

"I'm—I'm fine."

My heart is going to implode at any minute, and my stomach is consuming itself, but other than that I couldn't be better.

"I need to talk with you about Maggie, Matthew."

"Aye, so you said."

Just get it over with.

He cleared his throat. "I'm in love with her. With Maggie," he added inanely.

Well, that's getting straight to the point, all right. It might have been better to ease into the subject a bit, not hit her father over the head with it.

The other's expression never changed. "I know you are."

Jonathan stared at him. "You *know?*"

Matthew nodded. "*I* know. But does Maggie?"

Still trying to recover from his surprise, Jonathan took a moment to respond. "Why, yes. Yes, Maggie knows. But how did you—"

"I'm neither a blind man nor a fool, Jonathan. And I suppose Maggie fancies herself in love with *you,* does she?"

Jonathan nodded. "She does, Matthew. I mean, she seems convinced that she is." He tried to discreetly wipe his hands down the sides of his trousers, but Matthew followed the movement with his eyes.

"I can almost anticipate your concern about this, Matthew. That's why I wanted to talk with you right away, so we could discuss… everything."

"I know a lot of men marry younger than themselves, of course," Matthew went on as though picking up a thread already in place. "And most of those marriages seem to work well enough. But I'm not entirely comfortable with Maggie getting herself into such a situation. Surely you can understand why."

Jonathan had just been squashed. He had to find his backbone and find it fast or this was going to end badly. And he couldn't let that happen. Maggie thought he could handle anything—even her father. He expelled a quick breath. "Matthew, I'd be lying if I pretended not to understand your concern. But will you just hear me out, please? There are a few things I hope you'll consider."

Matthew nodded, but he had that fixed set to his mouth that usually meant his stubborn streak had locked into place.

"It's true, of course, that I'm quite a bit older than Maggie—"

"How *much* older, by the way?"

"Jonathan swallowed. "Ah…about fifteen years, actually. Nearly sixteen. But you and I both know couples right here in town with an even greater difference in their ages, and their marriages are solid."

Matthew gave another nod. "That's true."

He was being just a little too agreeable. Jonathan wasn't at all sure he trusted that mild tone of voice.

Again he reminded himself that Maggie was most likely counting on him, not her father, to come out the victor in this match. And in that instant, Jonathan realized that the only way that was going to happen was if he were totally, unequivocally straightforward with the man sitting across from him.

"Matthew, I'll be honest. If Maggie were my daughter, I probably wouldn't want her to marry a man so much older than her either. I believe I can understand any objection you might raise, except for one, that being if you were to question my love for her. I love Maggie more than my own life. Indeed, I would give *up* my life for her in a heartbeat.

"If she'll have me, I'll be the best husband I know how to be, and I believe I have the ability to be a very *good* husband. I will never hurt her, Matthew. Nor will I let anyone else hurt her. I'll protect her with my life. And I vow to you that I'll make her happy."

Matthew had not changed expression throughout this entire discourse. Did that mean he was getting through to the man? Or was his mind already made up and he was simply letting Jonathan bleed himself out for absolutely nothing?

Jonathan chose his next words with great care. "I'm not ignorant of the likelihood that I'll…pass on before Maggie, given our age difference. If that concerns you, I want to reassure you, should that be the case, I'll leave her well-provided for. I have a little money, you see. Well, more than a little, actually, by way of an inheritance from my mother. Maggie will be taken care of financially, whether I'm…dead or alive. But as long as I *am* alive, I will make it my life's mission to see that she's the happiest, safest, most thoroughly loved woman in Skingle Creek. In the county. In—"

Matthew put up a hand. "I take your point. You needn't belabor it." He shifted in the rocking chair. "Now, Jonathan, you know I think you're a fine man, as good a man as I've ever known. I respect you, just as the whole town does. Maggie could do a lot worse for herself, that's true."

Jonathan's hopes rose a little, and at last he caught a breath.

"I don't like the difference in your years, I won't deny it. But I wouldn't fight you on that alone."

His hopes slipped a notch.

"Here's what concerns me more. You're a well-educated man—a *gentleman*—clearly from a fine family, with some money behind you. And because of that, I can't help but wonder just how long you're likely to stay in Skingle Creek."

Jonathan started to protest, but Matthew cut him short. "No, hear me out. I've never understood what you're doing here, man, in the first place. And to be frank with you, I've never believed you'll stay."

Again Jonathan tried to object—and again Matthew waved him off. "The thing is, we've lost Nell Frances to a man who moved her away from us. We lost Eva Grace as well, for some years. Aye, she's home again now, and I intend to make sure she *stays* here. But it was hard not seeing her for so long a time in between visits. As for Ray—well, the boy's too young as yet to know which way he'll go. But there's something I know about Maggie that I wonder if *you* know."

Jonathan waited, no longer so impatient to counter with his own argument, but curious now about what Maggie's father was getting at.

"Maggie, you see, belongs to Skingle Creek. She may not know this herself, but both her mother and I have known it for years. The girl loves this town, no matter how peculiar and unaccountable that might seem to some. When she was away at college and off to her job in Chicago, we could hear it in her letters. And now that she's home again, I see it in her eyes. Maggie *belongs* here. This is her place—not only because her family is here…but because her *heart* is. You take the girl away from here, and it will eventually *break* her heart. She's not a city girl, Jonathan. She'd wither up and die in the city if she knew it was forever." He paused, then added, "We'd lose her for good. And so would you."

Jonathan waited until he was sure Matthew had finished. Then he leaned forward on the sofa and locked eyes with the man. "Please hear what I'm saying, Matthew. I love Maggie. But you're my friend, and I would never lie to you. I have no intention of ever leaving this town. I'm here because God *put* me here. Maggie knows all about that, by the way. And I'm well aware that you're right when you say she belongs to Skingle Creek."

He paused, knotting his hands together as he continued. "But so do I, Matthew. I belong here. And though I can't promise you that God will never call me away from here, I *can* promise you that that's what it would take to make me leave this town—a call from God."

Jonathan realized as he went on that he had never in his life opened his heart to another man, not even to his own father, as he was opening it to Matthew MacAuley. He could only hope it didn't work against him.

"I love it here, Matthew. I love the town, the people—it's home to me. It's *been* home to me for years now. Just as it is to Maggie. And I know in my heart that I belong here just as surely as she does. I can't give you any more reassurance than that."

He stopped, flexed his fingers, then asked, "What else?"

Matthew looked at him. "What else?"

"What other reservations do you have about my marrying Maggie?"

That green-eyed stare sharpened still more. "That's what you're asking then? To marry her?"

"Nothing less."

"What about Maggie? Is that what *she* wants?"

Jonathan got to his feet. "I believe it is, yes. I believe Maggie will marry me if you give us your blessing."

Now the strong Irish chin came up, and the eyes narrowed. "And if I don't?"

"Matthew—I told you. I intend to make Maggie as happy as I possibly can. And I know full well that if we have to get married without your blessing, it will mean her forfeiting a part of that happiness. It will hurt her terribly. And it will hurt me. That's why I'm asking your consent...and your blessing." Jonathan swallowed. "As I said, your refusal would hurt both Maggie and me a great deal." He stopped. "But if she'll have me, Matthew, I intend to marry her anyway."

Slowly Maggie's father hauled himself up from the rocking chair, wincing with the effort. When he straightened to his full height, he topped Jonathan by an inch or two. Enough to make Jonathan feel suddenly small...and, strangely enough, very young.

For a full moment more, Matthew drilled Jonathan with his piercing green eyes. Then at last he cracked a smile and extended his hand. "Aye, then. Marry the girl if she'll have you. And it will be with my blessing."

Jonathan again wiped his hand down the side of his trousers before grasping the calloused, bone-bruising hand of Maggie's father. "*Thank you,* Matthew! I give you my word you'll not be sorry."

Still flashing that thoroughly Irish grin of his, Matthew gripped Jonathan's hand even tighter. "And I will give *you* fair warning that if you don't live up to that pretty speech you just made for me, *you'll* be the one who's sorry."

Maggie stopped in the doorway, looking cautiously from Jonathan to her father. They were both smiling. She expelled the breath she'd been holding and took a tentative step inside the room. Then another.

She saw it right away. Something new, something…different had risen in his eyes. The old hesitancy, the hint of reservation, the *questions* that had been there before—they were all gone. In their place was *certainty*, assurance.

She couldn't take her eyes off him. Not until her father broke in with a gruff directive: "I'll be leaving the two of you alone now—for fifteen minutes and no more." He paused. "And, Maggie, don't lock up until your brother gets home."

He left the room, leaving them to stand and stare at each other.

"He doesn't seem to be angry," Maggie finally said.

Jonathan went to her, took both her hands in his, and pulled her a little closer…though not *too* close. "No, he's not angry."

"What did he say?" she choked out.

His smile warmed her skin and her heart. It was like being bathed by the sun.

"He said that we have his blessing."

She should say something. But all she could manage was a whispered, "Oh…"

"Even so, fifteen minutes isn't nearly long enough for a proper proposal."

"Oh…" Maggie said again.

"When a man proposes, he wants it to be memorable, after all."

"I expect so," she said quietly. "How long…*would* a proper proposal take, do you think?"

He seemed to consider the question. "An entire evening, to do it up right, I'd say."

"A whole *evening?*"

He nodded. "At least. Unfortunately, I can't see him leaving us alone for that long. Can you?"

She pulled a face. "Not unless he's sound asleep. And I've always suspected he sleeps with one eye open."

He tugged her a little closer. "But he could hardly object to a restaurant filled with other people, now could he?"

"I don't suppose, but—a crowded restaurant?"

"I'd have to drive you home after dinner. We can make it work."

"All right. But…when?"

"Considering our time limitations—and the busy, difficult week we've just gone through—I suppose we should wait at least a few more days, until the dust settles, so to speak."

She nodded, albeit reluctantly.

"In the meantime, it might be a good idea to have a brief rehearsal."

"A rehearsal?"

"Exactly. You see, Maggie, I had my heart set on kissing you good-night for the first time tonight, but your father would frown on that without a proposal in place and a mutual commitment. Don't you think?"

"He wouldn't approve," she agreed, again reluctantly.

· She felt the hands holding hers tremble slightly. Or were they *her* hands that were trembling? She couldn't really tell, what with the way he was holding on to her. She felt a little dizzy. If he hadn't been clasping her hands so securely, she thought her legs might buckle right out from under her.

But he was holding her steady, with his hands…and with his eyes.

"Remember now, this is simply a rehearsal," he said softly.

She nodded, her heart giving a jubilant little leap.

"So, then…Maggie…my love…will you marry me?"

"Yes," she said. Just to make certain he'd heard her, she cleared her throat and said it again. "*Oh, yes!*"

"Soon," he said.

It wasn't a question.

"I should hope so," she said. "We've put this off long enough."

"I was thinking of December. During our Christmas break from school."

"That soon?"

"*Soon?* At this moment, December sounds like a ridiculously long time away."

"There's a lot to do to get ready for a wedding, Jonathan—"

"*Maggie...*"

"But I can manage."

His eyes were actually dancing. She knew hers were too, in spite of a few tears swimming in them.

And then Jonathan kissed her, just the corner of her lips, with a lingering, unspeakable tenderness.

It was as if she had been blessed.

He drew her into his arms, closer now, and kissed her again, rather more thoroughly this time.

In that moment, every wish, every daydream, every prayer for the future that the young Maggie...and the grownup Maggie...had ever harbored in her heart came true.

Epilogue

A Night to Remember

O holy night, O night divine...

Placide Clappeau

⌒

Christmas Eve, 1904

Jonathan took one final, thorough look around the classroom that on this Christmas Eve would become a holy place: the chapel for his and Maggie's wedding.

Most couples in Skingle Creek were married in the church or at home, but he and Maggie had decided they would be wed in this building, in the school that had played such a vital part in their lives for so many years. With the help of a few friends, an altar had been constructed at the front of the room, directly in front of the rough-hewn, unpainted wooden cross that had been nailed to the wall when the building was first erected. Jonathan had always been thankful that a cross, the constant reminder of his Lord's sacrifice, and another carved in its likeness, graced both classrooms in the school.

Garlands and wreaths of dried wild flowers added gentle touches of color to the otherwise rustic surroundings. Flickering lanterns and candles bathed the room in a soft, golden light, gilding the simplicity of the setting and its furnishings with a loveliness that brought an ache to his heart. He had wanted to bring as much beauty and warmth as possible to this special night—his and Maggie's night. God's night.

They had chosen Christmas Eve for their wedding not simply because the Christmas break would allow them to be away from school for a time, although that was the practical side of it, but because this place, this time of year, held special significance for both of them.

The memories of another winter's night came rushing in on him, as he'd known they would. On that night many years ago, this same room had been the setting of a miracle, one that had saved—and changed—his life. And Jonathan believed with all his heart that tonight this room, so dearly familiar and so simple in its lack of pretension, would host yet another miracle that would change his life.

He walked up the aisle that had been cleared of desks and chairs for the occasion. With a lingering look at the wooden cross on the wall, he knelt at the altar and began to pray to the One who had brought him to his knees on a daily basis throughout most of his life.

His prayer issued from a heart so filled with gratitude and love it threatened to overwhelm him. He prayed to be the man Maggie believed him to be, the husband she deserved him to be, and one day, please God, the father he had always hoped to be.

He stayed as he was, on his knees, until Ben, his closest friend and pastor, placed a gentle hand on his shoulder and roused him.

"It's time to get you behind the scenes, my friend," said the pastor. "We have guests arriving. I think you'll be surprised by how many. Your bride will be making an entrance before long."

Jonathan got to his feet and shook hands with his long-time friend and followed him to the supply closet leading off the room.

His bride...

Another miracle.

Fifteen minutes later Jonathan cracked the door of the closet just enough to get a look at those who had come to witness the wedding. He caught his breath at the sight of the chairs, already filled, and the steady stream of people filing along the back of the room to stand and watch.

He turned to Ben. "It looks as if the whole town is here!"

"I wouldn't be at all surprised," Ben said, smiling broadly. "These people love you, Jonathan. And Maggie."

Jonathan turned around quickly, unwilling to let even his best friend see the emotion welling up in him. Allowing himself another look into the schoolroom, he saw Maggie's mother and Eva Grace, now large with child, sitting in front. Maggie's other sister, Nell Frances, was also expecting and had reluctantly stayed in Indiana.

He keenly felt the absence of his own family, but his father was no longer able to travel, and his sister, Patricia, wouldn't leave him. He and Maggie would see them soon, though, on their honeymoon trip to Lexington.

There was Dr. Gordon, seated right behind Eva Grace. And the Rankins, the family of Maggie's friend, Summer, who had died in childhood. Even Dr. Woodbridge and his wife were here.

And Carolyn Ross. Carolyn, who had come to both of them weeks before and wished them well. Carolyn, who had also suggested that she was considering giving up her employment at the school "to try something new."

But Maggie had asked her to stay. "Please don't leave. Jonathan needs you to look after all the things he *can't* look after and to keep him organized. I'd like you to stay…and be my friend."

So Carolyn was staying. And Jonathan and Maggie were both glad.

And then there were the children—from the smallest to those in their teens—it seemed the entire student body of Skingle Creek had aligned themselves in the back of the room. Some who had just entered were shaking the snow from their coats and hats.

"It's snowing!" Jonathan whispered to Ben. "Oh, Maggie's going to love this! She hoped it would snow tonight."

"I suppose you prayed for that too," Ben said dryly.

"I tried to cover everything."

"You did well."

Not for the first time, Jonathan withdrew the ring box from his pocket and opened it to reassure himself. The gold ring, woven in an Irish braid, caught the light from a nearby lantern and glowed like a promise kept.

Maggie's only difficult moment came when she looked up at her da and saw the dampness in his eyes.

"Well, Maggie," he said after clearing his throat. "You're quite sure, are you, that this is what you want?"

"I am, Da," Maggie said. "And I want to thank you for giving us your blessing. It wouldn't have been right without it." On impulse, she slipped her arms around her father's neck. "I love you, Da," she choked out. She must not weep. She *would not* weep.

Her father tipped his head to kiss her, ever so gently on the cheek, then lifted her chin to search her face. "And I love you as well, Maggie *a gra*. You're a good daughter. And you'll be a fine, good wife to your husband."

For the first time Maggie wished she had not foregone the bridal veil. It would have concealed the treacherous tears welling in her eyes, threatening to spill over.

Her father offered his arm. "I'm sorry you'll be walking down the aisle with a lame man at your side," he said gruffly.

Maggie managed a fierce look for him as she took his arm. "In truth, I'll be walking down the aisle with the most handsome man in town," she said. "Except for the groom, of course."

"Of course."

At that moment, her brother, Ray, opened the door to the school-room, and she saw him…Jonathan…standing at the altar.

He was achingly handsome in a dove-gray suit, his flaxen hair gleaming in the soft light. He looked like a prince.

"It's time, Maggie," said Da.

She was a vision in ivory lace and a satin sash, a princess with a crown of dried wild flowers, a wonder with a smile that lit the room and set his heart ablaze.

Jonathan drew in the breath that he had lost at the first sight of her, and then reached behind him for his flute. He had been unwilling that she should walk the aisle without music. And, unconventional as it might be, it seemed only right that *he* be the one to make the music.

He saw her eyes glisten in surprise as he lifted the flute to his lips and began to play "The Irish Wedding Song." He found himself pray-ing again, this time that he wouldn't collapse and spoil the music.

He couldn't take his eyes off her. He followed her every step as he continued to play.

Once before, on that same winter's night so many years ago, he had played…not a flute, but a tin whistle. A penny whistle that somehow, in the grip of divine power and unspeakable grace, had become an elegant, shining instrument of exultation and praise. He had played it for his God…and he had played it for Maggie. And for an entire room filled with people who loved him.

And now he played again, for his God and for Maggie…in the same room filled with many of the same people…people who loved both him and Maggie.

Finally her father took her hand and placed it in Jonathan's before stepping away.

"Dearly Beloved," Ben Wallace began. "We are gathered here together…"

Dear Readers:

If for any reason you missed the story leading up to *The Wind Harp*, be sure to look for *A Distant Music*, book 1 of the Mountain Song Legacy, in which Maggie MacAuley is first introduced as a preteen, and Jonathan Stuart as her young schoolteacher.

The story of the penny whistle referred to in *The Wind Harp* is a very special part of that first book.

And watch for book 3—*The Song Weaver*—to be released in the fall of 2007, as Maggie and Jonathan's story continues.

God's blessing upon you all,

About the Author

Widely recognized for her award-winning historical fiction, BJ Hoff is the author of The Mountain Song Legacy series, The American Anthem series, and the Emerald Ballad series. Her bestselling historical novels have crossed the boundaries of religion, language, and culture to capture a worldwide reading audience. Although she writes of early America and the people who helped build the country, her stories of faith and love and grace are timeless.

When asked about her own story, BJ points to her family: "They're my favorite story."

A former church music director and music teacher, BJ and her husband, James, make their home in Ohio, where they share a love of music, books, and time spent with family.

If you would like to contact the author, you may write to BJ:

BJ Hoff
Harvest House Publishers
990 Owen Loop North
Eugene, OR 94702-9173

Or visit www.bjhoff.com

HARVEST HOUSE
PUBLISHERS

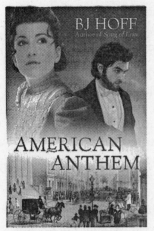

BJ Hoff offers another thrilling historical saga that will capture the hearts of readers everywhere.

At the entrance to the city, an Irish governess climbs into a carriage and sets out to confront the man who destroyed her sister's life—a blind musician who hears music no one else can hear...

On a congested city street, a lonely Scot physician with a devastating secret meets a woman doctor with the capacity to heal not only the sick...but also his heart...

In a tumbledown shack among hundreds of others like it, an immigrant family struggles to survive, and a ragged street singer old beyond her years appoints herself an unlikely guardian...

So begins *American Anthem,* a story set in 1870s New York that lets the reader step into another time to share the hopes and dreams and triumphant faith of a people you'll grow to love...a people readers will never forget.

"An eloquently told story that weaves history, music, faith and intrigue...an absolute pleasure."

—CHRISTIAN RETAILING

"The story gently unfolds with intriguing characters, and the sound of music, which Hoff manages to make fly off the pages with her glorious and passionate descriptions."

—CHRISTIAN LIBRARY JOURNAL

Originally published to strong sales several years ago, this new edition combines three of BJ's best novels into one saga-length volume.

The mysteries of the past confront the secrets of the present in bestselling author BJ Hoff's magnificent Song of Erin saga.

In her own unique style, Hoff spins a panoramic story that crosses the ocean from Ireland to America, featuring two of her most memorable characters. In this tale of struggle and love and uncompromising faith, Jack Kane, the always charming but sometimes ruthless titan of New York's most powerful publishing empire, is torn between the conflict of his own heart and the grace and light of Samantha Harte, the woman he loves, whose own troubled past continues to haunt her.

Originally published to strong sales nearly a decade ago, this new edition combines two of BJ's best novels into one saga-length volume.

"The Song of Erin contains some of my favorite characters. This story—and its people—hold a very special place in my heart."

BJ HOFF